adp

THE SENTIMENTALIST

Also By Stavros Stavros

The SIRENS

THE SENTIM- ENTALIST

A NOVEL IN FOUR PARTS

STAVROS STAVROS

The Artless Dodges Press
www.TheArtlessDodgesPress.com
Cleveland, Ohio

The Sentimentalist
A Novel By Stavros Stavros
ISBN 0981993931
EAN-13 9780981993935
copyright © 2010 Artless Dodges, Inc.
Published by The Artless Dodges Press
Cleveland, Ohio
www.TheArtlessDodgesPress.com

Cover design by T. Maven
www.TrashMaven.WordPress.com

"… To be sure it is the body which disturbs us: an arm or a half-exposed breast or perhaps a leg. But we must realize at the start that we desire the arm or the uncovered breast only on the ground of the presence of the whole body as an organic totality…"

- Jean-Paul Sartre, *Being and Nothingness*

A PSYCHOLOGY OF PYGMALION

OR

SENTIMENTALITY: AN INTRODUCTION

The sculptor Pygmalion, detesting women, resolved never to marry and devoted himself instead to his art; despite his purported misogyny he nonetheless applied himself tirelessly to a statue in the image of a woman, working until the statue's beauty was unrivaled by any woman of flesh and blood. Having finished his work an odd fate befell him, for overcome by its beauty he fell passionately in love with the stone figure. He devoted himself to his creation as a newlywed husband devotes himself to his bride: he caressed the statue, dressed it in colorful garments, kissed its lips. The statue, being of course only a statue, did not respond, and Pygmalion was miserable. He prayed to Venus that he would find a woman like his statue, and find some relief from his misery; Venus, sensing the sculptor's true wish, and impressed with the original circumstances of his infatuation, instead brought the statue to life.

Young Pygmalion, lavished with praise, dwelt in the radiant womb of his mother's love. It was she who watched and applauded him when, at play, he formed his first inglorious towers in the indifferent mud; it was she who kissed his soiled hands! As he fell asleep it was she who whispered in his ear: he was the best and brightest; none in the world could match him! Never had a woman been born who was worthy of him; no woman could love him as his mother loved him!

(And as he grew older it was she who cast disapproving eyes on the girls he brought home to meet her: she had given him everything; wasn't her love enough? What was her love to him if it could not keep him from common girls: girls who could never love him as she loved him! For she loved him with her whole heart, her whole being, her whole life and every ounce of blood that continued it: no love could rival a Mother's Love!)

3

The child Pygmalion, lacking the experience with which one informs perception and determines behavior, hid behind his mother's legs and fled the confronting world. But this retreat was not disinterest: he watched the world as an explorer watches the savage races of an unfamiliar wilderness, observing their rituals and approaching them only after their war cries have ceased. But of course one can learn only so much through observation, and a child understands little of innuendo; later the man looks back on the child he was and finds there a collection of inaccurate postulations and absurd conclusions which, though ridiculous in hindsight, were nevertheless drawn from careful (if uninformed) observation.

Oh happy delusion, when one imagines childhood as a carefree time, a time unencumbered by anxiety! Truly one is never more anxious than when one is a child, when the world is vast and wholly incomprehensible! The child Pygmalion struggled frantically to understand the meaning behind form: what did this mean? And why was this? His mind produced countless questions which his observation could not answer, and the world remained a collection of nonsensical gestures and unintelligible remarks.

How much simpler it was to wield hammer and chisel, pen and ink: lost in the world of his own creation he knew the circumference of every form. Sheltering beneath the canopy of his mother's affection he painted the sky and everything beneath it with the myopic bias of his own limited understanding. Bolstered by his mother's praise he mistook his perspective for veracity: yes, only the artist saw clearly; only the artist saw the truth behind appearance! Women were loathsome, deceitful, the owners of faults beyond measure; their beauty was a screen concealing artless advances, selfish love, spiteful tricks, irrational thoughts, disjoined humors... How he longed for something truly beautiful, something whose beauty was not tainted by an inner ugliness!

Pygmalion the absolutist, the first sentimentalist, begged Venus for a woman to match his Galatea. What happiness, when her new-animated lips (those lips so often kissed and yet so unerringly indifferent!) responded! Overcome with joy, he failed to notice her confusion; anxious to bed her, he ignored her odd indifference. Here was his perfect woman, his gift from Heaven! Watching her sleep, he felt an overpowering love (a love he had held in check, a love he had been waiting his whole life to bestow on another: a love always stopped in its early stages by his own repulsion (for look at the way she chewed her food; listen to her horrible laugh! Truly, he could not love this one!)), a love which, though overwhelming, had as little to do with Galatea herself as his repugnance did the women on whom it was visited.

Yes, sentimentality: that phenomenon by which the emotional need of the viewer takes precedence over the reality of the object; sentimentality: the excessive and inappropriate infusion of meaning, the incorrect alignment of form and content; sentimentality: a child's perception, the stain of immaturity, sister to stereotype, father of prejudice, the soul of dramatic irony!

What happiness: to surrender the child's frantic and broad assertions about the world for the nuance and subtlety of true understanding! What joy: to abandon these delusions, to marry form with content, to live without sentimentality!

THE FLOWER OF THE COMING GENERATION

The Flower of the Coming Generation

He received a letter stating that his grant proposal had been accepted: in its twenty-seven year history this award had never been given to a first-year student; congratulations! They looked forward to reading his manuscript at the end of the semester. He folded the letter and returned it to its envelope; he went back to his room to call his mother.

He passed other students as one passing the footlights of the world's stage, he felt their eyes upon him; here he was: the great writer in their midst! At the beginning of his career, perhaps, but no matter! Those with attuned eyes had already discerned the invisible caul upon his head. Yes; he had within him a voice that could not be silenced: a greatness that could not be ignored! The decision to award him this grant reflected more than the opinions of the faculty on the review panel: it was the verdict of the institution, the judgment of a world into which he had been welcomed, which stood upon his arrival and saluted him as the Flower of the Coming Generation.

Yes; he paused on his walk, took pen and notepad from his pocket, and wrote *The Flower of the Coming Generation*. Overwhelmingly satisfied with himself,` he continued on to his room and called his mother.

His Life's Great Reporter

She was overjoyed; she was so proud of him! But then she had always expected great things of him; she had always known that he would be a great writer! Even as a child he had written the most wonderful stories. And then there was that story they put in the school newspaper; did he remember? Of course he remembered; of the stories he wrote in high school, it was one of the few he had allowed anyone to read. His English teacher had encouraged him to submit it to the student newspaper; the story had been published and generally praised.

The thought of it now filled him with staggering embarrassment; the story was laughable! The characters were undeveloped; the conflict was contrived and naïve! Why had he had this character say this or that? And that horribly predictable affair! He wished that he hadn't submitted it. The thought that, to many back home, the story still represented his talent and marked the beginning of his aspirations horrified him. He could imagine their conversation: he had been awarded a grant to write? That was wonderful! But then of course he had published that wonderful story in the high school newspaper; how could anyone forget? The story was like a badge of immaturity, pinned forever to his chest.

His mother went on: yes, she had just loved that story! She would have to call his old English teacher and let him know. And had he called his grandparents? He knew how much his grandmother loved his stories! She would call his grandmother herself; they had some catching up to do! And of course she would have to tell this friend and that friend; but oh, she was so proud of him!

He was filled with a sudden repulsion; he wanted nothing more than to hang up the phone. He wished he had not called! The happy blush he had felt at his mother's pride had rapidly dissolved into something resembling disgust; he was certain that, if he did not hang up soon, he would begin to scream at her. What was it about her pride that so revolted him? It was her insufferable desire to sing his praises! Didn't she understand his self-conscious discomfort; couldn't she respect his wish to be anonymous? His wish to be seen as the great writer was wholly dependent upon the existence of a crowd unaware of his presence.

But it was more than that: yes, there was more to it than that! The anecdotes about himself others reported back always bore the embarrassing stamp of his mother's ignorance. His mother said he was doing this or that; it was so wonderful that he was doing this or that! How often he found that, attempting to explain himself, he was muted by his mother's version of his life; how often he winced to find that, while he was away, his mother had said this or that!

And yet there was nothing to be done: by speaking of him in his absence she retained the final word. He was certain that, returning home, he would be overwhelmed with questions from acquaintances displaying their imperfect vision of his life produced by his mother's incomplete understanding. And yet, despite her continued failure to comprehend, she nevertheless refused to remain quiet: how maddening! For as long as she lived she held the intolerable authority over his actions. Not as their director; no the reality was much worse! Her authority over the happenings in his life arose because she cast herself as their reporter; yes, she was the great reporter of his life!

He imagined how, coming from her, the assessment that he was the Flower of the Coming Generation would sound stupid, grandiose; he imagined with horror a future in which his mother, asked by strangers about her son's success, would explain that she had always known he would be a great writer, ever since he was a small child writing wonderful stories.

This prospect seemed wholly unendurable. Making some vague excuse, he ended the conversation and hung up the phone.

The Shameful Garb of Immaturity

Anxious to dispel thoughts of his mother, the Student left his room and crossed the campus to the Girl's apartment, where he entered through the unlocked door. The Girl was on the couch watching television; she moved to make a place and when he sat she lay back against him. What was she watching? It was a report on the famine in Ethiopia: the screen showed a group of people waiting to board a truck. Some were too weak to climb aboard themselves, and had to be helped by attendant soldiers. A well-known Newscaster stood before the scene and explained that for many families the promise of relief was bitter-sweet, as thousands of lives had already been lost in what some were calling a biblical famine in the twentieth century. The Student kissed the top of the Girl's head. He had something to show her: he took the letter from his pocket. She sat up as she read it, and embraced him when she was finished. She was so happy for him! Wasn't he glad now that he had applied? She had told him that he would win!

Yes, it was true: she had encouraged him to apply! This fact suddenly confronted and pained him: now she, too, wished to claim an intolerable authority over his life! How dare she: when the application had been his own, the writing sample his own, the interview and anxiety all his own! It was suddenly very clear: he should not have called his mother, should not have come here; the only appropriate celebration was to forgo celebration, and begin writing immediately. Now, instead, his achievement had been lessened - almost instantly! - by the unwelcome intrusion of their claims upon it. By seeking their praise – like a child! – he had in fact invited their impious steps inside the ethereal temple of his progress into and status as the Flower of the Coming Generation.

Yes: to seek their praise was to don the shameful garb of immaturity. No! Rather it was to thoughtlessly slip the costume of maturity and reveal the naked child beneath! He wanted nothing more than to take the letter from her, to hide it back within his coat, to beg her to forget his having shown it to her.

She handed back the letter and again lay against him on the couch. Did he know what he was going to write? Did he have any of it written? Would he let her read it? She was so happy for him! He folded the letter and placed it in his pocket. He silently reproached himself for having shown it to her, and vowed to himself that no one else would see it. No, he had nothing written yet; when he had something worth reading she would certainly be the first to see it! She did not say anything. On the screen the Newscaster was interviewing the Ambassador from Ethiopia. How dire was the situation? The Ambassador responded that the situation was indeed very dire.

The Student Hopes to Never Be a Boyfriend

She had talked to her mother today; her mother had asked how her new boyfriend was doing. And what had she said? She had said that he was fine, that he was waiting to hear back about a grant that he had applied for. That he wrote the most wonderful stories! He watched the screen, where a classroom full of starving children were being led in song. So he was her boyfriend, then? Wasn't he? He kissed the top of her head. He didn't know; didn't boyfriends buy flowers and chocolate? Didn't they throw their coats over puddles so that their dates' feet would stay dry? It didn't seem like the right word. She wove her fingers between his; he wasn't her boyfriend, then? He shifted beneath her; it was not that he was not her boyfriend! He just didn't care for the word, that was all. Why not? Because the word had an unhealthy, bourgeois and provincial feel. Boyfriends and girlfriends held hands, they argued over forgotten anniversaries! They spent hours on the telephone, and fought over the stupidest things. The word stank of the silliest bourgeois fantasies: one could not imagine Jean-Paul Sartre and Simone De Beauvoir ever having called themselves boyfriend and girlfriend!

The Girl Offers a Subatomic Parallel

She did not think so; she thought it was a nice word! It always made her think of a movie they had watched in science class in middle school: hundreds of molecules floated around an empty space, and then two bonded and floated around together. It was right around the time she'd had her first boyfriend; the association had always stuck with her!

The Student laughed. But in those bonds, more often than not, one atom took more than it gave! Didn't she remember? She shrugged; that did not matter! The image was inexorably tied to the dawn of her own secret life; when she was with him the image was never far from her thoughts! When she'd broken up with that boyfriend she'd felt lost, and had been overwhelmingly relieved to find another. As though her perception of herself had fundamentally shifted: she was unstable without a bond! She laughed.

The thought of her first boyfriend, and the tone that had entered her voice as she described the association between the film's depiction of molecular bonding and that first relationship, irritated him. How could it not? And what had she thought? That by describing how the label of boyfriend had been infused with pleasant connotations by another would make the mantle easier to wear? Further, the unspoken but nevertheless (in his mind) apparent suggestion that he existed as one in a series – let alone a series that would continue after his eventual but inevitable departure! – wounded him. How could it not? And why had she said it? Surely, to wound him! Yes: she wished to wound him for his refusal to wear the label of boyfriend. It could not be written off to mere thoughtlessness: any license she gave herself to be thoughtless was a direct refusal to acknowledge the impact of her words! He fell silent, and felt the rise and fall of her stomach beneath his hands. How many others had shared the intimate knowledge of her breath? Five? Ten? A dozen? More? He could not bear the thought! He rose from the couch and went into the bathroom to calm down. When he came back she asked him what was wrong. Nothing was wrong: he merely had to use the bathroom! He had been thinking about it: very often one atom robbed the other of its energy, and then departed! Perhaps she was right; perhaps it was a fitting metaphor!

She was sorry; she had not meant to upset him! He shrugged; it did not matter! He sat down on the couch. The television showed an emaciated couple packing their belongings into a trunk. The Student did not like thinking of her with others! Was that wrong? Was it wrong to want her all to himself? She lay back against him and again wove her fingers between his. Well, she was with him now! Wasn't that what mattered most of all? He didn't say anything.

Did He Know What He Was Going to Write?

The Girl changed the subject: did he know what he was going to write? They were both watching the television screen, where a child had fainted from exhaustion. He had a few ideas. In any case, he knew what he wanted to write about; he was as of yet unsure as to the details of plot and character. But those were wholly secondary to the meaningful subtext! That was the thing that no one seemed to understand! Writers wasted their time and that of their readers cluttering a story with colorful characters, unprecipitated happenings, strange locations; they gawked at the jugglers of the world to better ignore the void beneath his tight rope! They wrote so that their books might be a pleasant lark, a distraction, an opiate! But reading should not be easy: truth was neither pleasant nor easy!

But what, she asked, was the truth he sought to capture? That man's limited ability to understand his own existence was coupled with his boundless need to know it; that incomplete knowledge carried with it inherent isolation. These were the only truths! That man would live and die as one bound within four walls, and quickly be forgotten; that his heart's expansive and ceaseless protest at the injustice of his entrapment and his ignorance produced no response from his indifferent captors! Yes: that life was a cage of years, a tightrope walk on a line made of years!

But then, she protested, what about love? One need not live in isolation! He shook his head; even the most intimate of lovers remained secret strangers. Or had she never experienced, with any of her dozens of boyfriends, that profound horror: what was the other thinking? And what was he going to say next? No: no greater distance existed than that which arose between the intimate. What passed for love was, rather, the basest impulse: it was surrender to that unripe desire to infuse one's life with undue gravitas. Love was just another name for self-importance! But it was still only the juggler upon the high wire; it was the placebo which calmed the soul when the horror of truth became too great. But, like all placebos, it was merely a delusion!

The Tragedy in Ethiopia

The Girl did not say anything. The image on the television changed: it was night, and the starving shuffled in line through a lit doorway. The Girl pressed back into him: God, it was so sad! She almost could not believe that something so horrible could happen. Didn't he think it was horrible? God, it was so horrible!

He replied that this tragedy was not important, as all tragedy ended up forgotten, buried in the dump heap of history. He was certain that hundreds of races had been erased by conquerors, diseases, and disasters. And yet: where were their monuments? No one remembered them; they might as well never have existed! Those forgotten lives were indistinguishable from those lost to the famine: did she know the names of the dead? Of course not! They were an abstract, buried in a mass grave beneath a headstone marked *The Tragedy in Ethiopia*. The fact of their own knowledge or sadness - the conversation they were having at this moment - did little to alter history's amnesia. One day they and all of their memories would disappear completely; irrevocable tragedies crying out for justice disappeared completely!

Yes, history was the dump heap where events were discarded and stripped of their attendant gravitas; on the scales of history all of the famine's collected dead could not outweigh a flat tire or a forgotten anniversary. To say that the famine was tragic was to view with undue reverence the progress of human history: in the end one had no way of knowing the meaning of the Ethiopians' starvation.

Suddenly something strange happened: the Newscaster paused in her explanation of how for many relief had come too late to clear her throat and wipe a tear from her cheek. The Student scoffed; was the Newscaster crying? Yes, she was crying! The Newscaster took a breath and finished her report; the Student laughed and his laughing disturbed the Girl, who sat up. What was funny about the Newscaster crying? She could not see anything funny about the Newscaster crying!

He was not certain how to respond; why had he laughed when he saw the Newscaster crying? He honestly did not know! The fact that he had laughed seemed abhorrent to him now. And not just to himself; he anticipated his peers' disgust. And yet in the moment laughter had seemed the only appropriate response; he had seen her crying, and laughed without thinking! Yes, laughter was the mark of his unique perspective, was the view from his exalted place as the Flower of the Coming Generation!

Asserting this, it became easy to explain his behavior. Didn't she see? The crying Newscaster was ridiculous! To be uniformly moved by tragedy and injustice was to spend one's life ceaselessly weeping; he was certain that by now the Newscaster had moved on to another assignment, and was troubled not at all by visions of starving Ethiopians. And yet now her image was forever linked to their hardship! It was as false a performance as any given on television. No, perhaps it was worse! Because the Newscaster likely had no inkling that her performance was false; he was certain that she did not know what had come over her and, congratulated by her colleagues on a wonderful, compelling report, had begun to think of herself as a beautiful person, with an inner reserve of profound compassion! More than likely her tears' origin had nothing at all to do with anything she had seen on her no more than cursory tour of this tragedy. But now, he was certain, she would be exalted as the holder of some unique perspective, a wonderful reporter worthy of honors: the network would parade her as the face of their conscientiousness and in so doing net millions of viewers, each hoping to share in the profoundly moving experience of watching a grown woman cry for strangers half a world away!

She did not see why he could not believe that a Newscaster could be moved by the subject of her own report. He did not have to be cynical all the time! He said that it did not matter. The whole conversation had struck him, rather suddenly, as unbearably stupid. Sorry that he had come, he explained that he had a class to go to. He would call her afterwards. She asked him what time he thought that would be. He didn't know; did it matter? Well yes: if he was not going to be late, she would wait to eat dinner with him. He told her not to wait.

The Student's Jealousy

Walking to class, the Student lost his jealousy. His former emotions seemed petty and ridiculous; had he really, only moments before, been wounded by the mention of her first boyfriend? What did it matter? He had his own romantic history, after all! Further, she seemed to carry nothing but a nostalgic fondness for the boy; truly he was impassioned - possessive, jealous, mad! - to be thrown into such agonies. Yes, it was his curse to feel more deeply; it was his burden as the Flower of the Coming Generation!

Nearing the classroom, he was certain that he adored her more than ever. He felt flooded by unrestrained affection; he was certain that his heart would burst! Yet he was suddenly troubled; he knew that, were she seated before him, this feeling would quickly dissipate. How odd! With her he was anxious and uncomfortable, prone to jealously! It was only in her absence that his heart embraced her.

Of course: thinking of her he possessed her completely; the only words she spoke were his own! Having permitted - initiated, created! - the moments that now informed his thoughts of her she was no less a fantasy; the Girl his heart embraced was his creation and little else! Why else was he so irritated by her off-hand comments, her reverence for the weeping Newscaster? They constituted little more, to him, than refusal to conform to the mold of the Girl whom his heart embraced! Yes: in his mind he controlled her and was free to adore her without restraint; seated before him she might, in the next moment, declare her intention to leave him for another.

How ridiculous; he quickly dismissed these thoughts. Of course it was the Girl herself whom he adored; even those things which, a moment before, seemed only refusals to conform to his image of her piqued his adoration. She was so cute when she said this or that; he just loved the way that she did this or that! Reassured, he opened the door and entered the classroom.

Golden Pins

The class was already in progress when he arrived. The Professor stood before the chalkboard: it was a matter of historical fact that Cleopatra, to pass the time, would stick the breasts of her slaves with golden pins; what in their reading had stuck in their own breasts? What had caused them to cry out?

Pygmalion On Trial

A student sitting near the front spoke up; she found the myth revolting! It was overwhelmingly disheartening to think that their own society grew from such misogynistic foundations. The fact that he went through life disgusted by women, only to be rewarded for his unrealistic expectations of them, brought to mind the current loathsome vogue in which older men leave their wives – the mothers of their children! – for younger women and are not only not ostracized, but widely admired by their peers! Myths such as this one served only to foster and perpetuate unhealthy gender relations.

The boy sitting beside her spoke up; he agreed! Superior Pygmalion never learned his lesson: he was rewarded not by divine justice but by divine mercy. Were they really supposed to believe that Pygmalion, having received the woman he pined for, did not eventually – if not immediately! – become dissatisfied? He was sorry; the myth failed on the level of story! The primary discord – Pygmalion's inability to find satisfaction – was never resolved. It was deus ex machina of the worst kind, in which the gods' intervention signaled the end without resolving the plot.

Another student agreed: she did not like Pygmalion, and did not want his prayers answered! Further, she could not imagine what kind of life awaited the statue. Pygmalion was smug, arrogant, disdainful: he was the prototype for the superior artist, in love only with himself and his own ideas, childish enough to demand that the world alter itself for his satisfaction! She could hardly think of a less likable character!

The Student Feels That He Is Pygmalion

While they were speaking the Student became indignant: who were they to judge Pygmalion in this way? They obviously did not understand Pygmalion's dissatisfaction, and so twisted it to allow for their immature impulse to vent their opinions in the guise of criticism. But they did not understand the artist's inherent dissatisfaction with the world! Yes, the creation of a woman was merely a metaphor for every act of artistic creation: it had little or nothing to do with women's faults!

As they spoke he became more and more convinced: truly, they understood nothing! It became very clear to him that only he, as an artist, had any right to speak. What did they know of the impulse to recluse oneself, to labor meticulously at one's craft, to demand more, more, always more? Yes, only he understood Pygmalion: only he knew that wondrous and horrible refusal!

The Professor Responds, or *The Perception Which Demands the World's Surrender*

The Professor had to admit that he also found the myth troubling! But perhaps for different reasons: Galatea had form – a form so beautiful no earthly woman could match her. And yet – how Pygmalion wept! For when he reached to touch her he found content absent; he infused his statue with undue emotion and grew wretched when his fantasy was not fulfilled. Like a child, thrown into a tantrum when refused a toy!

And yet Pygmalion was regarded as a gifted artist, a master of his craft! Yet his art was an expression only of his immature desires: feeling slighted by the world he went to his room to sulk and, in sulking, produced a statue of uncommon beauty. He went through life with a perception which demanded the world's surrender: a perspective that reflected the world exactly as it was not and refused to look beyond itself!

And yet this was not so uncommon: in his own life he saw it quite often! Every few years there would be a student who would surround themselves with themselves in just this same way: feeling slighted by the world they would condemn others for their shortcomings, disengage from their fellow students: they would decry the state of the world from their self-appointed zenith, and preach the importance of their own quest for truth! And yet, what was this truth they sought? Not truth at all, but the universe's recognition: they wished to produce a thought - as Pygmalion produced his statue! – that, held up before God and man, would elicit some response. But this was hardly truth: cloaked in the heady banner of art was the child's frustrated nihilism; the truth-seeker was tugging at the world's apron strings, begging it to watch!

He was surprised, in fact, that he had never come across any literature on the subject. To think that the common man knew of Oedipus from Freud's remarkable work, and yet knew little to nothing about Pygmalion! Certainly the sculpture's name belonged to a recognizable complex, if someone would only take the time to describe its characteristics.

... Or Not

Or perhaps he was being too hard on poor Pygmalion; perhaps he misjudged the self-appointed truth-seekers and artists! If Pygmalion was guilty of anything, perhaps he was only guilty of an abhorrent sentimentality; what other name was there for the inappropriate alignment of content with form? To feel such staggering love for a statue; how ridiculous! But then again: weren't they all a little sentimental? Weren't they all guilty of some undue flourishes of emotion? Didn't they all hold some secret corner of themselves in which they gave themselves over to emotion, let themselves feel more than circumstances warranted? It was wonderful to feel blessed or cursed; it was only human to see oneself upon the world's stage! It was grand to fall in love! The feel of her hand, the heart's palpitation at the first kiss: these were mere poetics, of course! But what was the reality? The mere congress of salivary juices? Where was the fun in that?

One has to wonder, for example, at one's own relationships! Does one see one's other truly, or is one blinded by one's own need? Or is it even possible to see another truly? And what is the true self that must be seen? Does one see oneself truly? Perhaps one views oneself with even less insight than one views another! He often wondered about the friendships and romantic relationships that sometimes formed between great thinkers: did Jean-Paul Sartre and Simone de Beauvoir, for example, fall into these same traps, or did their extensive meditations on the nature of perception and Truth lead them to some more perfect union? And if it did not, what hope was there for the rest of them? It was certainly something to consider!

The Poet's Constant Vigil, or *In Defense of Art*

The Student spoke up: surely the Professor was not making the case that all art was sentimental, that all content was inappropriately assigned! It was true, perhaps, that Pygmalion was ridiculous in his wretched love, but one could not dismiss all artists based on his case alone! The Professor could not honestly believe that all art arose from some infantile impulse, that this or that poem or painting was merely a misdirected infant's cry for its mother's breast! Nor could he imagine that the Professor so readily dismissed the quest for Truth; surely, the Professor had to admit, great insights had been made by artists: insights that for lack of a better word could be called Truth! It was true that the artist had to be keep a constant vigil over himself, lest he fall into mannerism and sentimentality. But the artist was not alone in his need for vigilance! One became sentimental a hundred thousand times a day: each memory, each anticipation, each perception carried millions of assertions about content linked to but not mandated by the form they presented. One could certainly call each of these sentimental!

The Professor's Father, Living

The Professor nodded: of course, the Student was right! Everyone was guilty of sentimentality to some degree. But it was the extremity, in Pygmalion's case, which interested him! Taken on its own, as a normal part of daily perception, it was largely harmless; taken to extremes it caused problems! When, for example, one used sentimentality as a guard against forgetting - when one assigned an emotion to a memory, and made the memory only the feeling - one hastened the death of that memory, for once the memory became a sentiment it was lost behind the screen that had replaced it. By guarding against forgetting, the true memory was forgotten that much sooner!

He would give an example:

Some years earlier he met his father for lunch, and greeted him with cheer; he was glad to see his father! But his father seemed distracted, and replied to the Professor's questions, jokes, and comments half-heartedly. When the Professor asked what the matter was, his father explained that he'd just spoken with his brother, the Professor's uncle. They'd been sharing recollections, and arrived upon an event that his father did not remember: as young men his brother had refused to drive him somewhere, and now wished to apologize. The Professor's father could not recall the event in question, and had replied that certainly it was all right, and hardly mattered now. This, however, had failed to satisfy the Professor's uncle, who insisted that the Professor's father forgive him. It troubled the Professor's father to see his brother so agitated, and made him wonder if perhaps old age was catching his brother: if perhaps, after all these years, his brother's mind was going!

The entire incident might have fallen from the Professor's own memory, had he not encountered his uncle the next week and, explaining his father's perplexity (and thinking that he might investigate for himself his uncle's mental state), inquired after the episode in question. His uncle was quite obstinate, and explained with great clarity and in exact detail how he had refused to drive his younger brother, an act to which he could attribute no other cause save his power to do so and the malevolence it had, in that moment, inspired in him. It was, perhaps, an insignificant moment, and yet the regret he'd almost instantly felt had remained with him. Attempting to assuage his uncle's obvious lingering guilt, the Professor had assured his uncle that his father was more than happy to forgive him, that indeed his father hardly recalled the incident and that what memory there was troubled his father not in the least.

Perhaps all of these incidents - the exchange between brothers as young, and then old, men, and the Professor's experience of both - came to little, and yet in the days and weeks that followed the Professor had found himself preoccupied: how many of his own exchanges, he wondered, grew strange and powerful and disparate connotations in just this same way? He could clearly recall how, as a young man, he would throw himself into agonies of self-doubt and self-evaluation over the contents of the slightest interaction with a revered mentor, or the object of some other youthful infatuation. His words and actions took on, in his own mind, worlds of meaning wholly out of joint with their (he was certain) insignificance to their recipients. And how strange it was to consider that now (he did not think he was flattering himself to say) he might hold that same revered position in someone else's mind, and inspire just such self-evaluation and doubt, while in truth he gave most of his students (he hoped he was not disappointing anyone!) very little thought, assuming that they were as involved in their own spheres as he was in his.

He asked them to consider what apparatus it was by which the memory of a day or an hour or an event became merely a facet of a sentiment that pertained to many years. They felt that this or that person did not like them: could they site dates and events? Or was it merely a feeling, a sentiment, a compilation of experiences fused into a unified *sense* of reality? And how, once an event became part of this sense, was the event changed? Was it distorted by the screen through which it was now viewed, or altered by the attendant memories with which it was grouped? Was sentimentality only the mind's way of coping with too many memories? Or was it something more troubling? Was it bad that a thing became a timeless abstraction of itself, uncomplicated by specifics?

The Professor's Father, Deceased

And then his father died! The Professor remembered the viewing; he clearly recalled his horror at the unnatural way the body moved when the coffin was bumped. And yet what was a body, but form divested of content? After all, a body was only muscles and bones, minerals and elements! The thoughts that ran around the meat of the brain and which were called the most essential self were nothing but electrical impulses dancing across a circuit board. And soon enough they ceased dancing! Did the same essential self still live in the muscles and bones, the elements and minerals? Of course not! And yet it was with the oddest sort of morbid sentimentality that they ordered him buried in his favorite suit, and were certain that he appreciated the words they spoke over him. Perhaps there was no greater sentimentality than that of the living for the dead!

The Professor's Friend as Pygmalion

It was nearing the end of the hour. The Professor looked over his notes; if there was nothing else, then he would leave them with the following story. His friend came to him in an ill humor: the girl he was seeing refused to perform one very specific sexual act. All of his other requests she honored! The Professor had reassured him; this act was no great thing! Its pleasure was inferior by far to many of those acts which she had performed and continued to perform without hesitation. Yet his friend was resolute; he could never again be satisfied bedding her, having discovered this boundary!

How long and how passionately his friend had spoken of it! Finally, to change the subject, the Professor suggested that his friend change his tune: he should beg for something more extreme, and let her imagine that he was growing bored in bed. He then instructed his friend to cancel a couple of dates, but not in an off-hand way! Each time it was necessary to provide a satisfactory reason for the cancellation. But – and this was most important! – he should not indicate that the alternative he was going to was in any way less desirable than the date he was missing. He should let her believe that it was all the same to him! Then, when he was with her again, he should answer vaguely about their time apart. But he should not obviously evade he questions! If he allowed his thoughts to wander, the Professor told his friend, the girl would suspect that he was growing bored with her. In very little time, he assured his friend, she would amend her perversions to include those acts he so yearned for.

However, the oddest thing had happened! For not long after their conversation, his friend's relationship had ended. Suspecting that his advice had played a part in it, and fearing his friend's annoyance with him, the Professor made to avoid his friend. But they'd met, by chance, soon after in a bar. His friend had already had several drinks, and stopped him as he made to leave. His friend was glad to see him! Citing his fears, the Professor confessed his avoidance. His friend, however, laughed; the Professor had no need to worry! He'd ended the relationship himself; it was the strangest thing!

He had followed the Professor's advice exactly, and had asked for the most perverse thing he could imagine. He cancelled three consecutive dates, and allowed his thoughts to wander when he was with her. He found that, by feigning boredom, he actually was bored – pretending to be bored gave him the liberty to act as he felt! Further, when he allowed himself to imagine the limits of his perversions, he found that they did not even begin with the act which, for months, had seemed the be-all and end-all of his sexual possibilities. He was, at the time of his telling, seeing three women, each more perverted than the next, and could hardly have been happier.

The Class Is Dismissed

Everyone laughed, and the Professor stacked his notes; that was it for today! He wished them all a pleasant weekend. The Student went into the lobby and called the Girl; had she eaten dinner? She thought that she was not supposed to wait for him! Did that mean she'd already eaten? What did he think? Why was she doing this? All he wanted to know was if she'd already eaten! He was calling to see if she wanted him to bring something back; perhaps he should not have bothered! Was she hungry? Did she want him to bring her something? She didn't care. That was fine; he hung up. The other students were leaving, and he joined the crowd of them as they exited the building. He took the letter from his pocket and read it over once again. No one took any notice. The two beside him laughed at something; he was disgusted by their self-involvement. How could they leave a class such as the one they had just attended and return instantly to themselves, their own base thoughts? The answer was obvious: they had no regard for philosophy or art; they were tourists in the realm of the intangible, the eternal, the profound! They could never understand the heart that beat within him: the heart that sought to deconstruct, to understand, to know! No: theirs was the shallow and gaudy spectacle of life; they would never know what it meant to dwell amongst its mysteries!

The Letter, Reexamined

Yes; he stood as one atop a line between poles, slung above a raging void which threatened always to consume him. The horrors of life at all times confronted him; he was not made for this world! The slightest thing sent him reeling in agonies of self-doubt; his self-importance was matched only by his self-loathing! And here was the letter in his hand; horrified, he folded it and returned it to his pocket. What had he hoped? That someone would see him reading the letter, and ask after its contents! Hadn't he privately hoped that the Professor, perhaps having heard of his achievement, would publicly praise him, congratulate him before the class? Hadn't he felt a secret disappointment when class ended and his accomplishment went unheralded?

Why did he imagine that his achievement merited their regard? Truly it was of no great consequence! And to think that, hours earlier, he had looked upon himself as one appointed to some near-sacred post: the Flower of the Coming Generation! How ridiculous; how laughable! And yet he had looked down upon his peers, sneering at the ways they were unlike him. But how effortlessly they went through life! They who did not see themselves upon a line slung between poles; oh God! How ridiculous he must have seemed before the grant-awarding panel, speaking of the artist's duty to truth, of the veiled profound! His grandiose tone, his lofty and ill-defined ambitions paraded his unmistakable and unending naiveté. Doubtless the award was the result not of their esteem but of their indulgence. Yes: they had laughed at him later and, finding his passion remarkable and his project acceptable, awarded him the grant with condescending beneficence and the lowest possible expectations for the work he would produce.

Inexperience

Yes, he was just like Pygmalion! Inexperienced Pygmalion, despiser of women, who knew little, who viewed the world with disdain from his hermitage, who laughed at those who engaged with life and struggled amongst its complications! But of course a moment of action was worth more than a lifetime of thought: living in the world granted one a position superior to all of those reclused from it, all of those who snickered from their garrets and dreamed of immortal vindication against the world which wounded them!

Yes: he had railed against sentimentality as the enemy of art, but what was his own work if not sentimental? What else could it be, when he had no experience to draw from, no engagement with the world to lend it substance? Who was he to presume to write with authority about anything at all? The Flower of the Coming Generation, somehow endowed with the insight to transcend experience, to know more deeply, feel more deeply? Ha! Looking out into the world he saw only his own assignations - this thing was this or that; these people were such and such! – and mistook these for Truth!

Yes; he had divested the world's forms of their content, and reassigned them with his own! There was no worse sentimentality: no more obvious immaturity! The products of his labors were irrevocably stained by his undeniable inexperience: they were an embarrassing jumble, an unreadable mess, a monument to his wretchedness, indicative of nothing redeeming!

A Painful Blunder

He returned to her room; finding her still on the couch he lay down beside her and wept. What was wrong? He shook his head; nothing, everything, himself, the world! He didn't know; he didn't know! The world was an unbearable place; he was certain that he could not endure a lifetime! He was hounded by tireless thoughts; his mind endlessly bedeviled him! She had no idea! Whatever was good or pleasant he could not help but dismiss; whatever was mean and brutish shone, in his mind, with the luster of irrefutable truth! How he wished he could be like others: others who saw only what was before them, who felt only the low animal reactions their immediate experience produced! But no: the world disintegrated under his scrutiny; even in his horror it remained only grist to the ceaseless mill of thought!

She had been listening quietly, but now gave a laugh; he thought life was easy for everyone, and difficult only for him? Life was not easy for anyone! Others felt just as he felt; he was not the only one! And what did he mean, he was certain he could not endure a lifetime? And was she, too, dismissed with the pleasant and the good?

He was startled by her outburst, and stopped crying. He began to formulate an explanation: that was not what he meant; his criticisms did not include her! But thinking of these explanations he became almost instantly annoyed. Why should he have to explain himself? And who was she to demand his silence or his discretion? He had meant the things he'd said! He'd spoken only truth! Further, he'd spoken to her as one speaking to one's closest confidante; he spoke with trust that his emotions were sacred, inviolate! How painfully he had been mistaken!

He was filled with hatred: yes, he hated her; she had betrayed his most intimate trust! He could no longer stand to be near her. He rose from the couch and, cursing himself for his blunder, left her apartment.

A Bisected Mannequin Left in Her Place

His telephone was ringing as he entered his room. He exclaimed a spiteful laugh; so she was calling already, sorry for what she had said? Well she could keep her apologies for a while! He let the phone ring. What a poetic scene! The Girl calling in a panic, hoping to find him at

home, so sorry for having hurt him! And he: mute, resolute, stoical; even if they reconciled there were sure to be
irrevocable changes! Yes; the boy became distant and the
Girl, realizing this alteration's origin, cursed herself,
begged him to let her in! She would never again speak to
him as she had; she had not understood, then, the depth of
his pain!

The answering machine picked up; hello? Was he
there? It was his mother! Listen: she'd been thinking!
What if she and his father drove down tomorrow and took
him and his girlfriend to dinner, to celebrate? She wanted
to do something special for him and besides: she wanted to
meet his girlfriend, and see where he went to school!
Okay? So he should call her back and let her know! She
loved him! Goodbye!

He thought suddenly and seemingly without provoca-
tion of something that had happened that morning: the
Girl, rising from bed, had climbed over him and turned so
that, kneeling on the edge of the bed, her naked rear was
uppermost as she reached to the floor for her clothes; her
organ, blatant and uncovered, held gracelessly aloft and
viewed from an odd angle, had failed to inspire in him the
slightest longing, was wholly and surprisingly divested of
its enchantment.

His disinterest had startled him: a few hours earlier that
place had consumed him, had interrupted his every
thought! Now it seemed unremarkable, almost inhuman: as
though the legs, rear, and organ belonged not to her, but to
a bisected mannequin left in her place!

She turned and, seeing that he was watching her,
blushed; she had thought that he was still asleep! God, but
that must have been a sight to wake up to! She covered
herself with the blanket. The image had remained present
to him for hours, filling him with an odd and unintelligible

disgust. He'd turned with uncharacteristic vigor to his class work, hoping to flush it from his thoughts. It was a relief to remember that, seeing her again that afternoon, the image had not come instantly to mind. Recalling it now, he envisioned a dinner scene in which he, his mother and father, and the Girl's bare legs, naked rear, and blatant organ sat at a table; his mother, too polite to say anything, nevertheless regarded him with obvious disappointment.

He wanted desperately to explain that he felt nothing for the bare legs and blatant organ: presented in this way, they failed to inspire in him even the slightest longing! His mother shook her head: they were going to have a nice dinner; they would talk about it later!

He burst out laughing: what a strange thing to imagine; what a ridiculous scene! He called his mother to confirm the arrangements.

The Paragon of Tolerance

His mother was delighted; where did he want to go? She would call and make the reservations! And if that place was full, was there a second place that she should try? But she was practically beside herself; she and his father were so proud of him! And they were so excited to meet his girlfriend! He interrupted: the Girl was not his girlfriend! His mother was confused; oh, she was sorry! She'd been under the impression that they were seeing a lot of each other, spending a lot of time together! But perhaps she was guilty of leaping to conclusions! The Student relented; his mother was not wrong! It was only that the word stank of the petty and the bourgeois; it lived in high school hallways and on telephone lines between vapid blondes gone comatose over their latest crushes! It was a horrible word, a philistine word! His mother apologized; she had not meant to upset him!

He had a sudden, clear sense of his mother: earnest, affectionate, yet painfully simple! Her perception seemed to penetrate no farther than the obvious world: this thing was this; this other thing was that! A girl he was seeing a lot of became ipso facto his girlfriend! The spectrum of possibilities, the subtleties of relation were all seemingly negated by the assignment of that name! The Girl was not his girlfriend: she was more! The Girl was not his girl-friend: she was less! And yet his mother's satisfied mind desired no greater understanding; he could imagine only too clearly her polite disinterest should he try to explain.

No: his mother's world was fixed, stagnant: the things that arose were recognized only by their resemblance to those forms, those precepts, which preexisted their appear-ance, which were sewn together to form the very fabric of her perception! No more room for new experience! No more room for new understanding!

And yet: what horror! For the world that surrounded her was dull, false, closed: a world in which the proud par-ents took their son out to dinner to celebrate his accom-plishment! How silly it seemed: how arbitrary! And here he stood before her; he saw and understood her at a glance!

Seeing her thus encapsulated he pitied her; yes, he pit-ied her as one pitying the physically handicapped. For what was she guilty of but a spiritual handicap, an inability to see beyond herself, beyond the closed circuits of her own thoughts? He was convinced that, had his mother wit-nessed the report from Ethiopia, she too would have seen only a woman weeping for the world's unintelligible hor-rors. Yes: this was this; this other thing was that! Any speculation otherwise, he could expect, would be met only with her polite but final disinterest. What could he do? Even Christ could not unstop the ears of the indifferent!

Lauding himself privately as the paragon of tolerance, he assured his mother that it was of no great importance. Certainly the Girl was his girlfriend; he could not wait for them to meet her! Basking in the glow of his own altruism, he ended the conversation and hung up the phone.

The Student Declares That He Is Above Reproach

But now: how best to approach the Girl? The fact that it was his mother on the telephone and not her seemed an intentional oversight; as though she had not merely failed to call, but had decided not to, to punish him! How obnoxiously didactic! For a moment he could hardly stand to think of her. A wave of violent repulsion took hold of him; he threw himself face-down on the bed. This repulsion quickly passed, and was followed by a surprising calm. He felt wholly detached from and indifferent to his life and its situations; he felt terribly sleepy!

And why not: he could now see that he had not slept well during the last week, wracked as he was with anxiety over the award's announcement. But – at last! – the week was finished; he felt the letter crumpling beneath his body, and was filled with profound relief. His former irritation, his impatience with the Girl – even his fervent defense of art! – struck him now as silly: why did it bother him that his mother was the reporter of his life, or that the Girl had other boyfriends before him? Neither reduced him in the least! And yet he had railed against each as though to admit its existence was to forever surrender the fortress of his self. How like a child!

He knew just how to approach the Girl: he would act as though nothing had happened, as though the recent memory of the episode did not trouble him in the least! Yes: to admit his behavior was to in no way surrender the fortress of his self! True he had wept, had left her apartment without a backward glance, but what of it? He was passionate, was prone to moods: he was an Artist! Such eccentricities could not be thrown out without also discarding his gifts, his unique perspective!

Perhaps only a madman would act in such a way, but then: perhaps he was a madman! What of it? One could hardly call the world sane! Yes, his behavior was in perfect harmony with his being: he was the great writer in his youth, the Flower of the Coming Generation! In the decades to come such episodes would comprise his legend. Yes: his ardent dismissal of the weeping Newscaster was akin to Hemingway's stoic bravado; Kafka, too, was hounded by familial difficulties! Yes: each incident, viewed through the inaccurate lens of public sentimentality, carrying the full weight and status of history, would paint him more clearly: deeply flawed, perhaps, but above reproach!

The Collapsed Person

He would show her, with his manner, that his felt his actions were above reproach! He left his room and went downstairs. There was a commotion in the lobby; someone had collapsed. A crowd had gathered around the place. An ambulance was backed up onto the sidewalk outside, and paramedics were loading the collapsed person onto a gurney. What had happened? No one in the crowd knew for certain: the collapsed person was a diabetic! No, the collapsed person had epilepsy! No, it was none of those things; someone who knew the collapsed person had said that they had neither. Most likely the collapsed person was only drunk; perhaps they were drugged! Perhaps it was an allergic reaction! Perhaps it was dehydration! Whatever it was, the collapsed person did not appear to be breathing! The paramedics were in a fantastic hurry; they lifted the gurney into the ambulance and drove away at tremendous speed. With the ambulance gone there was nothing else to see. The crowd began to disperse; a few students stood beside the door. One of them was crying; should they go to the hospital? They should go to the hospital! Could anyone drive? The Student left the dormitory and headed for the Girl's apartment.

The Speaker on Environmental Ethics

But the Girl was not at home. He started back to the dormitory but then remembered: the biology department was hosting a speaker that night in one of the lecture halls; a week earlier the Girl had suggested that they attend. He had demurred: that night was the night he would know the result of his grant application, and he did not want to commit to going; what if he was in a foul mood? Certainly she had gone without him! He headed toward the building where the lecture was being held. He would no doubt arrive as the speaker was finishing, and catch her in the lobby; he would show her, with his manner, that the events of the past few hours were of no great importance, were, in fact, completely forgotten!

The speaker was far from finished. He spoke at great length about the need for conservation; he cited numerous instances of man's disastrous impact. His voice trembled with emotion; he struck the podium with his open palm. His speech was punctuated by the audience's passionate applause. He sighed heavily into the microphone; he thanked them for their enthusiasm, even though it broke his heart! It broke his heart because he knew that most of them would leave the lecture hall with no intent to change! And he knew that others would change for a while: for one, or two, or in some cases six months they would take shorter showers, would ride a bicycle or take the bus instead of drive! But in every roomful of students he knew that there were only a few who would take his message to heart, who would change for good! Yes: he thanked them for their enthusiasm now, but his thanks came with a challenge! Would they be one of the hundreds who changed just for a little while, or one of the few who changed for good? He slapped the podium with his palm; he thanked them all for coming! The audience stood and applauded. The Student went into the lobby to wait for the Girl.

A half an hour later she had not come out. He was certain that he could not have missed her; perhaps she had not come after all! He took a look inside the lecture hall and spotted her; she was standing in front of the stage with six other students, talking to the speaker. He went back into the lobby to wait. A while later she was still inside. He looked in; she was one of only three students left. The speaker checked his watch and then hugged each of them. She started up the aisle, and waved when she saw him. The Student left the doorway and went out into the lobby to wait for her. But she did not come immediately over to him; she walked with the other students to the door. When they had gone out she hurried over and embraced him; had he heard the speaker? And wasn't he amazing? God, she'd never felt so inspired!

The Student scoffed: poetics and rhetoric! Certainly the speaker had made some decent points. But his message was marred and reduced by his ceaseless emoting: one could hardly discern his point amidst his overwhelming mannerism! Good God: his approach was that of a revival preacher, his tactics the same as those used to whip the ignorant into a tumult of religious frenzy! Of all the obvious propaganda: of all the artless manipulation! And to lament that his audience would not change: how laughable! What more could he expect, when he played solely to the emotions? Emotions were essentially transient! What could his audience have but the most fleeting response? Indeed: he could hardly keep from laughing at the speaker's lament!

Lysistrata, or *The Student Admits His Mistake*

He followed her back to her apartment. She undressed and got into bed. He undressed and climbed in beside her. He touched her, but she gave no indication of having noticed. His parents were driving down tomorrow; they wanted to take him to dinner and wanted her to come. They really wanted to meet her; they wanted to meet his girlfriend! She did not say anything.

He was sorry! He was sorry for what he had said. All right? Was that what she wanted? He was sorry for having mocked the speaker. He did not realize she cared that much! What more did she want him to say? He was sorry!

He waited for her to say something. She did not say anything. After a while he began to suspect that she was asleep. He whispered her name; she gave no indication that she had heard him. He shook his head; of course she would not make any response, even if she were awake! He turned to face away from her. A while later she bumped into him and he woke up. But she was only climbing out of bed; he watched her leave and heard her go into the bathroom. He tried to stay awake until she returned, but dozed and woke with her already back in bed. He was not certain how long she had been there, and did not want to wake her if she was already asleep.

The Collapsed Person, Revisited

She had a breakfast meeting with one of her professors, and was gone when he awoke. He dressed and went back to his room. On the stairs he recognized one of the students who had stood beside the door as the collapsed person was taken out. What had became of the collapsed person? The other shook his head; no one had any idea! The collapsed person was not intoxicated, nor did they suffer from any medical condition. The doctors were really puzzled! They had ordered a number of tests; the collapsed person would be in the hospital all weekend. The Student really should go and visit! A bunch of them were headed down later in the afternoon; he could ride with them! The Student explained that his parents were coming, and he did not have time.

The Student Feels That Existence Is an Overwhelming Sadness

Yes, his parents were coming; he shuddered at the thought! The prospect of an evening spent enduring his mother's constant and meaningless praise, his father's ridiculous, undue, and inappropriate gravitas, filled him with dread. He could hardly stand to be around them! Yes: his happiest day was the one on which he was finally able to leave their place for this one; his greatest joy was watching them drive away! Finally his own life could begin: a life uncordoned by their example, incentives, and reproach!

Yet he himself had agreed to – had invited! – their visit; he'd called his mother as soon as he learned the results of his application. How odd! He shook his head in disgust. He had sought out her praise like an anxious child; what the hell was he thinking? The only appropriate celebration was to forgo celebration, and begin writing immediately! Yet the impulse to tell her was so powerful as to negate any refusal he might have felt; he could not help but call and, like a child, seek her praise!

And there was the difficult truth: he could not help it because he was indeed a praise-seeking child!

He saw himself standing upon the threshold of this thought; here an average mind would turn back, would refuse the painful sight of its own mechanism! But his was not an average mind! Yes: what he felt now was the impulse to self-preservation; here was the first trick of many his mind would use to hide from him the truth of his own being! But he would not be tricked! Yes: the shudder he felt at the thought of their arrival was not at their failings but at his own: it was not his mother's affection nor his father's gravitas which pained him, but the unendurable shame of having invited both, having so artlessly sought their approval!

Walking beside his parents the other students would see not the great writer in their midst, the Flower of the Coming Generation, but a child attempting to drape itself in the ill-fitting garb of maturity. His former bearing and gravitas, his criticism and praise, the authority he had claimed, were all that of a child at play in a world of adults: self-important, ridiculous, laughable!

What could he know of life, he who disguised within his over-loud etudes a child's hunger for its mother's praise? Nothing: he knew nothing of life! Yes: his prose was false and uninformed! He had fooled the panel; he had fooled himself! But the truth was now too obvious to ignore; entering his room he again threw himself down on the bed and wept. How he loathed himself! He was a pompous, parading child, laughed at by the world! How could one such as this write anything worth anything? Of course he could not!

Yet he had been certain that he was the Flower of the Coming Generation; he had looked down on others from his self-exalted place above them! He had walked through life in the all-encircling haze of this profound delusion; oh God, he was insane! He could not bear it; he gasped for breath. He was falling; yes, falling into the inescapable void! He was nothing: the self he sought to assert upon the world was only unfounded claims and over-grandiose poetics! Oh black despair! He clutched the blankets to his face. Existence was an overwhelming sadness; sorrow oppressed him! What a blessing it would have been to have died at birth, to have never been born at all!

Galatea, or *The Student Feels That He Understands the Girl*

He understood the Girl; he knew what misery it was to love him! Love? Yes, love! They had not yet spoken the word, and yet it was obvious to him now: she loved him, and he loved her! Yes: he felt a love more powerful than anything he had ever experienced; he felt a love which cared nothing for itself! He felt a love which devalued the world; she stood opposite a raging void! Only by clinging to her could he keep from falling. And he knew she felt the same; yes, he knew it beyond any doubt! Even if she did not understand herself he knew. And yet he had made it so hard for her to love him; he knew clearly her frustration and pain! She stood opposite the raging void, and yet he gave her only the narrowest ledges on which to stand, the smallest edges on which to cling! Yes: his acceptance of her love was necessary! What horror, to love a stone! How could he have been so heartless? How could he have been so blind? It was inexcusable; there was no excuse!

Yet she had loved him regardless; he was filled with admiration. She possessed a strength he could never achieve: the strength to love at the expense of oneself, to continue to love when one's love had gone unnoticed, unacknowledged! This strength seemed to lie at the root of her being; it was with this same strength that she had been moved by the speaker on environmental ethics! Yes: to invest oneself fully when the problem was so vast, so overwhelming, was something he was certain he could never do. The risk of failure was too great: to care was to risk a broken heart! And yet she did; he was awestruck by her. How horrible, that it took this same courage to love him; how could he ceaselessly threaten her with a broken heart? He was filled with disgust.

"Her Love Was a Courageous Love…'"

He suddenly panicked: what if this understanding toppled into a mess of disjointed thoughts and logical strands leading nowhere? It often happened that an idea evaporated before he had time to commit it to paper; would the same occur, before he'd had a chance to speak with her? He left his room and ran to her apartment. Was she there? He had to speak with her!

She opened the door; he stepped inside and embraced her. She laughed; what was this? He loved her; he loved her! He was sorry; he was so sorry! He was stupid and crazy and he knew how hard it was for her to care about him and he was so grateful that she did and he did not know what he would do without her! He was sorry for what he had said about the speaker and he did not think it was stupid and he loved that she got excited about it and he did not ever want to discourage her ever again because her love was a courageous love and if he did anything to extinguish it he would be committing the worst sin that he could imagine!

He broke down into sobs; she led him to the couch and lay down beside him. After a while she touched him and he stopped crying. They undressed; he said again that he loved her and she replied that she loved him as well. Afterwards he said that his parents were arriving soon, and he had to get cleaned up. They agreed on a time to meet for dinner. He rose from the couch and got dressed. He left her apartment with the sudden, clear sense that he had to get away from her as quickly as possible.

The Student Reunites With His Parents

They were standing in the lobby when he returned. He hugged his mother: he was sorry, but did not realize he was keeping them waiting; he had not expected them for another half an hour! His mother shook her head; it was all right! It was their own fault; they'd made very good time on the drive down. His father took a picture of them. Could his son believe they'd made the drive in just under three hours? And on a weekend! The Student said that he could not believe it.

His mother grew suddenly serious; was he feeling all right? They'd been speaking with the woman at the front desk; had he heard anything about a student collapsing in the lobby? Apparently some student had simply collapsed; the woman at the front desk had called the ambulance! No one seemed to know what was wrong with the collapsed person; it made his mother very nervous! She knew that he thought he was invincible, but if the student who collapsed was sick then he had to be very careful! Dormitories were notorious for enabling the spread of disease; she didn't want anything to happen to him! Could he blame her? She was his mother; she loved him!

His father looked him over; did he have any different clothes? The restaurant where he'd made the reservation did not allow blue jeans. And did he have a collared shirt? He could not imagine that a restaurant that did not allow blue jeans would allow tee-shirts! They certainly had time to go and pick one up for him if he did not. Although – damn! – they could as easily have brought him one from home! If only they'd thought of it. They would have to remember, next time, to bring an outfit for him.

But how was he? They had not seen him in ages! It really was something to see: his son, the college boy! No - he excused himself - college *man*! Yes, his son was all grown up, ready to start a life of his own; it was hard to believe that not long ago he was just a little guy! He shook his head; it really was amazing! One day, when he had children of his own, his son would understand.

What time were the reservations? His father checked his watch; not for a little while! There was plenty of time for him to show them around. And his mother was dying to meet his girlfriend! And pictures: his mother wanted them to take lots of pictures! They left the dormitory. Walking across the quad his father stepped off the path and got mud on his shoes. He cursed loudly; he had not brought another pair! His wife hurried to his side; if he waited until the mud dried, he could scrape it off and then wash away whatever was left with a damp towel! He spoke to her sharply: the shoes were suede; he could not merely wash the mud off! Well she was certain he could have them cleaned when they got home; yes, why not worry about it when they got home?

His father did not seem to be listening; he turned his back and kicked the muddy edge against the grass. The Student looked around, and was grateful to see no one he recognized. He made a joke: did the restaurant allow muddy shoes? Perhaps neither one of them would be allowed in! His father looked at him with obvious annoyance.

The Soiled Shoe

There: the mud was coming off! Now if they would just give him some room to walk on the path, maybe it would not happen again! His wife apologized. She would let the men of the family go ahead! She fell in step behind them. Why didn't he tell them about the grant? She knew his father wanted to hear about it! His father looked up from his shoes to nod his head. Yes, he wanted very much to hear about the grant! He thought it was fantastic; he was so proud! He went back to watching his feet. He leaned against a tree and ran the soiled edge back and forth across the grass. He looked up; he was listening! He inspected the top and sides of the shoe.

His Father's Injury

Wait: she wanted a picture of them! She told the Student to move closer to his father. The Student did as he was told. And she wanted to see where his classes were held! And where did he get his mail? And where did he do his laundry? And was he getting enough to eat? Sometimes it was hard to eat a balanced diet with a college student's lifestyle; she had just been reading an article about it! Was he getting enough variety in his meals? And had he had any cause to visit the medical center? And did the medical staff there seem competent?

Wait: she wanted a picture of them here as well! The Student was not smiling in that one; she wanted him to smile! The Student did as he was told. His father's arm was heavy across his shoulders. His mother aimed the camera. Everyone hold still! She took the picture, and the Student slipped from beneath his father's arm. His father gave an exclamation of pain. His wife let the camera dangle from the tether around her wrist, and rushed over to him. The Student asked what was wrong. His mother explained: his father had hurt his shoulder the other day, moving some of the Student's things into the basement. His father clasped his shoulder with the opposite hand, and slowly circled the injured arm. He stared at his son with a look of anger and annoyance. His wife, standing beside him, rubbed his back; was he all right? Was it all right? He shook his head; he didn't know! He made a circle with the arm and grimaced in pain. The pain seemed to reverberate through his wife as well.

It was all right; he undid one of the buttons on his shirt front and worked it into the cuff of the injured arm. This was what they did in the Air Force for a makeshift sling! There: he relaxed his arm. His elbow dropped to his side and the pinned wrist pulled open his shirt where it was not buttoned closed, revealing a diamond of white undershirt. He smiled at his son: nothing to worry about! But now he wanted to hear all about the grant; he thought it was just wonderful that the Student had won! He put his uninjured arm around the Student's shoulders as they began to walk.

Punctuality

49

His father checked his watch. But now they were running short on time; the Student had better go get cleaned up! They did not want to be late for their reservations. He left them at the campus coffee shop and hurried back to his room. Once inside he called the Girl; was she going to be ready to go to dinner soon? And what was she going to wear? It was only that his father had made it very clear that they should look nice! She said that she would look nice.

He hung up, took a shower, and changed his clothes, then hurried to her apartment. She answered the door and he rolled his eyes; that was what she was wearing? Yes: what was wrong with it? He threw up his hands in exasperation: nothing, it was fine! Could they go now? His father was very easily upset when it came to punctuality! She had to go back inside to get something first; he closed his eyes in obvious frustration. She came back out and closed the door. He hurried her across the lawn to the coffee shop.

He could see his parents through the coffee shop window: his father checked his watch with an expression of obvious irritation. The Student felt a sudden wave of hatred. He slowed to a casual walk. His father, seeing him, stood from his chair, his sleeve still fashioned into a makeshift sling.

The Student stopped and turned to the Girl: he was sorry, she looked beautiful! He had no excuse for the way he was acting! Being around his parents was very stressful for him. Could they just have a pleasant evening? She could be as angry with him as she wanted afterwards; she could hit him and call him names! But he needed to know that she was on his side. Facing all of them at once was too much for him to handle. She gave no indication of having heard him; she stood still and stared straight ahead. He really was sorry; he began to explain again, but was interrupted by a strange noise. He turned around; his father knocked three more times on the window, then pressed his watch to the glass. The Student took her hand and led her inside. In the hallway outside the coffee shop she stopped him and hugged him; she was always on his side!

His parents came out of the coffee shop. The Student introduced everyone. His father offered her his left hand and apologized: they'd had a little incident on the tour! He looked meaningfully at his son, then checked his watch; well, they really should be going! They did not want to be late for their reservation. They walked to the car, and his mother insisted that the Student sit in the front seat. They waited while his father unbuttoned the cuff from his shirtfront. The Student turned on the radio, but his father turned it off: he was certain that everyone would rather get to know everyone than listen to the radio! The Student turned to the window and listened to the Girl as she answered his mother's questions.

The Tragedy in Ethiopia, Revisited

Had they seen the special report about the famine in Ethiopia? The situation over there was really unbelievable; it had brought the Newscaster to tears! It was enough to break one's heart! Sometimes she thought it should be a requirement for college students to learn what was really going on in their world. Did the Girl get the feeling that her fellow students were well-informed about world events? Did they know about the tragedy in Ethiopia?

And what did he think? He laughed: he thought the subject was ridiculous! Oh, it made everyone sad when the pretty blond Newscaster shed a tear for the starving Africans: it made him sick! He whole-heartedly assured them that the Newscaster felt nothing for those dying around her. How could she? She did not know them at all, did not speak their language, had not heard their stories! She was there to wear the mask of tragedy; they were paying her to cry!

Sentimentality: it was the worst kind of sentimentality! They wanted tragedy? There was no shortage of tragedy in daily life! Every silence between couples was a tragedy; every minute failure was a tragedy! And yet it was the situation half a world away - and with which they had no personal experience! – which was imbued with undue emotion; it made him laugh! They knew nothing of Ethiopia or of starvation; on what grounds did they feel anything? This tragedy was not theirs to claim!

The Collapsed Person, Re-examined

Or the collapsed person: his mother knew nothing of the collapsed person! And yet she had immediately responded with a swell of emotion: he had to be careful; dormitories were notorious for enabling the spread of disease! And yet there was little grounds for this response: the cause of the collapse was unknown and perhaps unknowable! Her heart had leapt to its own conclusions, and the rational quest for understanding fell by the wayside. But to live like this was to live in perpetual ignorance: it was to look at the world always from inside the half-distorted lens of one's own emotional certainty about truth, regardless of the reality! He was certain that, were it later revealed that the collapsed person was drunk, or otherwise incapacitated as a result of their own doing, his mother would not admit this fact entry into the over-partial realm of her worldview.

The Student's Father Intervenes

That was quite enough! He would not sit idly by while the Student insulted his mother! The Student was incredulous; what had he said to insult her? He was speaking in generalities; any citation of his mother's behavior was not an indictment, but a suggestion! His father interrupted him: the Student knew very well what he had said; he would have no more of it!

The Student Is Disappointed

The Student turned and stared out the window. The conversation in the back seat resumed. They arrived at the restaurant and went inside. The Student sat, but his father cleared his throat and remained standing in order to assist the Student's mother in taking her seat. The Girl, obviously unsure of what to do, looked from the Student to his father. The Student rose, but his father arrived at her chair before him and assisted the Girl himself.

The Student, still standing, excused himself; he left the restaurant and took a seat on a bench outside. He felt certain that the Girl would come after him. Yet he knew this certainty to be unfounded: the bathrooms were beside the entrance, and it was likely that she'd assumed, as he was certain his parents had, that that was where he was going. Still, he could not shake the feeling that she would somehow know where he was, and pursue him. But after ten minutes it became clear that she did not, and was not coming. He rose from the bench and went back inside.

The Flower of the Coming Generation, Revisited

His father met him in the entryway. What did he think he was doing? They'd been three hours on the road to spend some time with him! He did not know what his son's problem was, but he expected him to get over it and be pleasant for the rest of the time they were together. That was not so much to ask! The hand on his injured arm was hooked into his suit coat pocket, and the elbow hung limp against his ribs. Had he made himself clear? Had he? He expected to see his son a changed boy when he came back to the table!

The Student said that he had to go to the bathroom. His father did as well. They went into the bathroom: his father went to the urinal and the Student went into the stall and closed the door. He stood, staring at the toilet. He could hear his father breathing. The sound was amplified by the tiled walls. Then that sound was joined by the hiss of his father's urine. After a while this sound stopped. It was followed by a long silence. Then he heard his father go out. The Student closed his eyes and imagined that his parents were gone. He wished that they would go; he could no longer stand to be near them!

But when he opened his eyes the rest of the evening still lay before him. He left the stall and considered his reflection in the angled mirror. His father was right: he looked much better in the outfit that he was wearing now than he had in what he was wearing when he met them. This observation somehow exhausted him. He leaned heavily against the sink; he did not have the strength to face them! Perhaps it was ridiculous, but then: what of it? He was too weak to face the world; he would make no apologies! Flowers were also weak; yes, flowers were too weak to survive very long, lived best in well-kept beds, thrived when doted upon, leached components from the base soil to produce a single, beautiful, transcendent bud...

He'd been more right than he'd realized, to call himself the Flower of the Coming Generation! Yes: that was exactly it, for more reasons than one! For a moment he stood in reverence of his own intellect and insight. Certainly his was a mind unlike any other; the panel had been correct to award him the honor!

Thinking this, he felt much better. He left the bathroom and went back to the table. His arrival was followed almost immediately by the arrival of the waiter. He ordered with complete indifference. How did he want that prepared? However the chef saw fit! And what kind of dressing? Whichever one the waiter preferred! And what to drink? Champagne: they were celebrating! The waiter looked at the Student's father, who laughed apologetically and said that water was fine. The waiter took the rest of their orders and went away.

His Life's Great Reporter, Revisited

An uncomfortable silence followed the waiter's departure. His mother turned to the Girl; she was so glad the Girl had been able to join them! She'd been so hoping that she would get a chance to speak with someone who'd read her son's more recent work; her son did not let her read anything anymore! Honestly: she had not read anything he'd written in the last four years! Could she even imagine? His own mother!

Had she read any of his earlier short stories? Oh, but he must let her read this or that story! And had she read this or that one? She had not? Why, then she would tell the Girl all about it! It was the most wonderful story; his mother did not know where he got his ideas! They were so proud of him; yes, they certainly were proud of him!

Listening to this, the Student was filled with hatred; yes, he hated that the award gave them pleasure! The award offered them an intolerable intrusion into his most secret inner life; no one would fault them their graceless intrusions into the most private regions of his being! How was his writing going? And what was he writing these days? It was none of their God-damned business! Yet the public nature of the award gave them the right to ask: it was wholly intolerable; he could not bear it! He wished that he had never won the award; he would just as soon give it back! Yes: he would rather relinquish the award and work in private, and never again admit to having written a single word.

The Student Again Feels That He Is Pygmalion

The Girl answered that she had read some of the Student's more recent work and that his mother should be very proud: the Student was a very talented writer! Of course she did not have to tell them; it was obvious! After all: he was the youngest recipient in the history of the grant; that was certainly something! But disregarding the Student's more material successes, she was certain he felt a greater pride at the success of each individual piece; which was to say that the Student was amazingly adept at both setting lofty goals for his stories, and achieving them! What she meant to say was that artists were plagued with a chronic sense of failure: one could never achieve in the physical form that which was seen so clearly in the mind! And yet the Student seemed unhampered by this condition: the clarity and control he displayed in his writing, the skill with which he maneuvered his reader through a story, his ability to create an ending both satisfying and surprising, never failed to amaze her. Honestly: she stood in awe of their son!

How odd! For he instantly recognized the Girl's words: he had said these same thing to her. The explanations of his desire to maneuver a reader, to create a surprising and yet satisfying conclusion, to set lofty goals were all his own! Hadn't he expressed to her the artist's chronic sense of failure? And hadn't he used these same words?

He looked at the Girl; she smiled warmly at him. Her smile seemed not her own: no, her smile was a compliment to her praise, done in accordance with what she could only assume to be his unvoiced request for admiration. He saw, in that instant, not the Girl but some creature of his own creation: tamed, silenced, taught to speak, lauded for some behaviors and chastised for others, altered, recast, distorted, revised! Her praise came at his request; even his silence held a request! And it seemed that between himself and the Girl stood a vast distance: a distance taken up by the insulating buffer of his demand that she become, in his presence, something which she was not.

Yes: he had surrounded himself with himself; he had altered her until she'd become his mirror, his twin, his Galatea! Yes: his was the perception which demanded the world's surrender; marching beneath the heady banner of art he'd given free reign to his own worst impulses. And nowhere was it more evident than in his relationship with the Girl! Yes: he consistently forced upon her an image of herself exactly as she was not; how frustrated he became when, at some heedless moment, she let her true self show through! His irritation with her over the news report from Ethiopia, his jealousy over her previous boyfriends, his hurt at her impious response to his angst: what were these but the tantrums of a child, unwilling to accept the world as it was? And what did a child know of life? Nothing: a child knew nothing of life!

Dinner

His mother continued to praise him until the food arrived. The Student did not care for what he had ordered, and ate only as much as his father demanded. The waiter asked if anyone would care for dessert or coffee. His mother repeated the question to him; did he want any dessert? The Student said that he was fine. The waiter boxed up what was left of the Student's dinner.

Where did they want to be let out? They could drop them anywhere. The Student replied that the campus coffee shop was fine; his father pulled up to the curb and his mother got out to hug him goodbye. She was so proud of him! And it was very nice to meet the Girl! And she would see him soon! But he should not hesitate to call! His father called his goodbyes from the driver's seat. Then his mother got back into the car and they sat next to the curb, waiting for a line of cars to pass. Finally there was an opening, and his father pulled into traffic. The Student wiped his forehead in an exaggerated display of relief. The Girl gave an obligatory smile, but did not say anything. She turned and began to walk in the direction of her apartment.

A Problem

The Student caught her up; what was wrong? Was something wrong? Had his mother said something to her? Of course: he knew it! She was always ruining things; he should have told them not to come! The Girl interrupted him; it was not his mother! What was it, then? She did not want to talk about it. What was it? He had to know! It would be better if she did not say anything and besides: she was certain that she would feel differently tomorrow! She was only tired now. So could they please just forget it?

He could not forget it. If something was wrong he wanted her to tell him! What was it? What was it? They arrived at her apartment and went inside. He waited in the living room while she went and changed her clothes. But when she came out she did not offer any explanation, and he again asked what was wrong. She fell, exhausted, onto the couch. Couldn't he just forget it? It was not important!

It was important: how the hell could she say that it was not? He did not know why she insisted on playing these games with him all the time! He'd spent the last two hours dealing with his parents; he was exhausted! Why did she have to make him work for this, too? Why couldn't she just say what she was thinking, instead of this bullshit? What the hell was it? What the fuck was wrong?

It was him: he was always complaining! No one understood him, no one thought his work was good, no one supported him! And yet here were his parents: proud, loving, full of praise, supportive! He waved a warning finger and shook his head: she did not know them; she did not know what she was talking about! But this warning produced no effect, and the Girl continued regardless: her own mother never asked what she was doing, never showed the slightest interest! And yet he never heard her complain, never heard her blame her mother for her own failures!

And the funniest thing was: she was not even mad at him! No: she was mad at herself; she always did this! She always placed her experience below others; she always assumed that others had it so much worse! No matter what: even if her problems were clearly worse or deeper, she always assumed that life had been harder on the other than it had been on herself! She had all of this anger and hurt that she never let out, because she had convinced herself that it was not important enough to mention! And life: life had convinced her, her parents had convinced her! She always thought somehow she was getting past it; she always thought that a new relationship would bring with it a new dynamic. But here she was; it was funny! Six years later she was still fourteen years old, convinced that no one would ever give a damn about her stupid little experience, her stupid little feelings!

Hypocrisy

He was filled with shame and this shame produced an almost immediate rebuttal: why hadn't she told him how she felt? And why was he on trial? He'd never attempted to voice his problems at the exclusion of hers; he owned no part of the fault! Further, the thought that, as he had complained and wept, she was, in her mind, privately tabulating his hardships against her own humiliated him. How ridiculous he must have looked, all of those times he came to her to vent his anger or sorrow: how laughable his tirades! And with what self-satisfied tolerance - what smug charity! - she had listened, comforted him, all the while smirking at the smallness of his problems, the immaturity of his angst! Hypocrisy: it was the worst kind of hypocrisy!

Oh, he had not known that her life was so difficult! He was so sorry; he had not realized how bad she had it! Could she ever forgive him? Because obviously it was his fault: not knowing what she had not told him was his fault! After all: who else's fault could it be? It could not be hers: everything she did and said was perfect! Would she tell him about her old boyfriends? He loved to hear about them! Perhaps she would rather laugh at him when he came to her in despair! Or maybe she would rather keep her secrets in all of their hypocritical glory; any of that would be fine! Everything she did was fine! It made him laugh; yes, it really did!

Hypocrite? Yes, hypocrite: she misrepresented herself! She remained silent in the guise of understanding, and yet she was not interested in understanding! Her silence was the bait with which she lured out his most painful secrets; she was stockpiling his faults to use as ammunition against him! He was stupid to have trusted her!

The Student's Thoughts Are Spoken Back to Him

She was a hypocrite? He should look at himself! He spoke about engaging with the real world, claimed to seek truth, and yet he knew nothing of the world! He surrounded himself with himself: the only ideas he heard were his own, he saw in others only that which he recognized in himself! He railed against the world not for its objective failings, but for its refusal to adhere to his wishes. This person should have said this or that; this person should not think this or that; this thing was done poorly for this or that reason! He'd elevated his subjective aesthetic to a realm above the objective world, and devalued the world for its failure to rise to his standards. But the world was the world: he could not demand the world's surrender!

He did not do that; he refused to believe that he did that! No? Look at their relationship: in the time they had been together she had been wholly transformed! She could not say this or that thing, could not display interest in this or that idea, could not like this or that book, this or that movie, this or that song: she was no longer herself but only his clumsy rendering of her! He said that he loved her and yet he knew nothing of the kind of love she felt for him:

the love that would alter itself to become pleasing in its beloved's eyes!

He began to reply but, startled at hearing his own thoughts from earlier that evening spoken so succinctly, he closed his mouth. Yes, she was right: he was a hypocrite!

He felt suddenly exhausted, and sat down on the couch. After a while he excused himself, and went into the Girl's bedroom. Lifting the receiver of the telephone which sat on the bedside table he dialed the office number of the professor who had overseen the panel. He identified himself to the answering machine, and expressed his intention to relinquish the award. He was at a place in his life where he felt he could not live up to his obligation, and did not want to deny someone else this opportunity. While he was honored to have been selected, he had come to the difficult conclusion that to accept the award would, in the end, do him more harm than good, both as a writer and as a person. He thanked them for the honor and hung up the phone.

"The Sound of His Own Words..."

The sound of his own words had brought tears to his eyes: what profound nobility, what stoic resolve! In the dark bedroom his sacrifice seemed to hang in the air all around him: a masterpiece! In the decades to come such episodes would comprise his legend; Sartre, too, had refused awards! Yes: each incident, in the garish and inaccurate light of public sentimentality, carrying the full weight and status of history, would paint him more clearly: the great writer, the Flower of his Generation!

Later, after they had reconciled, after his tears and apologies, after they had made love, he left her apartment. In the parking lot outside he passed a group of students.

He passed these students as one passing the footlights on the world's stage. The night was warm, and the quiet buildings and hanging stars seemed to weep with the poetry of his failure and loss.

SIMONE ET JEAN-PAUL

"...He often wondered about the friendships and romantic relationships that sometimes formed between great thinkers: did Jean-Paul Sartre and Simone de Beauvoir, for example, fall into these same traps, or did their extensive meditations on the nature of perception and Truth lead them to some more perfect union?"

- you were my heart yes my true beating heart and when I felt you beating within me I lost all control and went mad for days running through the streets and holding discourse with all those who would listen I was a mad young man for certain it was that God-awful play I saw you through the curtain with bare arms and half-exposed breasts and what madness what can one know of another with only the knowledge of bare arms and half-exposed breasts it is a silly thing but I could not be happier no could not have been happier than later after your presentation on Leibniz when I asked you and you were cunning but agreed not for the night I had suggested but another night to shortly follow and what chance did I have knowing that you had cunning and bare arms and half-exposed breasts and I could not help running through the streets no could not help it how could I help it

- remember the winter that the spring could not seem to overtake and we did not rise from bed no not even for coffee nor toast but stayed the whole day and there was no you nor I nor subject nor object and your body was my body and my body was yours and what value does it have you said what value does it have and I wept you were bent on your postulations pressed your lips to the lips of postulation and you asked why I was crying you were young but so was I and I could not have loved you more nor felt that I received less love what value does it have and I had no answer then nor have any answer now as my pleasure in no way reduces our love's worthlessness I suppose and no eternal ledger I can hear you say it now no eternal ledger each word a hammer blow on your chisel and little pieces of me falling and I prayed each time that you were finished but no not finished never finished never going to be finished even as an old woman pieces falling away and even now with no more bodies I see your hammer poised

- and did you love me too when you pressed your lips to hers did you love me then I saw you smiling before they took me by the arms and removed me from the premises although I was not such a disturbance as they acted no not a disturbance at all but only a sad and heartbroken boy because you smiled and then they dragged me from the premises but that was what you wanted wasn't it because you came running after me and the joke was on her wasn't it because you were only using her to get to me yes that is some comfort if it is true but who knows what is true and I imagine that if you knew you would not tell but I do not think you know yourself because you are thoughtless yes insufferable crawling through life with your parts pressed to the earth leaving a trail yes behind you yes but you cannot help it can you and in that case I suppose the joke is on both of us I like Hephaestus and you like Aphrodite and I can see by your eyes that you understand but what could I do with your cunning and your bare arms and your half-exposed breasts but turn mad and run through the streets

- but you had me then and there was no more I nor thou did you not see or only refuse to believe it but it is hard to love one who does not see you how many times did you correct my thinking in what image did you hope to cast me like Pygmalion whom you detest yet resemble I was a marble prisoner beneath your ever-working chisel who am I really you do not know but know only the image you have and the unintelligible hurt you felt when I was not all that you'd hoped when I was bare arms and half-exposed breasts and you'd decided before a word was spoken between us that I was the one ridiculous sentimental man I would laugh if I did not love you so but you do not know that I love you no do not know it because I love you only as I love you and I loved you when I pressed my lips to hers and his and hers and hers and I loved you yes even

when they touched me loved you loved you could not help
but love you

- but I could not help but wish to consume your body
yes clutch it to me clutch it to me clutch it to me and for all
I understood I never understood enough to stop myself
from clinging

- hell is other people yes and how do you imagine yes
how do you imagine that made me feel am I your hell was
I your hell oh do not answer that and I know there were
many times when you would have been happier away from
me and I would not let you go nor admit it to myself nor
take responsibility thinking always that if a break must be
made then it must be yours to make but perhaps it would
have been better to have the break regardless of its author
yes and I think of what you could have done much more
that you could have done and sometimes I do not know if I
should have let you stay

- but not now no not myself no longer subject how can
there exist object when subject is interred beneath earth
and stone prophetic worms not withstanding no more existence to precede essence only essence which outlives existence and hell is eternal disembodied discourse how funny
I never imagined it would be this way no never in my
wildest imaginings

- but I see you as I saw you always wearing the red cap
the one I bought you looking young and handsome in as
they say the full flower of youth or does that only apply to
the female of the species with such anatomical similarities
to the flower but of course the flower has a stamen which
is masculine in no subtle way hermaphrodism in botany
marvelous subject and must study when there is more time
there's a laugh never more time than now and yet no botany to behold this deforested afterlife no library in which
to study illiterate afterlife only ourselves yes ourselves and

memory but you were in the full flower of youth with proud teeth shining at my approach and I felt the swell as we kissed beneath the bridge in the hidden place you showed me felt the swell and put my hand upon the place and every hole wants for filling I'd heard my uncles say when the children had been ushered off to bed and they thought we could not hear every hole wants for filling as bung wants for tap as bore wants for peg as grave wants for corpse I see you now as I saw you then not handsome no no one would call you handsome but you looked exactly like yourself and is there anything prettier you looked exactly like yourself and I wanted you then but for the sake of propriety and what else is love what else is love you cannot say that is not love and with him it was not the same no not the same but you know that you must know or is it as they say the same with the lights off no I cannot imagine that it is the same and one way or the other it is not the same for a woman or at least it was not the same for me and even after many times it was not the same and it is funny do you remember when we were young and said yes it certainly makes sense and yes doesn't it make sense and after all it is only sex and what does it mean it means nothing if you do not want it to mean anything and besides monogamy is a construction and like all other constructions has no inherent worth and we were so bright yes weren't we laughing at everyone and their hang-ups the way young people always think that they know better yes we said we know better and after all it is only sex and you will see it will be just the same afterwards no nothing will change no nothing at all everything will be exactly as it was before and you said to bring him to dinner later that month a friend of Simone's is a friend of mine and I asked you in the coat check room to go easy on him and you said that you would and I made you promise twice but what good did that do of course it did no good at all

   - and everything I said counted for nothing my insults counted for nothing because he took first the check and then your hand and of the long walks home that was among the longest thinking yes now we are very rational and smart and bright and man is something to be transcended after all think of Nietzsche and everything will be the same afterwards yes just exactly the same I ran out to the first one I could find and did not bathe afterwards hoping that you would smell her when I saw you again but then it was two days or more and most of her scent was gone or at least you made no mention of it and what did you do in those two days I always wondered did you best our record of a whole day spent in bed when spring was still winter I bet you did I bet you did and I could see how men were moved to murder yes and all my condescension about brutes committing crimes of passion thrown right out the window with baby and bathwater and oh yes hell is other people listening to you go on and on about him knowing that I made my bed and now would have to lie in it and then the time you came to me I have a surprise for you you said and I could not see her but she was standing behind the door yes I said this is a surprise and you put your arms around my neck you are not mad at me are you and no of course I'm not mad this is what we agreed to isn't it of course it is how could I be mad it was my idea after all and nothing has changed between us and I agreed that nothing had changed and then we two and then she and we became three and when I awoke in the night I could tell just by the sound of your breathing which one you were now isn't that something I suppose it is something or maybe not who the hell knows what is anything I have a surprise for you and yes it certainly was a surprise

but she did not like it did she no she did not and even
when we were eating breakfast the next morning she did
not like it and when I left to pay the bill and came back I
could see from across the room could see that she was
smiling to have you all to herself did not want me coming
back oh no not ever and you wanting to make her happy
did not want me to come back either whether you knew it
or not really makes no difference but I saw her smiling and
went out another way because I loved you then and love
you now and loved you before and we had agreed hadn't
we yes we had agreed that we would not let it change us
but I am Jean-Paul no longer nor ever was but now have
no existence to precede essence only essence which has
outlived existence and if I am myself then am not body
interred beneath stone but also am neither works nor image
and Jean-Paul has achieved his capstone so what I am only
memory of myself no new memory to make in timeless-
ness and I cannot now remember the six years that passed
between our reunion nor seem to remember your arrival
although I still know that they both occurred how very
strange like becoming old again yes a very strange hell
that one is not aware of and soon I will not remember this
sensation or what it was exactly that I have already forgotten

   - and when you went away to war my heart oh my
heart was nearly broken for fear that I would never see you
again and all of this need to be rational and avoid the
grandeur of goodbye which you regarded as bourgeois and
any display of public affection I could not kiss you on the
platform as they called for you to board because you
thought it was bourgeois to treat one's own life as a great
romance no you said lets not have any goodbyes or final
kisses as though something could be said some final thing
could be said that would say it all everything you ever

wanted to say said in one perfect statement one spasm of the vocal chords exhalation of vapors and that is all it is isn't it and after all no movie cameras rolling nor eternal ledger only you and I and the memory of this moment which will expire with us and probably before no let us say nothing oh why say anything we both know you said we both know and yes we both knew and you were right then because I knew yes and knew that you knew and they called again for you to board but it was hard yes very hard to pretend for your sake because you were going off to war that I had no bourgeois impulse to run after you kiss your face press myself to the front of you so hard all the brass buttons on your uniform leaving their mark upon my skin no do not let him see you cry I thought and whatever was between you cannot be said nor killed nor stretched to breaking by distance and when word came that you had been captured I thanked God yes thanked God though I knew you did not approve and I did not approve myself but not mauvaise foi no only the best kind the best kind they sent word you had been captured and what else could I do I missed you so and thought of you always and laughed yes laughed at myself because I was just like all of the other girls with sweethearts away at war crying laughing gossiping how ridiculous I thought every time I saw them and sat with them how ridiculous and still I was one of them crying laughing gossiping and wishing you were home wishing you were back with me back in my arms back in my bed and it makes me laugh to think of it now and even then I sometimes laughed at the sentimental girl I had become in your absence but it is exhausting to be vigilant constantly vigilant unrelentingly vigilant against oneself and the girls saying my Francois has sent a letter home to his mother but none to me and my heart is broken my Jacques has not written at all and I do hope that he is all right if anything happened to him I would die my Peter has been wounded my Christopher writes me with promises of marriage and you with your brilliant letters always so brilliant so mercilessly brilliant and some nights I would have given anything for a letter in which you stumbled over words for love but then of course I was not missing you no not really you but a Jean-Paul who was not you my brave soldier away at war and sometimes it was hard not to forget with the propaganda and everyone speaking all the time of our brave boys away at war that you were still my Jean-Paul just my Jean-Paul nothing more than Jean-Paul and what I felt for you did not make our story a wartime romance I imagined you laughing and laughed myself but it is so hard to remain how should I say it not removed because it is the sentimentality that is the removal yes it is hard to keep from stepping back your absence was so much to bear then and again when you died and for six years I had only your absence it is hard to keep from stepping back what a comfort it is to step back and to think oh my love the great love of my life oh how tragic and to let go the complexity which requires so much attention but then without that then it was not really us was it no not really us but something else a story to be told after we are both dead and oh they will say the great love story of Jean-Paul and Simone not knowing that the Jean-Paul and Simone of whom they speak do not resemble us in the least but it is so hard to stay there right there down amongst the bodies

   - your presentation on Leibniz I remember yes remember well yes doubt that I will ever forget but having forgotten so much already who is to say what will remain when it is all over with more than I imagined would be as the body is now interred beneath the stone and yet I am certain that to forget your presentation of Leibniz would be to forget myself the moment I began as they say but that is not it at all perhaps it is but only slightly but I became myself after your presentation like a baptism perhaps or is that too bourgeois you have a man's intelligence your father always told you and we laughed about it later how bourgeois to think that a woman must be less intelligent made as they are for the bearing of children only for the bearing of children and so a woman looks only toward the children converses with children remains a child how often it does work that way intelligent like a man he told you and I remember yes remember and after the tremor along my skin as I approached imagining that you would assume yourself more intelligent in light of your triumphant presentation trying to formulate some intelligent response which you dismantled yes dismantled no you said not like that at all but like this and allow me to explain and laid it out so clearly and younger than me too by three years and I wanted you yes wanted you all to myself you with the bare arms and half-exposed breasts and cunning yes cunning so very cunning a man's intelligence your father called it and I laughed thinking of all the stupid men I had known but then I suppose that one never understands anything of others yes one is always a sentimentalist knowing only his own sentiments no matter how closely they resemble reality yes unknowable reality what more is there to know of reality than one's own sentiments nothing one cannot know anything more of reality than one's own sentiments inescapable subjectivity how are we to be held accountable for making into object that which is not subject I always wondered was it you I was seeing or something else something of myself and perhaps that is true all love then only self-love the marriage bed only a grandiose masturbation imagining that somehow we have escaped necessary subjectivity objectivity but the joke is on them yes the joke is

on the lovers and when I adopted Arlette now here another
strangeness because you said no one understands the parent like the child and what you lack in lineage you make
up for in other ways you laughed other ways yes and I was
always uneasy after the paperwork went through although
it meant nothing of course it meant nothing how could it
mean anything just a piece of paper after all saying that
she was my daughter and still I felt so odd the next time
the time right after and the times after that felt so very very
odd even though it was not incest no more than Claudius
and Gertrude were incestuous and yet what did I know of
Arlette perhaps nothing probably nothing and at least no
more than I knew of you or anyone else the world remains
a secret hidden in plain sight which we cannot discern with
our own eyes now that's a laugh isn't it when they captured me they took my boots and made me march and I
was certain that after they saw that they had put the fear
into me they would return them I was cold and the ground
was hard and sharp in places but I never saw them again
my boots I mean and the soldiers looking at my feet it was
the oddest thing not with hatred loathing or disgust but
with absolute indifference as though they themselves did
not have feet as I had feet and could not and would not
imagine what it would be like to have their boots taken
from them such incredible inempathy yes man's essential
state of inempathy and all empathy just for show but how
can one have empathy one cannot have empathy because
one cannot know the experience of object and even if one
could one cannot know it as the object-as-subject yes essential inempathy is perhaps more honest and they hit me
when I fell behind saying that I had to keep up and I explained that if they would only return my boots I could
walk much faster

- and sometimes sitting with you I never felt less understood as though you just refused to hear me and I thought I was going mad or losing my mind repeating myself over and over thinking if it is so clear to me it must be clear to him and if it is clear to me and unclear to him then perhaps I have crossed over yes always a fine line we talked about always a fine line when one is busy deconstructing deconstructing peeking through seams and windows always a fine line between that and madness and oh God I thought if he does not see what I am saying then maybe I have crossed over and the thought of all those women with their reproductive organs removed as therapy they said for hysteria and if I went mad would I still be Simone and would I still object one day thinking perhaps I am other perhaps I am mystery and the only thing to do is remove all the secret parts yes just like the doctors think go in with a silver spoon the way children do at Halloween with pumpkins yes the body a great orange pumpkin filled with mystery and only when it is all scooped out can the light shine through but no you understood all along and only refused to understand refused you were such a little boy sometimes the oddest juxtaposition all of those fine ideas and sometimes all you used them for was cutting me down cutting me down you and your hurt little boy's feelings with all of your big words no better than Hitler all of your strength focused on some infantile obsession some latent neurosis about unclean Jews it is funny when you think about it and says a lot for a system of checks and balances but of course checks and balances did not stop the Americans from committing their own genocide and anyway boys with guns killing killing killing and you with your big words telling me how wrong I was it's funny to think of the ideas I quit for you thinking that it would make you love me more it seems silly now and seemed silly at the time but then again what does not seem silly it's all pretty silly absurd Albert would say and it would not have mattered then if they had scooped me out like a pumpkin is scooped out no would not have mattered in the least and let us remind ourselves that there is no eternal ledger in which all of these kind acts of charity and sins cardinal venal et cetera are recorded I could have lived many years thus castrated and been very happy I'm sure

- and words yes the summer that I realized words were useless and writing writing always writing writing but all of it I realized worthless and words just so many words and what are you reading my lord words words words but what's the matter between whom yes and I went home and cast my books upon the floor and trod upon them very dramatic perhaps but nonetheless I did it laughing all the time to myself the joke was on me and later when the letters began to arrive letters yes hundreds of letters so many that I stopped reading them but the first ones were better than any admirer's praise oh God yes better than any critic's glowing review and then the bomb in the entryway and they placed an officer in an unmarked car across the street for a whole month and had him follow me everywhere I went and all the while wondering how many people had read my books and of those how many had done anything at all about their contents and glad I had trod upon them yes because they deserved to be trod upon and I with them remiss as I was for so many years ignoring my responsibility thinking that to write was just as good yes I said it's just as good but no of course it is not and think of the illiterate and those with no access and it's almost a crime yes almost a crime that I did nothing for so long writing writing always writing such a fool and how far out ahead was the media telling it like it wasn't and all of us scrambling to catch up and I should have seen it sooner no more need for the printed word and only my own nostalgia and habit to keep me writing no no more need for the printed word

- and our love like something I did not have to look for but found by chance which seemed not to be chance afterwards with each small tiny simple step which led to our first encounter now so beautiful in the remembering sickled o'er with the pale cast of thought and now history and our history forever and ever amen and it is like there is an eternal ledger isn't it when you think about it that way yes hard to believe that those tiny steps vanish along with their beauty the beauty only you were aware of hard to imagine yes that they vanish completely when you die

- and those moments frightening moments lucid moments when you are not yourself but only someone else's thought I still remember the first time I stumbled upon a letter my teacher had sent home Jean-Paul is such and such and my God that's who I am not myself and the first time hearing my voice played back or myself on the television God I remember the first time like it was yesterday the strangeness yes my God how strange to live in your body but also live in fractions in all those other minds the sum total of which makes the whole of you as much of you as anyone will ever know and the two so very close the you that you are to yourself and the you that you are to them so very close and yet never close enough will never can never be closer than dissimilar in many respects isn't that funny no perhaps not funny at all or only funny when you got used to it maybe that was it that nothing got better but only became familiar and I remember such rising choking or perhaps drowning anxiety as a child when I was certain someone had misunderstood I went to such great lengths to explain yes explain what it was I had been saying what I meant to say was this or that and everyone always nodding because it did not matter to them what I was trying to say child that I was and what could I know that was worth such effort to relate anyway but nothing really changes when you get older does it no nothing really changes and they were still looking at me with such paradoxical attention yes attention coupled with refusal to hear or admit modification to their own understanding yes still looking at me with such attention when I died

- but there were times yes weren't there times when we were one yes just simply one no more Jean-Paul and Simone but JeanPaulSimone only one and inseparable never-to-be-separated all those times just think where we awoke and found that we'd had the same dream perhaps it was only as you said later the suggestible state that follows sleep but I did not care because I wanted to believe and yes self-enforced ignorance but it was a beautiful ignorance at least more beautiful than the explanation you gave and what did you dream my love that is very strange yes very strange I dreamt a similar dream in which something similar occurred and more remembered as more was revealed as though we shared a mind yes and all of those ideas whose implications were found by committee and we could not say it was I or thou to refine this idea because you spoke the words as they sprang to my lips and I spoke them as they sprang to yours and that old cliché we've been married so long that we finish each other's and perhaps it is just that but sometimes I did not think so did not want to think so could not think so even if I had wanted to and no eternal ledger you said and just life and death and within life the transcendent but the transcendent in life transcending nothing more than oneself such hubris you used to say yes that was your word hubris to think that it must be divine because it touches something beyond the minor scope of our own thoughts yes it must reach to

heaven thinking that we are so close that God must live on
the floor above us yes hubris that sonata was simply divine
and you would laugh later and say so let me see if I am
understanding you correctly your experience exceeded
your expectations and so it must be close to God and
laughing and all of those society women you offended it is
only a figure of speech you know and why ruin a perfect
evening with such unnecessary hostility but you had your
standards yes but weren't we one I remember the first time
I was riding in a train car watching out the window as we
passed trees and fields and hills and river and houses and I
was not myself but trees and fields and hills and river and
houses part of everything and nothing and no more Simone
only trees fields hills river houses and you were beside me
the whole time I'd never experienced that with anyone else
near but only in solitude and I awoke in amazement wondering what it meant excitement running all along my skin
we are one we are one I thought I dissolved and he was
there and I did not weep because I knew that when you
asked what was wrong I would know that I was Simone
and you were Jean-Paul Jean-Paul who did not know why
I was crying Jean-Paul in his seat and I in mine two bodies
again oh I could not bear the thought but yes what did you
dream my love and that is very strange I had a similar
dream and yes I am just remembering that occurred in my
dream as well and what do you think it means what do you
think it means what do you think it means and all of those
youthful displays of affection when I could not stand that
our love for each other would exist for no one but ourselves no eternal ledger you said and that which is not seen
disappears for whom did our love exist only for ourselves
and that was somehow not enough stupid it was so stupid
but I could not help it no could not help throwing my arms
around your neck and the silence that followed when eve-

ryone knew yes horrible silence and why is that one of the other boys liked me you said and things would change if he knew about us but how could he possibly not know it was as obvious as the nose on your face but still you insisted I pretended that I was hurt accusing saying that it is because I embarrass you isn't it you the great intellectual who always espoused the Grecian ideal yes platonic love and all of that the love of the mind and all of that and dirty yes it was dirty did you think it was dirty and no of course not and come now you cannot really think that you embarrass me and no I did not but refused to admit it watching myself play the wounded yes enjoying being wounded when all along it was so nice and so wonderful that you did not want to tell wanted it to be only ours I know that now and knew it then only ours and no one else's and that when they knew it would change but it had to change how could it not change those first few days so beautiful and left alone by chance and no one suspected a thing nor would have believed I hardly believed myself but no you are embarrassed by me I said and you saying that is not it at all and I know you understand don't you see how things will change afterward when they know everything will be different it always happens that way but I so wanted to tell them wanted them to know our love only three days old and still like a dream and so afraid that it would go as quickly as it had come and would be like it had never been you were putting on your coat and I cried yes such a perfect melodrama I could hardly believe and afterwards was so ashamed such a perfect melodrama please don't go I am sorry am I to be inhuman and forget that I want you forget that I want you all to myself to be mine only mine always mine and want them to know that you are mine you must be reasonable you insisted must be reasonable these people are our friends remember and oh I embarrass you all brains and nothing like a woman no not like a woman like your women and I understood always that with me you were always Jean-Paul always forced to be yourself because I loved you so and to couple without love is one of life's great mercies and with the others you were not Jean-Paul just as with mine I was not Simone and what a relief unending relief holy relief to be only a rush of sensation yes God oh and free from the burden of thought no one asking what do you think about this or that or sitting through I found the performance very satisfactory on an aesthetic level but felt that they failed to do proper justice to the play's metaphysical aspect God no none of that no more of that and how many times did I sit and marvel at your ability to go on and on with your careful articulate answers and your polite interest I myself could hardly stand it but you hardly seemed to mind yes and what I relief to slip free of yourself with a rush of sensation I understood and understand but why can't we tell them I insisted as though I could feel myself losing grip of still-recent memory and wanting to tell them refusing to understand no eternal ledger after all and when I threw my arms around your neck I felt such weight wonderful weight and they knew yes they all knew everyone knew like diving deep into a pool and feeling the water pressing in on you on all sides and feeling marvelously held in place it is so hard to describe their silence like that weight and even when you politely disengaged still that weight and nothing could lessen it not just two memories yours and mine but all of them perhaps no eternal ledger but still it was something still something yes something like permanence I loved you then I loved you so because there was nothing you could do you were mine yes all mine they knew and the weight God yes and did not need to say anything no nothing more needed to be said they understood and moving on I remembered then why they were our friends and loved them all and waking the next morning with you there beside me I wept yes you did not know that did you I wept and watched you sleep God yes you my Jean-Paul mine here yes my own my very own dearest my own mine but don't you know that for me there is always but now how is it called a black hole surrounding you and no matter where I am I feel myself being pulled it gave me great pleasure to cease my resistance it was so easy and when you were with one of them it was as though I was trapped in a room all the world was a room and I was being pulled in just the same way only I came up short against the walls can you know what that is like I don't imagine that you can you were always the center of your own world I suppose that was part of the reason I fell for you always the center of your own world and nothing could move you not even the Germans no you said we are staying in Paris and I agreed on the same principle but knew then as I know now that my agreement was unnecessary as no you said we are stay-ing here and at one time only myself in my own head and later only you when I closed my eyes always there always a tiny unstoppable anxiety an errant ignored thought I wonder what he is doing wonder where he is wonder who he is with and if I thought about it too long going crazy really crazy making myself mad with speculation and yet helpless to stop myself always thinking and still no relief when I was with you only more anxiety for the times past when we were not together and whatever happened then making a lie of the present how could I open myself to you when I did not trust where you had come from maybe you had another one tucked away somewhere nearby where you would go after and talk about me laugh about me I allowed you to go but did not allow your dirty little secrets that was our deal wasn't it to never lie but how do you keep from lying one lie always breeds another and if the first was said to spare my feelings then certainly the next dozen were said to spare yours but nothing the same between us when I could not stop myself from wondering where you were and who you were there with and certain that you would not tell me later or at least not the whole of it so mistrusting your explanations I was a mad woman certainly but only as much of one as you made me I thought of drowning myself but was not certain that you would understand imagined some attendant lord saying she drowned yes alas and you stumbling upon my funeral already in progress and do you see what a ridiculous sentimental fool you made me by your absence laughing about it later myself and glad that I had told no one nor written it horrified that someone would find it out

- and isn't it funny you said and have you ever had the experience of writing a word and your pen goes dry you retrace the word until the ink comes but as you are doing so the word loses the thought it was attached to becomes just another word now you are thinking about the lousy pen and you find that you cannot remember quite how to spell it and on top of that even when you are careful and make sure that you have spelled it correctly the word looks strange is this right I used to ask you and of course it is you'd say you know as well as I do and yes of course but how do you spell this word and then the fumbling reading over the last line trying to find the thought again but it is no use yes I think it is gone forever and it is only later and with great relief that you realize just what it was you were trying to say thoughts are so elusive and words so imperfect I love you you used to say and what does that I mean I asked cruel I suppose but wanted to know what does it mean and if your pen ran dry as you were writing it would you still remember the thought behind it as the ink began again to come

- and there were times yes so many times I felt as though you tolerated me out of politeness that it was all superego with you unless you were in bed yes life as the superego was the price you paid for our time in bed you did not ask for my ideas but listened when I spoke them and if I did not speak them I was always afraid that if I did not offer them you would not miss them out of politeness yes you were always so polite I felt certain that behind your polite mask you were tapping your foot an odd feeling yes very odd and the times when you were thoughtless some part of me always rejoiced saying yes I knew it yes I knew that was how he felt and later when we forced the reconciliation I always clung to that feeling that I was right yes I knew you felt that way knew you didn't love me as I love you and I made it so hard for you I am sorry made it so hard for you demanding that you convince me the opposite of what I was certain that I knew

- but don't you know that I did love you God I loved you loved you yes love you and you asked me to prove it all of the time but would never believe me no not ever only in glimpses did I know that you understood it was such a chore sometimes I admit it was a chore and one which required monumental effort I am not ashamed to admit that I faltered yes faltered often I defy anyone to do more than I did they could not did not never did never were able to you knew that I loved you and then went to such great lengths to make me say it yes say it over and over God how I tried and believed yes that is the ridiculous thing each time convinced that now I would say it in just the right way yes the right way to make it stick a painting placed prominently so that you would see it often I wore the trousers you bought me until they were worn nearly through you see I have hung the painting you see I am wearing the trousers the ones you bought me but no never enough not enough some hole at the bottom of you where it all drained out as I toiled to put it in the joke is on me I suppose yes the joke is on me for believing that your un-stoppered heart could ever be filled I had a good laugh about it once I threw up my hands and laughed there was nothing I could do no nothing at all but laugh you were going to believe me or not and what could I do and you yourself everyone laughing oh he does not know and yes they were right to laugh he does not know he does not know and you had a good laugh too didn't you but oh you said no I would not with you if I was with another and I believed you I suppose it was my fault for believing and that party where you came with her I saw her looking for you all night yes but oh no I thought not with her of course not with her how could it be with her and when we went upstairs thinking no now it is obvious not with her and I suppose then it was as much my fault as yours yes my fault for believing you and when I confronted you later you cried and cried and of course I had done more harm to you than you had to me and of course you had earned the right yes earned the right to hurt me you said as much yes that was the hub of the argument wasn't it wasn't it who had hurt whom more and no you said that does not hurt me of course it does not hurt me our love is too strong for that to hurt me and after when you were hurt you blamed me for believing you when you said that you did not mind no of course you did not mind why would you mind and oh I was foolish to believe you I knew it then and know it now yes foolish to believe you when you said you would not be hurt but then not speaking how could you speak having promised that you would not be hurt and no you said noth-ing is wrong nothing is wrong and it would just upset you to know I bit my lip until it bled yes and it had the taste of your silence I could have wept leaving your room yes wept as I descended the stairs numb from the head up and the waist down and all hollowed-out in the middle without the energy to weep and isn't it funny I wanted to telephone you the moment I got home not to talk it out but because I could think of nothing else to do had always called you and that was the first time I felt that you were gone and I did not sleep in agonies that you were gone yes out with another it being only just and only fair tit for tat and all of that walking the streets with nowhere to go feeling somehow certain in the most irrational way that I would stumble upon you with another hear you laughing spot you catch you in the act and all of my righteous indignation cut off at the knees by my own indiscretion laughing then because there was nothing else to do certain you were with somebody else and me sitting on my hands sitting on my hands knowing that you had every right to have one of your own equal partners we always said and equal now yes equal and to hell with you and to hell with him and to hell with all of it plenty of fish in the ocean isn't that what they say and I was young then yes young no reason to get bent out of shape over a woman and thinking I would simply throw all of my high ideals into the Seine no more nonsense about existence and essence no more dodges yes all they were was dodges didn't anyone see that they were dodges pretending to look past life to something else just pretending and I knew then it was all worthless myself no more engaged with reality than those kneeling before the crucifix saying our father who art in heaven and help me though this world of illusion and temptation saying to myself always this is not this nor is this other what it appears to be but only and always something else and yes wishing that I could chuck it all knowing that if I'd had my notebooks with my I would have thrown them from the bridge and what was any of it worth if I could not have you just life upon life and laughing yes thinking I was onto something and I hurried home to write it all filled with loathing yes impossible self-loathing because I could not help but write it could not help but turn it into an idea could not help but see myself the tragic figure upon the bridge like Oedipus having sewn the seeds of my own downfall and Oh God yes what a tragic figure am I such worthless dodges and I incapable of anything but observing my own infinite resignation and unable to do other yes I laughed at all the times I fancied myself evolved or enlightened a young man of twenty-two yes evolved and enlightened and oh God yes evolved and enlightened awake at four in the morning with pen in hand and you in another's arms

- but don't you remember later yes years later when it was good oh good it was good yes good wasn't it good with the war over and both of us working and all of our friends getting along and it was nice yes wasn't it nice and no one willing to admit that they enjoyed it so hellbent on misery and nausea that they failed to notice that it was nice but I knew you asked me why I was smiling and I said no reason and you and Albert waist-deep in some conversation and you thought I was laughing at you but no not laughing only smiling and when you fell in love with that actress I was so mortified she was such a terrible actress and you knew it too yes that was why you loved her wasn't it because she was always visible inside her roles like a woman whose slip is always showing visible behind her roles peeking out when she thought no one was looking couldn't help it it seemed but of course on the stage someone is always looking even when you are not the center someone always saw her such a terrible actress slouching between her lines or looking off in another direction thinking that acting only occurred when her mouth was forming words and we all agreed what a waste of talent the rest of the play became because once you noticed her you could hardly pay attention to the rest of it but you found her fascinating didn't you something you said about form and content and it almost broke my heart remembering how you used to tell me yes that you saw me through a curtain a form whose content showed through in snatches and no I never told you of course I never told you that I loved to hear that everyone loves to hear how they were fallen in love with it is only human loved to hear how you saw my bare arm and think how I almost did not wear that dress like somehow it was fate after all almost broke my heart you saying it is so fascinating the way she is this form and yet the content of the form so obviously differs it is like a paradox from eastern mediation to behold her and asking me didn't I agree and when I was silent you laughed and said you aren't jealous are you and no of course I'm not whatever gave you that idea and don't you know that when I speak of something like this actress I am speaking of it as if you were inside of me speaking it as well I do not go through the world as Jean-Paul but only as one half of we two and know that if it troubles you I will cast her from my thoughts no of course not of course not you may have your actress smiling but unable to breathe yes no oxygen in the small space between holding you close and pushing you away no air in the room where I was certain that to let you go would be to lose you and to hold you tighter would be to inspire your flight no of course I am not jealous what was one lousy actress compared to all that we had built together no she could never come between us no never of course not ever

    - yes Desdemona's attendant so lovely yes I never understood why they cast her too lovely more lovely than

Desdemona and certain to distract an audience even without her ceaseless fidgeting my God so endearing my heart flew to her immediately I was so taken by surprise expecting to fall in love with virtuous Desdemona as Shakespeare intended and finding myself only half-heartbroken when she died yes only half and my other half elated giddy and ridiculous did you see Desdemona's attendant and yes my God you all said how could anyone miss her I do not think she stood still for a moment she was upon the stage she must know someone to be given the part yes her father must be someone important and none of you could understand why I wanted to meet her could not keep myself from insisting my way backstage staying behind think he has finally lost himself but no not lost only bored to tears with the Moor of Venice my God and the plodding of tragedy which has already lost its tension through ceaseless repetition and restaging the actors like great marble monuments to their own characters plodding across the stage shaking the earth with their steps and she like a wood spirit on holiday from some production of *A Midsummer Night's Dream* stumbling upon the unfolding tragedy and handed a tray the travel spot redundant she outshone them all I could not find her and then did she was in the room the smaller parts all shared God you were wonderful women undressing around me I said you stole the show simply stole it she did not understand of course she did not understand her feelings were hurt thought that I was having a joke and indifferent women undressing around me no I said in earnest and introduced myself and would love to speak with you more and might I come by after tomorrow night's performance and take you somewhere she was hesitant but agreed my God so beautiful hiding behind her hesitation just as she had behind the tray and what crisis of confidence could I have certain as I was in all of her responses before she spoke them yes I knew her so well almost immediately and slowly working to unfasten the knots holding whatever armor remained until she was bare exposed before me my God yes so simple and I knew her and possessed her completely possessed her as one possesses a marvelous puzzle box whose many configurations have been exhausted not a partnership as such but something else I was certain you understood yes immediately certain because how can one be jealous of a puzzle box a puzzle box is a distraction and labors upon it lead only to itself I thought you knew was certain that you knew thought it impossible that you did not know that there was no Jean-Paul and as I pursued my puzzle box I did it always thinking that I was Jean-Paul and Simone always Jean-Paul and Simone and whatever delight I took in my puzzle box was your delight listen to what she said listen to what she did isn't that funny isn't that interesting and didn't you find it interesting too I was certain you did the night we went to dinner and you sat across from her I watched you devouring her with your mind that wonderful mind the mind of a man devouring her understanding her as I had explained her yes she was our pet some rare and exotic pet which gave us both delight wasn't that true yes wasn't that true

- but I wanted to feel it yes wanted to feel what it was to be subject seeking object had never known the feeling even as woman subject seeking man object becoming instead object-to-object a very tricky conversion would like to see any man try it and then speak of women as less intelligent beings no I do not think they could do it such absolute surrender to be surrounded by another's gaze and yes monsieur and no monsieur and of course you do not really think you can impress me with such bravado nor purchase my affection with gifts stringing them along

walking ahead with them hungrily staring at your back oh
it is a subtle game wanted to feel it yes wanted to feel what
it was to be the wolf walking in back of the chicken this
time and she was perfect wasn't she God yes perfect you
remember there were nights we laughed and said she must
have fallen to earth from a star there is no other such as her
so very strange and uninformed and yet so intelligent you
wondered where she could have been hiding for so long to
have grown to maturity with no sense for the world she
was wholly at a loss in Paris you paid her rent for years I
would not let you stop horrified at what might happen if
we were to put any demand upon her that she leave her
own sweet ignorance I showed her where the market was
and how to ride the trains she was so lovely I watched her
carefully repeating the steps as I had explained them and
thought yes this is what it is to be the wolf standing at the
chicken's back yes oh God yes and how can I describe it
for the first time as though I was not one in the crowd but
nowhere yes nothing no longer Simone but only the
thought of Simone and the thought of Simone only Simone's own thought and no one else's completely free
subject with she as my object I wept with gratitude then
she did not understand and asked me why I was crying I
pressed my lips to hers the easiest thing in the world my
hesitations all seemed foolish God yes and back to the
room you paid for feeling like the cat which has brought
the broken bird to its master's doorstep as an offering what
new knowledge I bring to you and one more way in which
we are not Simone and Jean-Paul but only SimoneJean-
Paul watching her as you watched her and pretending that
I was you or any man watching a woman the place she
went when she closed her eyes so mysterious and I wondered what she was feeling and certain that I did not feel it
the same as she and did I feel it that way and could I ever

her body so wholly encapsulated her experience a strange object like God whispering secrets in my ear and when I took her myself nowhere in the room and she something strange and alien moving beneath me

- there was a bowl of cherries upon the table I could only just see it which is to say that my eyes were only just level with the table bowl on top and cherries rising in a mound like a distant mountain peak and yes I wanted one wanted as many as I could hold so delicious the cherries my mother brought home from the market delicious because my mother had sanctified them with her approval yes these are the cherries I will bring home and she never picked a bad bunch and I do not know if she had a gift or if I was only blinded by love for her wanted one and reaching for it heard my grandfather's voice sharp reprimand my world which a moment before had been only wordless pleasure anticipation of wordless pleasure ethereal pleasure I was a thought drifting from room to room with no awareness of itself and then his voice sharp reprimand you are not to eat before dinner suddenly in a world so much larger than myself horrible feeling I never understood entirely how one can be so drawn out of oneself by another's presence and yes it is the subject becoming object and the strangeness of subject regarding itself as object but there is something else as well something I could never quite put my finger on and I suppose now it does not matter since whatever ideas are produced do not enter the canon of Jean-Paul the institution of Jean-Paul the institution I tried to avoid becoming but oh well every man becomes an object or perhaps life is only a long process of realizing that you are the object you have been all along existence preceding essence but also outliving it a corpse to be disposed of after all and then all of those books I wrote but not only subject-becoming-object something more realizing that you have a form when you were only aware of content and realizing also that the two are essentially linked to no one but yourself they did not care about my rapt anticipation of the pleasures of eating a cherry my mother had selected no I only a form God the most horrible feeling a form without a voice a small child attempting to spoil its appetite by snacking before dinner and no not it not it at all that was not it they did not understand no please and being misunderstood that horror yes but also that drowning horror realizing that they did not care to understand a bourgeois child fatherless child no content to speak of I came in and found him eating cherries the boy trying to spoil his appetite I wept with frustration and have never ceased weeping all of the words I wrote in books and spoke in lectures only tears shed in the hope that someone might hear and understand that I was not a child sneaking cherries

- and not the first wave but the second wave of Americans who arrived after the war and sat in cafes waiting for someone to ask them why they looked so glum do you remember how we laughed at them and used to pretend listening to them complain about other Americans and about how most of them knew nothing at all and the ones who knew anything were worse than the ones who knew nothing because it was all filtered through that lens of cowboy bravado God it was funny to see them there looking wounded and waiting for the world to notice a generation of pouting children you called them lost in the world because they had been raised with the knowledge that every time something made them feel bad their mother would make them a chocolate cake and now they had no chocolate cake and had no idea how to make any sense of themselves we would sit with them and I could watch you growing bored even the intelligent ones you had read everything they referenced and understood better too and when I picked up that one I think it was only to goad you my God you said doesn't he bore you to tears the American is the least integrated of the world's citizens all super-ego and id and nothing in between to speak of or speak with just a polite monkey you can sit with at dinner or some brute trampling across a muddy field with a leather ball and some high-minded references to Greece and the perfection of sport they would be laughable if they did not have most of the munitions nothing more dangerous than America's willful ignorance a marvelous thing that a slave owner could call himself cultured impressive powers of myopia and that was the difference between America and the rest of the world you said was that at least in Europe we saw ourselves too well to act in haste whereas Americans saw only what they wanted to see

- but the body which disturbs us arm or half-exposed breast or leg and the first time I saw a dead man in the war body which disturbs because it is body or because it is not body but rather organic totality of other and other-as-object but also other as the marriage of form and content though content remains elusive aware nonetheless of a form which is wholly saturated with content the wonderment of humanity and yet the problems that arise when one finds content unknowable and even to be being-for-itself-for-others is not enough to dissolve the final membrane between consciousnesses no one knew Simone better than I and yet the distance between Simone as I knew her and Simone as she knew herself makes laughable whatever claims I make to knowledge of her and yet no two were more in love more open than she and I and what horror it was to live with the knowledge that she was not truly as I thought of her as though returning to the western United States and finding that the mountains had unseated from the places they occupied in the skyline of your mem-

ory a profoundly disorienting experience and yes perhaps
that is it really what Albert called the wild call for clarity
really only man's innate animal need to orient himself in
the world and how can you orient yourself in the world
when your body is prone to the thousand natural shocks
and your mind can only perceive illusions the orienting
apparatus horribly compromised horribly horribly compromised because I never knew could never know Simone
as she knew herself always only and forever after an invention of the mind an organic totality invented from an
arm or half-exposed breast or perhaps leg every woman
like a Galatea yes every woman and every other thing as
well only Pygmalion's dreams shunning some things
clutching others to him the world itself something beyond
him and even to touch and shape the stone to make love to
hold to fix in place does not incarnate does not breathe life
into Adam's nostrils does not somehow fix content to form
knowing things only as we can it is a simple point I suppose and not a new one but it never ceases to amuse and
amaze me that the statements I know Simone and I do not
know Simone do not contradict each other a funny thing
you'd think the creator would have had more sense would
have more tightly tethered soul to body because sometimes
when you looked at me I had no idea what you were thinking what are you thinking I would ask and you would
smile and say of course you must already know and leave
it at that my heart always broke a little as though I had
seen Ithaca's shore and then your words had risen like the
unloosed winds blowing us farther and farther apart

- and dying yes like dissolving like what was it like I
suppose perhaps like a medicine capsule the casing disap-
pearing and then the contents all absorbed into the sur-
roundings but not of course the belly but the room and the
world a little capsule dissolving I felt like I was dissolving

and then it came and it was so pleasant even without hope or faith pleasant

- and Oh the great love story of Jean-Paul and Simone yes and did you know that they met at such and such a place and that such and such a thing happened and but oh the experts will disagree and they will squabble over our bones it is not pride that makes me say this but rather the knowledge that men must fight over meaning what did it mean when he wrote this God yes and what did it mean that her books were printed a year after his and we no longer anywhere to defend ourselves our closest friends all dead and dying or at least ignored because don't you know that it is possible to know someone for years and never discover their deepest secrets yes the experts will say digging for hidden meaning deeper meaning truer meaning and not no meaning if only they knew that there is no meaning to any of it but now worse for they will take our work's having outlived us as an indication of its immortality it makes me laugh to think of it they asked me once how I wanted to be remembered and I did not have the sense to say that the greatest tribute anyone could offer would be to forget me and all things past to dismiss the past because it is gone and that to cling to the past is to harbor undeserved faith in an eternal self a soul as it were yes I was a child and yes I was a teenager and even then my self was so clear no not cling to any of it you fools just forget me and everything I wrote and meditate on that my children meditate on its absence meditate on the nonexistence of past please I beg you that is the only thing to know about life the only great with all apologies to Albert philosophical question or if not question then at least dilemma the vast amalgamation of human memory only the contents of a piss-pot to be flung from the second-story window and into the street below where it may mingle with all other things forgotten by the amnesiatic universe every time I saw a statue or a monument it made me want to weep because it was so hopeless men were so hopeless and as long as there were monuments there would be wars and cruelty because life becomes worthless when we imagine that we continue after it is gone

- and remember when you said let's never stop growing no promise me that we will never stop and it is bourgeois to stop and become complacent and all complacency built on illusion yes must be vigilant against illusion like you said any artist too easy to fall back upon form and write good books and paint good paintings but then you look past form and there is nothing there the artist like a shark moving always forward to draw water through the gills yes the artist must feel just like that as though resting leads to suffocation or perhaps like a worm a mill for the earth before it and leaving a trail of soil behind yes an interesting thought the artist moving ever forward and depositing books and plays and paintings in his wake and to continue to consume and reproduce the same soil is to poison oneself and perhaps that is it yes we agreed to never stop moving forward and then later laughed about it remember how we were when we were young always needing to move forward and all that we did not know and yet thought we understood so much about the world and about each other worse than stupid because at least stupid can learn intelligent is proud and there can be no progress nor alteration and God yes we were so intelligent weren't we I always felt a little ridiculous in conversation when they asked how old I was the *agregation* not withstanding and how bourgeois we agreed to imagine that there are some things which can only be learned with age one more way to silence the youth but no of course some things one cannot imagine even if one has a clear picture of what one is after no some things I only learned with age or perhaps not age perhaps only familiarity and it took years for certain things to occur enough times until I had knowledge of them but was also older much older so much older and yes perhaps that is all they mean when they say that some things are learned with age just that some things are not taught until you are older even when you want to learn them when you are young I did not learn complacency until we had already settled into it and Jean-Paul I said one day we are not so unlike the bourgeois whom we have detested rising in the morning and going to our work even we too have found our complacency and you could not deny that I was right yes of course I was right but by then we had learned what it was to be tired my God yes tired and forward movement and growth can wait but for now I want to sit and not think about anything yes it took time to learn that feeling and do you remember how you came home that day in sixty-four in such a rage that they were speaking about you on the news and I was surprised and asked how you could imagine that they would not no one after all declines the prize as though you had intended to erase your name from the story entirely that reporter does not have any idea what he is talking about you kept saying to me and it is a sin to let those with no understanding speak at all I had never seen you like that and was quite surprised you who had been confronted by celebrity so often was it only that you did not want them to have the final word on your actions and by refusing the award had refused yourself a voice was that it I never really knew this reporter knows nothing one should not ordain to speak with such authority about things over which one has none and so odd to see you act in such a way I could make neither heads nor tails of it and people will see this and think this or that and that will be the final word to most of them such profound frustration I could not imagine what it was like to be you at that moment feeling this intangible devaluation against which you could not fight they will think me ungrateful you said and that is not it at all and my God I find myself in a situation where now I must defend myself against their unspoken accusations have vested them with obnoxious authority oh wouldn't it have been easier to accept the damned thing and then write something outlandish my own *Titus Andronicus* make them question everything they know about Jean-Paul yes and certainly no danger then of becoming an institution but too late now anyway and what will they think of me what will they think of me what will they think

- but you know as well as I do and knew it then as well that if we are not something then we are nothing never become object then might as well not exist like Kaspar Hauser only having never been found for example what then would he have been nothing perhaps there is another one out there right now howling at the moon but how are we to know pure subject is a ghost and we must all reconcile ourselves to being pure object if we are to get anything done in this world I should have known better than to decline deviance is only acceptable when it achieves its objective end these are not the trappings of the bourgeois but rather the trappings to the physical nothing to be done about it really and perhaps should have given up long ago trying to be both subject and object a hard thing to accomplish I always said but the truth of course that it is damn near impossible I am always impressed by politicians who can do it so flawlessly wish I'd had just a little bit of that but nothing to be done about it now no nothing to be done

- and all of those meetings my God I shudder to recollect them at *Les Temps Modernes* where I had to demand your opinions I would look at you and see that you were as the romantics would say a million miles away off in a day-dream but it was not a daydream with you was it no but a refusal to engage I watched you in your decline and the first time you called me by another's name I pretended to be jealous so that we would not have to admit what it was and in time realizing that you no longer spoke anything but my invention of your words telling the others Jean-Paul would say this or this but of course no you would not or at least not anymore no more Jean-Paul to speak of gone in amphetamines and all of your energy poured into your *Critique* and your testament to Flaubert and what was left of you where those three gave way into the rest of your life not much to speak of and the strangest feeling of all to see you sitting beside me and miss you at the same time yes to feel your absence and yet to see you not an arm's length away nothing prepared me for that and we all know that to live is to grow old and to grow old is to die and if it were only that God how merciful it would be yes mercy to watch the skin grow dry and fragile and posture stoop energy decrease and all of that which we imitate as youths shuffling forward our hands clutching imaginary canes and lips pulled tight over our teeth and laughing because we are ourselves and though the body is old there is another part of us which is in no way compromised and so we are untouched by age and thus imagine that we will not be touched when death comes to claim our bodies yes that would be merciful I watched you disappear slowly and then abruptly and so missed you before you were gone and them asking me what does Jean-Paul think about this or that and apologizing always he has been very busy with his work and no thank you for asking his health is very good and I will pass along your question and get back to you as soon as it is humanly possible already formulating Jean-Paul's answer they say that women tend to outlive men and only natural after all that one lead the other and I miss you already I wanted to say and sixty years is more than anyone has any right to expect but if there was any of me that was not Jean-Paul I did not know what it was and was horrified at the idea that one day you would be gone and I like a chair with half its legs removed would topple felt myself already toppling and it was only my clinging to the memory of you that kept me a phantom support and what would I do with myself if I ever lost you I asked when we were young and you laughed because what else can you do when you are young and old age is impossible in your own mind what can you do but laugh and I laughed too a silly question of course as impossible for me to imagine as it was for you having only this life and not any other from which to learn turning my merciless eyes to the widows not out of cruelty but only out of ignorance what mercy could I give after all I did not realize I was refusing them anything thought it was enough for them to ask of me a sympathetic hand no not enough and how cruel my God how cruel to imagine that I could sympathize and instead only managed to alienate them in their grieving my eyes speaking volumes about the world's inability to understand or offer comfort the dead husband walking the road to death alone and the widow walking the road of grief alone and never feeling more acutely the distance between the body which they held comforted and the heart which begged for relief O inexpressible grief made only more horrible by its isolation that is what they do not tell you when you are young yes and yes you will get old and yes you will die and lose your friends but they do not tell you that you will experience these things alone alone always and essentially alone not that you would understand them if they did

- but the first time rising in the morning still in a dream and finding it strange that my clothes were my own bed my own room my own and washing my face finding it strange that my face was my own and yes existence precedes essence but then essence comes to behold existence and it doesn't really matter then which came first but rather that the two stand facing each other or perhaps just that essence stands facing existence the oddest thing are these shoes my own and these trousers the feeling the same as when I slipped unnoticed into my grandfather's room and in his absence wore his clothes yes the same feeling of unfamiliarity and artifice feeling just that same way as I buttoned my own shirt and everything outside strange as well the familiar street and familiar sidewalk and familiar shops and familiar trees birds river lawns all of it strange there is a word for that what is the word they sent me home from school that day I had a fever they were worried that I would infect the other children and all of it strange yes so very strange I could not make sense of the concerned look on my mother's face no could not make sense of any of it and they put me down to bed and in the morning I lay awake looking at my clothes all hanging neatly in a row and unable to make myself feel again that they were strange they were just my clothes my mother said that I had been sick but that now I was looking much better yes my grandfather agreed I dressed myself and went out into the familiar world trying to recapture the feeling that it was all unfamiliar but to no avail I soon gave up fearing it hopeless and it was much later and only by accident that I felt it again I was in the city and saw a boy my own age I could have sworn was my twin separated from me at birth I had only just heard the story of how the musketeers replaced the king of France and my perception of my supposed double was horribly compromised I

watched him from a distance and suddenly had the sensation that I was watching not my double but myself the
strangest thing to behold oneself in one's totality and to
see him contain not the vast infinity of imagination the
world which lives by the senses but only his own organs
and minor concerns see the breadth of his aspirations con-
tained within his own tiny body I was horrified by my own
smallness my own totality the oddest sensation I followed
him at some distance fascinated he entered a house and I
waited outside but he did not emerge and so I returned to
meet my mother feeling split down the middle my existence going one way and my essence going another an odd
feeling indeed and difficult to explain it was obvious to me
then why I felt that the clothes were not my own and the
feeling I had when I beheld myself in the looking glass not
unlike the feeling of seeing him across the crowded square
I have often wondered having read those stories by Conrad
and Poe if I saw him at all or if he did in truth look
anything like me if I invented him as a child as a way to
understand what I was already struggling with myself as
both subject and object in the world now there's a thought
and brilliant Jean-Paul as a child already contemplating the
nature of existence no perhaps more likely the boy looked
quite a bit like me but I suppose I will never know and
who is to say that I did not invent all of it not only boy but
also house and crowded square and appointed time to meet
with my mother and the outing itself who is to say that it is
not my invention and that is the real horror isn't it subject
and object a product of history and history a derivative of
memory and the Cartesian nonsense about ideas in the
mind of God but we are here now aren't we and whose
ideas are we now I wonder having closed our eyes whose
ideas are we now

- the night your first play opened I held your hand as though we were lovers like any other and you were nervous yes but did not know that I knew you kept pushing your shirtfront more tightly into your waistband and my dear little being so like every other at that moment you never understood I loved you for your genius but loved you more when you tucked your shirtfront into your waistband and did not know that I noticed you doing it and did not notice that you were doing it yourself and I could smile and say nothing and love you because you did not know then that you were small yes small enough to fit into the palm of my hand small enough for me to hold completely and then when their applause came and you stood and waved you were Jean-Paul again and I applauded with them loving you as Jean-Paul and all night they bought you drinks and tried to impress you yes I loved you when you were him and I wanted to impress you as much as they even when we were past all of that still could not help but want to so certain that some charming student would come along and impress you more God yes that was the problem with loving Jean-Paul and was what made it so sweet to love you when you were tucking your shirtfront into your waistband yes no need to impress you or do anything but love you and I did not want that even though I agreed no did not want a love without affection and neither did you I suppose but what use did you have for my affection what use did you have for it when there were so many pretty young students buying you champagne and trying to impress you and I like the matron somehow though I never intended to be it was hell to watch you hoping that behind your smile they bored you terribly yes hoping that back in the car you would dismiss them with a word and tuck you shirtfront into your waistband a ridiculous thing to hope and especially ridiculous to hope against the evidence you

never grew bored of their praise did you and after all they
were very pretty it seemed like another lifetime in which I
had held your nervous hand as though we were lovers like
any other can you know what it was like to let you go
again and again and again silencing the objections that
rose within me knowing that to give them voice would
ruin it for you would ruin me for you I was your *Castor* a
name you called me saying I was tireless you were wrong I
grew so tired of feigning indifference of smiling when you
introduced me to whatever pretty young girl had bought
the last round tired yes my God so very very tired and
when they told me you had died I did not believe them and
went mad walking through the streets though of course I
had known it was coming for some time still there is such
a distance between the dying and the dead and even as a
sick man you were present as a dead man you were simply
gone there is no possible way to describe the way in which
I felt my mind recoil when I saw your chair empty and
caught myself thinking that you were in another room listing to myself without meaning to the other places you
might be inventing stories oh he must have been hungry
and stepped out for a moment it is almost lunchtime after
all it really was something to see the clockworks of my
own mind laid bare like that so apparent now the once ob-
scure I wonder if that was what it was like when they first
opened the chest of a living person and observed the beating heart saw the cogs of my own mind working yes he
must have been hungry and stepped out even though I
knew that you were dead knew where they had taken your
body even then I could not help thinking perhaps he has
gone down into the cellar for something and realizing then
as never before that Simone was only patterns of thought
running about the meat of my brain such an odd thing to
have obscured for so long I thought of writing a story

about it listing the chain of processes that fire in a character's mind in response to each of the stimuli he encounters
and showing in short fashion their limited scope I went as
far as breaking him down into primal drives the way the
mind does too and that's all we are isn't it just sublima-
tions of those desires I knew my own mind better at that
moment than I had at any other watching myself recoil at
your absence thinking he has just stepped out I will go and
have some lunch as well and perhaps catch him up later
and even when I told myself that you were dead feeling
hunger though I had only just eaten feeling hunger and the
desire to go and sit by myself in a café and prepare some
ideas to share with you when I caught you up again and
then later when there was no avoiding the fact finding myself angry with you for leaving yes angry as I had been
those times I came and you were out with one of your girls
feeling slighted by your death so ridiculous and yet the
feeling just the same and nothing to be done about it the
mind responding to stimuli along set patterns and in all of
our discussions on being never once realizing that being
was so innately ignorant that it was almost impossible to
make any reckoning of our apparatus the fallacy of trusting
the senses yes and the conscious and the subconscious yes
but also the mind in time always arriving back at itself and
acting with no understanding coming to conclusions with
no understanding just dumb animals attaching words to
sensations whose origins we do not understand whose progress we cannot see whose patterns we do not perceive I
never understood the rift between the higher and lower
mind until that moment your final discussion point perhaps
I thought later before realizing that to imagine your death
as a statement in a conversation with me was only to allow
myself the luxury of fantasizing your continuance Oh God
I could do nothing to stop it I still woke expecting vaguely

to see you later in the day every thought I had I made note of intending to share it with you later always coming to awareness of your absence with a renewed sense of loss a progressless sense of loss overwhelmed by its finality and vigilant enough at least to keep myself from conjecture ignoring the impulse to move away from the empty place you used to occupy in the world and in my world saying that is the way of the world or that is the nature of life or you knew this was coming and instead saying nothing thinking nothing and remaining wordless in thought and action yes wordless a fitting tribute and not unsuited to your passing you who called words a bourgeois escape I knew what you meant then as I had not before to say anything would be to move farther from and not closer to the truth of the thing and published my farewell certain that you disapproved but certain also that if you knew me at all you knew I disapproved as well but what else was I going to do you left me with so many hours in which to miss you what else was I going to do

    - yes a sensation becomes a thought becomes a passenger on a train riding a series of interlacing tracks to a limited number of locations far fewer than we would like to believe isn't it obvious we only have so many words for love and so many words for hate take all of the expressions of something inner and lump them together you would not have enough to fill your hat flowers on your birthday leisure hours spent fishing words spoken in anger the distinctions we make based on preference ignore the uniformity of the apparatus by which those preferences are formed and the notion of the self becomes only a series of claims made out of our inability to negotiate a world which acts upon us the self at the most basic level which yearns for its own procreation and survival lost behind an avalanche of words and thoughts and in no way cultivated yes there is a self but he is a beast striving after only the basest things all else is artifice and pretension the only true thing is the body all else a fantasy watch anyone as they slip into old age and you will see that only by your desire to see them as they were do they continue no part of them remaining but your memory which you affix to them long after any trace of that person has ceased and even in death such nonsense clinging to the image in memory the sense of a person imagining a heaven in which they continue oh the self is flimsy that is the horror of war men come back shattered not by what they have seen but by what they have done and can make no reckoning of God yes the horror of being is that it holds no parameters at all

- and do you remember the week we went to the spa in the mountains you said it would be good for us the mineral waters had restorative properties I went because you wanted to and the train ride I took by myself to meet you I felt ridiculous and certain that something had come up that would keep you from coming but took the train nonetheless and was so relieved when I saw you standing on the platform I'd never felt so loved you were tired and rode the rest of the way asleep upright in your chair and I edited the things you'd given me to read but I was useless as an editor at that moment so in love with you and my heart breaking with gratitude to you for being on the platform I could not have corrected you and the concierge so wonderfully indifferent to us did not ask our names and we laughed about it later saying it must pay well to be discreet in a place like this and wondering which of the men we saw around were there with their mistresses I had a great deal of work to get to and went upstairs and you came up with me anxious to get out to the spring I caught sight of you as you were leaving in your bathing trunks always so amazed by your body that it held you that this squat ugly body was Jean-Paul and loving you because you were ugly yes that something so ugly could be Jean-Paul after you were gone I felt foolish for refusing your invitation and changed into my own bathing clothes and stood before the mirror still surprised after all this time that Simone was this ugly body but more certain than ever that it was Simone and Jean-Paul always and essentially the fact of these two ugly bodies somehow an affirmation I went down and saw you'd already picked one out sitting too close to disguise your intentions it was cold and I had only a towel wrapped about me but the gooseflesh did not rise until I saw you laugh and thought no it would be better to go finish my work first yes it is always better to finish what you have started and then with the work done I will be able to relax we are all such wonderful liars when it comes to ourselves telling myself it did not bother me that you were talking with her and she not ugly like we were ugly or at least not like I was ugly it never was a hindrance to you though was it I should have written about that how an ugly man can get so much farther in life than an ugly woman yes not much in the world for an ugly woman but no of course that was not what was bothering me it was only the voice of the unfinished work calling from our room's open window and God it's funny to think about it now sitting at the desk in our room in my bathing clothes wrapped in a towel reading and rereading the same paragraph until you came back and Oh are you finished already I was planning to join you but then your writing called me back I guess I lost track of the time you see I've already changed into my bathing clothes but how was it and are you refreshed and my heart broke when you smiled and said yes I feel refreshed I could hear the excitement in your voice knew it from before knew what it meant and where it was going and that there was nothing for me to do but endure it I did not show it but said that is good then very good and this trip was all worth it if it makes you feel refreshed but for God's sake shower that mineral water stinks to high heaven it was a lie you sniffed but did not smell anything but shrugged and went into the bathroom I was relieved certain that I could not have kept it up for another moment and grateful when the shower went on because I knew I had a few minutes I put your writing away and changed my clothes rapidly but not rapidly enough because I saw it yes no way to avoid it my body so ugly intolerably ugly and the thought of yours in the shower through the wall no comfort at all and you came out and dressed and asked well shall we go eat and I imagined you anxious to go downstairs because there was a chance that you would see her again and God only knows what you said to her about me explaining that I was your friend or editor or assistant and should be no impediment I told you that I was not feeling well and thought it better that I stay behind and sleep worried that if I went down I would be sick for the whole week and maybe I could catch it now your disappointment could not hide your relief I watched you go and lay awake it seems impossible now but I am certain that I neither slept nor moved for seven hours watching the room go dark when night came the only light from the lamp over the writing desk and certain you were out with her marveling at you because you could work so quickly and eventually proud yes so proud because I was strong enough to love you this way and my God the lies I told myself and believed but nothing to compare it to after all no example to follow for our lives and so no way of knowing if things were what I said they were or if they were something else but I had strength enough to endure and that was something yes at least that was something and when you came back later alone I was so relieved and fantastically hungry and convinced you to take me out someplace to eat and nothing is open you told me except perhaps the one place and I convinced you to walk me there and took your arm feeling ridiculous and yet no less inclined to do so yes holding your arm making no excuses holding you and not willing to share too tired to sublimate or control myself yes too tired and half-mad with waiting and hunger I held your arm and loved you your ugly body and Jean-Paul and your laugh which raised the gooseflesh as I stood watching you loved you yes because there was no other way to take you prisoner

- and when we tried to form that trinity O what a mistake laughing about in nomine Patris et fillii et Spiritus sancti told her that she was the zeitgeist of the whole endeavor that she had some intangible and unrestrained quality some strength of personality some refusal to conform yes it was easy to love you and you loved her too but of course it was not so simple as all of that was it no of course it was not and how could it be after all the two of you and one of me an excellent lesson in geometrics for any student struggling with the subject one learns very quickly about angles in a situation like that angles and vectors I had never seen nor experienced nor contrived such maneuvers like a wonderful game we never stopped playing and even your jealousy and the artifice with which you attempted to disguise it all part of the game it really was fascinating to watch and she bouncing around the middle I admired you then watching your animal cunning yes fascinating to watch you maneuvered so deftly it seemed almost effortless and when you finally broke I was surprised having had no indication after all that you were suffering thought you were enjoying our game as much as I and that was it really wasn't it that it was not our game at all but only my game which you played to please me yes and I understood of course I understood but still asked what was wrong and acted surprised by your answer saying I had no idea that you felt this way no no idea at all and why didn't you say something sooner and that was a precious angle making you ridiculous in your suffering not my fault but your own for suffering in silence yes a cruel angle to pitch against you but I was having fun playing my game knowing that every moment you complained you felt me slipping more finally from you felt my heart fleeing to the one who demanded nothing from me and did not want to keep me yes felt it and knew it and yet said it is no matter and you do not need to worry and remember what you said when the game began that it would be fun knowing even then that you had said it only to make me happy but still nothing stopping me from throwing it back in your face and then insisting that we get ready for supper as we only had a little time before we were supposed to meet her I watched your stoicism seep up to the surface like ground water and you said yes of course please just ignore me I am being ridiculous I know and I forced myself to bestow upon you a kiss I did not feel a kiss uninspired by affection a kiss inspired by duty and a disinclination to change yes kissed you and followed you with my eyes into the bathroom until you closed the door and I fell back on the bed in relief knowing that you would say nothing for the evening and likely for weeks to come had likely bought myself a few weeks respite in which the battle in your mind would turn and turn back should you speak or should you remain silent and which was better and was I slipping away knew that your silence came at the price of your inner and constant deliberation and struggle and that at the moment I was willing to sacrifice your happiness for this game that we were playing yes the general sending another wave to the front it was cruel of course but perhaps the fact that it was cruel is less in the greater scheme than the fact that I knew even then that it was cruel but did it anyway waited for you as you readied yourself in the bathroom thinking only of her and what terrible fun it was and when we all sat down to dinner together thinking yes what fun the dozen other minds in the room slowly cooking as they watched us and wondered or did not have to wonder cooking under the flame of their bourgeois reservations and sense of propriety my God just immoral and yes my God just improper to conduct oneself in that fashion and feeling like we three made an island among them and a vast ocean lay between yes and the pitch of her laughter which never failed to reach the farthest point in the room it would have been impossible to ignore us and on the third bottle of wine impossible to ignore any of us you asked the waiter if you could borrow his apron and wore it like a veil held over your face obscuring your mouth and when she asked what you were doing pulled the veil away and gave her neck a nibble how she squealed and the waiter nervously asking for his apron back must have thought we would get him into trouble and how was I to know that you were unhappy when you played the game so well how on earth was I to know but of course I knew and going upstairs feeling again like we were an island and yet also that you were an island among us yes everyone is an island of course but not as you were then and I did not try to draw you back no knew that it was pointless but its pointlessness might not have been a deterrent would have made some attempt a year earlier but did not now did not care to and of course did not want to have another scene as we had earlier feeling sleepy afterwards and listening to her mumbling in her sleep the way a child mumbles in their sleep immediately into darkness no clinging to the waking world to keep her from slipping all the way down it never

ceased to amaze me and yes that is perhaps the best portrait you on one side and she on the other and she immediately to sleep with no reservations and you awake even
lying still I knew that you were awake and me somewhere
in between and in nomini patri e fili e spiritu sancti and
was God the one who went right to sleep or was God the
one who stayed awake and could not keep from worrying
it was obvious then as it is obvious now indifferent God
like a child who cannot be held accountable drifting off to
untroubled sleep and you awake like Christ in the garden
locked into an outcome you had not understood fully in the
beginning but now could do nothing to alter I pitied you
then yes pitied you because I saw myself floating above
you and comprehending everything about you the spiritu
sancti a horrible thing to do to someone you love but the
truth is that I did not care no did not care then working as I
was on just another angle in our triangle a wonderful angle
in which I bore straight down on you and pinned you to
the spot unable now to object or weep unable to do
anything I hoped but smile

- and the letters the other girls sent to their men away
at war how could anyone blame me for not feeling like one
of them one showed me a picture she'd had taken of herself something to keep him company and keep him away
from other girls she said but of course knew it was hopeless and asking me did I think it was all right or did the
officer in charge read all mail before it arrived I told her
she would have to take her chances a horrible thing I suppose looking back on it pitying her and her slight barrel
chest and small breasts and her face which no one would
call pretty but some would call nice yes I would call nice
and did I think the officer in charge would take the photo-
graph and black out whatever mention she made of it in
the letter she'd heard of them doing that and it had cost

quite a lot for what it was she could have had it done for cheaper but this man had been recommended to her by another who'd done the same thing and the man promised to destroy the negatives after and not make any other copies I went to his house she said and he took me down into the cellar where it was all set up and there pointing he said was a screen I could get undressed behind I almost ran out then but laughed instead and did as I was told emerging from behind the screen I was somehow not myself it was very strange but yes she said I felt not like myself he was so indifferent to me after all perhaps he is one of those but sat me down on just a crate thrown over with a blanket and turned on the light the brightest light my God and shielded my eyes how do you want to be he asked I did not know having never done anything like this and stood up straight and smiled the way I had when they took our pictures for the annual I was nervous yes so nervous do not think I took a breath the whole time and no turn like this he said making it easy this is how the other girls have me shoot them and before long feeling like a real pinup girl really incredible and then took me upstairs and gave me coffee while he developed the film a gentleman I never would have expected and then the walk home with the envelope tucked into the waistband of my skirt and hidden beneath my shirt certain that some policeman would stop me for being out at that time of night and find them and when I passed one coloring in the face I was so angry with myself giving myself away like that but nothing I could do about it but he only smiled to me and said good evening and after all a man my father's age all the young men being gone I hurried upstairs without greeting my mother and hid the pictures beneath my brassieres hoping that no one would look there but in a panic certain that someone would find them and it took an hour before I was calm enough to face my mother but now do you think I should send it and I cannot bear the thought of some stranger looking at me like that and being in someone else's daydreams you know how men are having you in their heads you can't do anything about it and they look at you different after but I suppose I will never meet any of those men but what if I should be walking down the street after the war is over and bump into some man who recognized me oh I would die of shame yes I believe I would die on the spot or want to die but for what did I take the pictures if I never meant to send them and perhaps to hell with all of that he might be killed fighting at the front and I would hate myself forever if I did not send them and no I was not like the other girls could not say I was like that and knew that you could be killed at the front as well and days later asked the same girl for the address she looked surprised it was almost funny no great beauty herself barrel-chested and with a face no one would call pretty wondering why I would want pictures like those or how I could imagine anyone would want to see them knew that I was not beautiful nor made any claim to be and had no intention with whatever photographs he gave me still she gave me his address I waited a week and then went half hoping that he'd been found out and shut down by the police yes hoping the decision would be made for me and how did you hear about me he asked a perfect gentleman inviting me inside and no use beating about the bush shall we go downstairs and the screen just as she had described and the crate thrown over with a blanket and afterwards coffee while I waited walking home with the pictures tucked beneath my shirt and I burned them without looking at them certain anyway that he had not destroyed the negatives as he had said he would but certain that I did not want to see them and that it was enough yes enough to emerge from behind the screen feeling the strangeness no other feeling like that ever and I loved you so yes loved you and wanted to love you as other girls loved their men away at war just a simple love an excitable visceral carnal jealous coy yearning anxious hungry love burning the pictures instead and writing you of my work my deep work my profound work my work which looked beyond the world of forms and into the world of meanings my work which got to the real truth of things knowing in the back of my mind that it was all a dodge and that if the bourgeois escaped life through fiction certainly we were guilty of escaping life through discourse and I knew I was not alive as that girl was alive in agonies and yet shyly proud of this testament to her body her being totally captured the content of her love perfectly expressed in the curve of her features of course my picture had not captured me at all could not capture even the impulse which drove me to his door wishing to love you as other girls loved their men at war no had captured nothing but a naked body divested of its meaning and so I wrote you instead thinking content would do in the absence of form no wonder you fell again and again into the arms of others having received from me no form to love only a disembodied consciousness hovering near an assemblage of meat and bone

- do you have a girl at home they all asked me an odd thing to explain so I just said yes and hoped that they would leave off but of course they did not nothing else to do after all but talk about home and what is she like what is her name what is she like in the sack huh tell us about that and did you make it with her all of that my God people like bad parodies of themselves and their questions less offensive than their presence if that makes any sense and perhaps it does not unless you have had to live in close quarters with people you are worried you will be bombed with and die with and thus be grouped with on the papers listing the details of the incident and meaningless yes I know but something within me objected to being lumped in with did you make it with her and what's she like in the sack stupid perhaps but one does not think clearly in those circumstances so I told them that you reminded me of certain passages from Boccaccio hoping that their ignorance would inspire their silence make them leave off but one can make no headway against such a unified front I could have wept with frustration finally the conversation turned from me such profound relief and ridiculous too for when I was captured I would have given anything to be back again wanted only to speak of you would have told them anything simply for the pleasure of remembering and of course the world we know is only a collection of perceptions and so the physical world remains secondary to the world of the mind but isn't it strange yes that a memory unspoken becomes insubstantial while a memory spoken becomes history and it was certainly odd but I felt you slipping from my mind and longed to speak of you and isn't it strange that the world of forms has such importance and yet no reality no not really any reality to speak of being only a collection of perceptions I felt you slipping away and would have given anything to be asked again if I had a girl back home and did I make it with her huh and would have told them everything so strange offering you up like the Eucharist gaining meaning only through consumption but no one to tell and half of those boys dead already and the fact of no eternal ledger was no argument against feeling like a bastard for finding them offensive and what would it have hurt to tell them about you except that I didn't want them to have you no not at all funny to think that later I wanted to tell them so that I could keep you and I suppose it makes no sense anyway and what makes sense in wartime no nothing makes sense and if I am to be forgiven for finding them offensive then perhaps it is only on the grounds that I was not thinking clearly in fear as I was of being bombed and listed beside them in the ledger of the dead

- and when you came home I felt my arms would break with clutching you yes thought I would embrace you harder than my body could endure and I would shatter against you a beautiful thought holding you and indifferent to the others at the station indifferent to the weather and the world indifferent to all but you my whole world you and nothing could be wrong no never again all of the stupid arguments over insubstantiality my God all the time I wasted wanting to best you in the argument and you on the platform like Odysseus returned from the dead so certain that I would lose you and now back in my arms I wept yes wept openly and had never loved you more would not no not ever never would no could not imagine and you no never and all my love irreducible by its impermanence or its meaninglessness or the absence of an eternal ledger nor the fact that I knew even as I embraced you that shortly we would both be forgotten and my sense of the importance of this moment was an illusion still I embraced you yes indifferent to everything but you and certain that the world could bugger off and I wouldn't mind saying it no would not mind taking that previously self-disallowed authority upon myself and telling them having no right to but willing to anyway and no longer any concern for the social contract or the dilemma of morality in a Godless world holding you yes indifferent to everything and certain that I could have died then happy ridiculous to think of it now but undeniable and felt you trembling too and certain that you felt as I did certain there was no impediment nor boundary left to cross what you felt I felt and words useless now yes useless and wished it never to end and in some ways I am still standing on that platform holding you no never released nor returned home but stood there fixed in eternity with my arms around you

- but do you remember as I remember the first time I saw you yes that terrible play and then afterwards speaking on Leibniz and I imagined from these few exchanges the organic totality of our relationship as one infers from bare arm or half-exposed breast the totality that is the body it belongs to and more than the body but also the person the self for whom the arm or half-exposed breast is a manifestation yes one sees a severed arm as an object divested of its humanity but a bare arm whose flesh is warm is something more one assumes both the totality of the body to which it belongs and also assumes the totality of the person we say resides within this body and thus the organic totality that is assumed is the totality of form and content which makes it also a fantasy of embodiment just as love yes involves a fantasy of embodiment wishing as we do to somehow grasp the elusive self hiding somewhere within the caverns of the body yes and yes it was in just this same way that I assumed the whole of our life together not as image no not as form but in its totality I imagined what it was to have you part of me and me part of you and our lives not two lives but perhaps a single conversation extending for fifty years into the future a conversation yes as one converses with oneself it is difficult to explain except to say that I saw all of it then and embraced you in my heart ridiculous perhaps but I was young yes young men may think such things at the sight of a bare arm or half-exposed breast I loved you yes sitting selfless in the dark of first the theater and then the auditorium where you spoke I loved you as only the anonymous can love and

Simone et Jean-Paul

lived our whole lives together before you were finished
speaking
  - but that day my God that day in late April with snow
on the ground and no heat in the apartment we stayed beneath the blankets woven together like strands of rope and
neither of us given to that sentimental impulse there was
nevertheless certain inevitable gravitas in which I let slip
that I loved you and you responded in kind but what value
does that have you asked the love of two people in the
vastness of an amnestic universe and knew that what you
were saying was true and important but knew also that you
were saying it because you were a scared little boy who
had never told anyone that he loved them before you
fought so adamantly for your postulation I wept and when
you tried to comfort me we made love again wanted to say
it when the moment came but knowing that it would only
cause problems I waited until you were asleep afterwards
and whispered it into your ear so that you would not object
whispered that I loved you loved you loved you and later
when you were gone I had that at least yes had the knowledge that I had said those things when you could not object
had told you everything I had to say it was not perfect no
not perfect but I had said it and in my youth I imagined
that it meant something there are certain stupidities it is
harder to escape and none so difficult as love when gravity
seems dense around you and everything is pulled toward
your center yes everything is vibrant and lovely and you
forget yourself and your obligation to your persona and are
just in love forgetting all of Nietzsche and Descartes and
Kant all thrown out to make room for this love which you
were not expecting love which demands all of your attention love which you cannot help but fall into and pleasant
yes my God the most pleasant stupidity I have ever known
better than oblivion and more permanent too and my

123

words like the juice of hebona in your ear coursing through all your smooth body something like loving an actor when you are in the dark audience I suppose my love somehow unstopped by my presence unrestrained and unguarded knowing how miserable you would make me and yet indifferent what choice did I have I was in love yes in love as the ignorant and the unlearned love in love as the stupid love clutching to one another with no understanding of themselves or each other only wordless yearning and grasping between them an unintelligible thing I could not help but be happy to leave off thinking and no longer Simone no not Simone not ever Simone never again Simone only that feeling always that feeling yes that feeling

THE NEWSCASTER WHO WEPT

"...Had they seen the special report about the famine in Ethiopia? The situation over there was really unbelievable; it had brought the Newscaster to tears!"

I

She still had a million things to do, and was not going to sit on the telephone waiting for him to speak. If he had something to say that could not wait until she got back then he should just say it! He did not feel right talking about it over the phone; could they meet for coffee? She replied that she might be able to squeeze in thirty minutes for lunch: if he promised to be on time she would meet him. Did he promise to be on time? He asked her why she would make him promise. Because: he knew as well as she did that he was chronically late! He said that he would be there. All right; that was fine; she had to go! She still had a million things to do; she loved him; bye-bye! She hung up.

When she got to the restaurant he had not arrived. She waited at the bar, watching for him through the window. After ten minutes she saw him crossing the street. She picked up and opened her menu as he came in and walked over. She shook her head: *this*! *This* was why she made him promise to be on time! She shook her head and waved the waiter over. Did he know what he wanted? What did he want? She ordered and then looked at him. He said that he was not hungry and the waiter went away. She scoffed: he was unbelievable, just unbelievable! He wasn't eating? It would have been nice to know that fifteen minutes ago!

He was not eating because he was not staying. He'd asked her here because he wanted to tell her before she left that he had been doing a lot of thinking, and had decided to move out. He'd given it a lot of thought, and had made up his mind. She laughed at him. What did he mean he was moving out? Just like that? He said quietly that he had given it a lot of thought. She had to have noticed how much they'd grown apart in the past year! They were both working all the time, and hardly ever saw each other: they were already living separate lives! She interrupted: he knew it was only until things settled down for her at work; things were just crazy for her right now! Did he think she liked being away from him all the time? Did he think she liked working these crazy hours? Look: she would be back in four days; there was no reason to do anything rash! When she got home they could talk it out: she was certain he would see that there was no reason to move out! He shook his head, then stood: he'd said what he'd come to say. He loved her, and wished her the best of luck. He kissed her on the cheek and then crossed the room, and she watched him through the window until he hailed a cab and climbed inside. When she turned back the waiter was coming with her salad. She ate and then asked the bartender if she could use the telephone. Ten minutes later the car from the station pulled up outside. The driver apologized: when she called he was away from the desk, and did not get the message right away. Oh, she did not mind waiting: she was sure that whatever he was doing was *very* important! She climbed in and he closed the door behind her.

The flight was surprisingly long. She ordered several drinks and fell asleep and was annoyed to find that, when she awoke, they were still in the air. She called for an attendant and asked how much longer it would be. The attendant checked her watch and replied that it would only be a few more hours. The Newscaster ordered another drink and then went into the bathroom. Looking in the mirror she was horrified by her appearance: her hair had flattened against the seat and there were dark bags under her eyes. Furthermore her face had an odd, puffy quality: she sucked in her cheeks, but found the look unnatural. Thoroughly frustrated she returned to her seat to find her drink waiting there for her. Taking the cup she called to the attendant and told her to remake the drink, using diet cola instead of regular.

Back in her seat she stared at her reflection in the window. God, travel was wrecking havoc on her system! She was retaining water like a sponge. But she knew why: there was no doubt in her mind that it was because of that horrible lunch. Yes, her mother had been right: one should never eat when one was upset! She had resolved to put thoughts of the encounter out of mind until her return, but now found little else to occupy her thoughts. Her head filled with a thousand arguments. He was just jealous of her career! She'd made it clear when they moved in together that for the next few years her career had to come first! She'd been very clear! He could hardly play the victim, giving her workload as the reason! Certainly there was another reason: most likely there was someone else! And now with all of the stress she was retaining water: he would ruin everything! Of course he did not want to break it off when she got back; oh no! He had to do it before, to sabotage her!

The attendant brought the drink. The Newscaster drank it quickly and then waved to the attendant. She would have another, with diet soda of course! The attendant went away, and the Newscaster turned again to her reflection. She sucked in her cheeks, and observed that in dimmer light this expression did not look nearly so unnatural. Perhaps they could fix the lighting when they were filming. Or: yes, she had the perfect solution! Her producer had repeatedly warned her to drink plenty of water: it was easy to get dehydrated in the desert! She would simply avoid water until it was time for them to film her.

What a relief: to think that this problem would be resolved, could be resolved by something so simple as not drinking water. Yes, she was resolute: she would not drink any water until the shoot was finished! Relieved by this solution she fell once again asleep.

Then the plane was landing and she woke up. Her producer came forward from coach and took her bag down from the compartment, then held up the line while she moved clumsily into the aisle. The attendant smiled indulgently at her as she disembarked. The ladder leading down to the tarmac was steep and her producer warned her to use the railings. A car was waiting and she got in the back and lay across the seat. Her producer sat beside the driver. They started moving and she fell asleep again. She woke up once and heard her producer saying Jesus Christ how awful. Then she was asleep and did not wake until they arrived at the hotel.

The cameraman was waiting for them in the lobby, and led them up to the suite. The elevator was broken, and they had to take the stairs. A team of bellboys carried their bags. She rolled her ankle stepping up onto the second floor landing and yelled at her producer; why the hell couldn't he find a hotel with a working elevator? She knew he was small time, but hadn't he ever heard of professionalism? The bellboys waited on the stairs below, holding the bags and blinking sweat out of their eyes. The cameraman and producer helped her up. She pushed them away and continued on unaided. She was limping and moved slowly, but no one would pass her. Finally they made it to the room. The bellboys left without waiting for a tip, but the producer chased them out into the hall. She sat down on the bed and asked the cameraman to get her some ice for her ankle. He left and came back, and explained apologetically there was no ice machine on their floor. The producer came back from tipping the bellboys and said that they should all get some sleep. She wanted to go downstairs to the bar, but decided not to because of the broken elevator. Why the hell didn't they get a room on the ground floor, if the hotel people knew the elevator was broken? The producer said that he did not know.

She closed the screen between the two rooms and lay down on the bed. The producer called that she should drink a glass of water before bed. It was important to stay hydrated! She rummaged through her suitcase, but could not find her nightgown. Eventually she found it folded inside another piece of clothing. By then the lights were out in the other room, and the cameraman and her producer were quiet. She changed and then went into the bathroom to wash her face. The sleep puffiness was gone, but her cheekbones lacked definition. She thought again that it was all his fault, that she always retained water when things like this happened. Giving herself one final annoyed look she turned off the light and left the bathroom.

She could hear her producer snoring. She climbed into bed but could not fall asleep. After some time she began to compose her report. It took some effort because she could not remember a lot of the details. She had heard them all in the production meetings, but had not been paying attention. She was reporting from – what was the name of the village? Reporting from wherever, where a new government initiative was underway: the military convoy they could see behind her was transporting residents from Ethiopia's famine-plagued northern villages to her more fertile southern regions. Or did "her fertile southern regions" sounded too suggestive? She laughed to herself at this joke. The military convoy behind her was transporting residents from famine-plagued northern villages to Ethiopia's fertile southern regions. She was reporting from wherever, a village in northern Ethiopia, where a new government initiative was working to curb the devastation wrought by famine. What they saw behind her was hope: hope that less dire circumstances could be found in Ethiopia's more fertile southern regions. But for many the promise of relief was bittersweet, as thousands of lives had already been lost in what some were calling a biblical famine in the twentieth century.

Thinking about the famine was making her hungry! She'd had nothing to eat on the flight: was it possible that she had not eaten since lunch in New York? Yes: she'd had nothing to eat since the salad over which he had told her he was moving out. An idea occurred to her: she would not eat until they were finished taping. They could get everything they needed in two days, she was certain, and it would give her an interesting inside perspective on the famine. Yes: hunger would give her an intangible quality that the viewers would immediately recognize. Further, it would give her cheekbones the definition they had been lacking.

She was very excited by the idea. People had heard of method acting, but she would be the first to try method *reporting*! She would be the portal through which the viewers would connect with the story: filmed on their own, the famine victims amounted to little more than an oddity. How were the viewers to know that the villagers had not always looked this way? And without that knowledge, how were they to feel anything about the story? The tragedy was in the difference between the healthy past and the sickly present; *she* would give them that contrast!

Yes, this report would be her finest: her rumbling stomach held the promise of future renown! She fell asleep, and awoke in the morning to the sound of the military convoy moving beneath her window.

She doubled her resolve to forego breakfast, and went into the bathroom to shower. Standing naked before the mirror she was pleased to see that her ribs, though visible before, were protruding slightly more than normal and that her cheekbones, even obscured by morning puffiness, were better defined than they had been the previous evening. Feeling very happy with herself she took a shower and brushed her teeth, remaining vigilant as to be certain that she did not swallow any of the water.

Her producer had ordered breakfast brought to the room. They did not have much time; the convoy was waiting for them outside. If she wanted something to eat she would have take it with her. She said that she was not hungry. The cameraman came in to pick up the rest of his equipment. They went downstairs and climbed into one of the trucks. Once they were moving the noise from the engine made conversation impossible. The cameraman had piled his equipment on the floor, and held it between his legs. She laughed; he looked like a strange bird that had laid a crazy egg! He looked at her inquiringly, and cupped his hand behind his ear. She shook her head and yelled for him to forget it.

They rode for two hours, and it was hot inside the truck. When they stopped her producer got out and told them to wait where they were. The back of his shirt was soaked through with sweat. The cameraman offered her some of his water. She said that she was fine. He held his canteen out to her: it was important for her to stay hydrated! She took it and held it to her lips, but pressed her tongue over the opening as she tipped it back. The cameraman seemed grateful: her producer had been on him to make sure that she stayed hydrated! She was a big girl; she promised that she could take care of herself! He shrugged; he was just doing what he was told. She knew; and anyways she thought it was sweet that he was looking out for her. The cameraman began checking his equipment.

Her producer came back and said that it was all arranged for them to film at the school. They would have to be quick, because he wanted to film some of the mothers at home before the children were let out. Then there was a town meeting. They would not have time to go back to the hotel before the meeting, but he had arranged it so that they could eat dinner with the soldiers. If they got everything they needed today then all that would be left for tomorrow was her greeting and sign-off, and shots of the convoy loading. He wanted the cameraman to remember that the report would only run for seven to ten minutes: he did need to save film, but he did not need a hundred shots of everything. He should just make sure they had options when it came time to edit.

They waited in the truck for half an hour, and then a pair of soldiers came and shouldered the cameraman's equipment. A third indicated that they should follow him. The streets were empty, and the producer explained that everyone was at home, packing. Every family was allowed one piece of luggage. There were several families that had agreed to be filmed packing. They would not have time to get to all of them, but he was confident that footage of one family packing was as good as another.

They went into the school. The children sat on the floor and the teacher stood in front, leading them in song.

The producer and the cameraman spoke together, and then the cameraman indicated to the two soldiers where they should put the equipment. Her producer tipped the soldiers. The cameraman began to set up. The Newscaster sat down on the bench that ran along the rear wall, and yawned. The cameraman dropped something and cursed, then looked around and apologized. Her producer said it was all right because the children did not speak English.

The teacher started another song, and the Newscaster put her head back and closed her eyes. God, she was hungry! Perhaps she could eat lunch, and then fast that evening and the following morning, and still achieve the results she wanted. But looking around she was filled with a sudden righteousness: what the hell was she thinking? These children had not eaten, so neither would she! These children with protruding bellies and eyes that bulged above sunken cheeks: yes! She took a notebook from her pocket and wrote *these children with protruding bellies and eyes that bulge above sunken cheeks.* That was good; that was very good! It was almost poetic. She would have to see where she could work it in.

The cameraman was almost ready. He spoke to the soldier who had led them. The soldier spoke to the teacher, and the teacher stopped singing. The children fell silent. The teacher, at the soldier's direction, moved four steps to her right, never taking her eyes off the soldier. The cameraman leaned back and then shook his head: no, too far! The soldier spoke again, and the teacher moved a step back to her left. The cameraman clapped his hands: perfect! The soldier said something, and the teacher started singing again. The children, having stopped, seemed to have a difficult time getting going again. The third soldier yelled something and then began to sing, and the rest of the children started. The cameraman shouldered the camera and switched on the light. The soldier who had directed the teacher began to sing as well in a deep, powerful voice. The teacher raised her own voice, and encouraged the children to do the same. The third soldier grinned and, satisfied, stopped singing. One of the children stopped singing and slumped to the floor. The children made way for the teacher, who rolled the child onto his back and stretched him out full length. She waved air into the child's face with her hand. The child opened his eyes and began to sit up. She spoke to him and he lay back down. When it was clear that he would not attempt to sit up the teacher returned to the front and started the song over. This time she sang it in the quiet voice she had been using when they first arrived. The cameraman wore a grin: it was beautiful, just beautiful! The child who had fainted remained on his back.

She watched her producer as he took the canteen from the pile of equipment and drank. He offered the canteen to her. She held it to her lips but did not take any into her mouth.

The cameraman moved around the room, getting shots from different angles. Her producer offered the soldiers a cigarette, and the four of them went outside to smoke. The cameraman moved around to the back of the room where she was sitting, and turned the camera on her. She crossed her eyes and stuck out her tongue. The cameraman laughed. He set the camera down and sat down on the bench beside her. Did he have everything he needed? He nodded. They sat, waiting for the soldiers and her producer to come back. The cameraman said he wondered why the class was still singing. Was that all they did all day? She said that she didn't know. She was pulling on her face, trying to feel the bones beneath her cheeks.

Her producer came in with the soldiers behind him. Were they all finished? He checked his watch. Perfect: that was perfect! He nodded to the third soldier, who said something to the other two, who picked up the equipment bags. The cameraman said that he would just as soon carry the camera himself. Maybe he would see something along the way that he wanted to film! Her producer said that it was a long walk to the next location, but that he could suit himself. The cameraman seemed to think it over, then handed the camera to one of the soldiers. If he saw something worth filming, there was no reason he could not get the camera back! Then they were leaving, and her producer turned and thanked the teacher. He raised his voice to be heard over the children. The teacher gave no indication that she had heard him. Her producer shrugged and they left.

The third soldier and her producer walked out ahead, the two soldiers with the bags walked behind, and she and the cameraman were last. The cameraman was searching in his vest pockets, and she laughed and said that he looked like a very lost fisherman. He looked at her with an expression of earnest confusion; he could have sworn there was a river around here! They both laughed.

Her producer had stopped walking, and they caught him up. He fell in step with them. The soldier said that they were going to visit three houses, the first one now and the other two after lunch. That should take them up to dinnertime, and then there would be a meeting where the soldier would address the villagers' last-minute concerns. There would be a tent set up for them so that they did not have to go back to the hotel tonight. Hopefully they would get most of what they needed today so that tomorrow they could take their time. She interrupted him: they were not going back to the hotel? She hadn't brought anything with her! What was she going to wear? And her makeup and hair? Yes: her producer had thought of that, and he'd had an idea: what if she wore one of the soldier's shirts? Think of how it would look! It would help convey the seriousness of the situation: there was no time for vanity on the front lines! Think of the impact it would have on viewers used to seeing her made up by a production team. The contrast in her appearance would be their most immediate point of entry into the story.

She attempted to imagine what it would be like, but was having trouble concentrating. Finally she agreed that it would be fine. By this time the third soldier was knocking on the door of one of the houses, and they hurried to catch up. Inside the house the soldiers set down the equipment, and the cameraman began setting up.

An empty chest stood in the center of the small room: the woman put something into the chest, and the man took it out again. They began to argue, but seemed to have little energy to do so. After a moment the man gave up and put the item back. Then the man put something into the chest, and the argument resumed. The soldiers went outside. The Newscaster and her producer followed them. The soldiers stood in a huddle farther down the street. Her producer went to talk to them about getting a shirt for the her to wear during filming. He came back and said that it was no problem. After a while the cameraman came outside and filmed the exterior of the house. Her producer asked if he was finished and he said that he needed five more minutes. Her producer told him to take his time. The soldiers came over, and the third one asked for cigarettes. Her producer handed him the pack. They took two each and went away.

Her producer took one himself and offered her the last one. He didn't know what he was going to bribe them with now: he had a carton, but had left it at the hotel.

The cameraman came out. He was done inside, but was thinking he would keep the camera with him, and get some footage of the town on the walk back. Her producer went to tell the soldiers that they were finished, and were ready to head back. The cameraman said that he hoped the other houses had better lighting. He asked for a drag of her cigarette. The soldiers came out of the house carrying the equipment. The cameraman shouldered the camera. They started back. The cameraman walked backwards, filming behind them. Her producer took the canteen from the soldier who was carrying it and offered it to her. She waved him off and instead caught up with the third soldier, and asked him if there was a telephone she could use. He said that there was not.

A village of tents had been set up in their absence. The third soldier showed them which one was theirs. The cameraman left to film the encampment. After a moment her producer left too, to see about lunch. She was exhausted from the morning, and stretched out on her cot.

How she wanted to go home, to stretch out on her own bed! But her flight home wasn't for another two days, and seemed impossibly far away. She couldn't imagine waiting that long! She was so tired of these locations, these crises, this life! It had occurred to her that he had been right: it was understandable that he could not live with her anymore; she could hardly live with herself either! She wanted desperately to call him, to tell him that he was right, to ask him if he would see her when she returned. She stood up

from the cot, thinking that perhaps one of the higher rank-
ing soldiers would have access to a telephone. However,
upon standing she felt overwhelmingly dizzy, and sat back
down. She had to call him! She stood again, and again felt
dizzy. Perhaps she'd rather rest instead: she would wait to
stand until her producer came to get her and would drink a
little bit of water, but only a little bit! Just enough to wet
her throat. Then, when her producer came, she would tell
him that she was too tired to go to the dining hall: the trip
had worn her out! She would ask if he would mind bringing something back for her, and then could get rid of it
when he was not looking. He would not understand, and so
there was no point in trying to explain it.

But her skin would look incredible after these three
days: she was certain that the sun and the fast's detoxify-
ing effect would work wonders.

The cameraman came back. His shirt was soaked
through across the shoulder where he had held the camera.
He sat down on the cot opposite and drank from the canteen she offered him. He looked upset, and she asked him
what was wrong. Couldn't she guess? The plight of these
poor people! Of course: of course it was really terrible! He
shook his head; he'd just seen soldiers throwing scraps of
food to the dogs that were hanging around the kitchen.
Food to the dogs, while the school was filled with starving
children! She asked him how old he was. He said that he
was twenty-four. He shook his head again. He was going
to get his lunch and take it up to the school. It was not
much, but at least it was something! He could not bear to
eat it himself. She nodded; she thought it was a wonderful
idea! In fact, she would do the same! Was he going to
bring the camera? The footage could be very compelling.
And besides, it was better to have it and not use it than to
want to use it and not have it. He agreed. They left the tent

together and she took his hand; she thought it was really brave of him to do this! They went into the meal tent, where the soldiers and her producer were already eating.

But the guard at the door would not let them leave. He called to another soldier, who came over and explained to them in English that they were not to go outside of the tent with their food. The cameraman asked him why not. The soldier replied that they did not want to deal with people begging at the tent for food. The convoy carried enough food for the soldiers for the duration of the operation. It was the job of the army to feed its soldiers so that the soldiers could do their job, which was to move the people.

The cameraman did not say anything. The soldier suggested that they sit down. He indicated an empty table. The cameraman looked past the guard, out through the tent flap. He handed his plate to her, shouldered the camera, and asked the soldier to repeat what he had just said. The soldier grinned, and repeated that he thought they had best sit down. The cameraman told him to say the other thing. The soldier did not know what he was talking about. The cameraman lowered the camera and took his plate. The soldier told him to enjoy his lunch.

They sat down at the table. It made her sick: just sick! She had entirely lost her appetite; she could not even think of eating! She pushed her plate away. The cameraman folded his arms on the table and did not say anything. Her producer came over and sat down. He saw what had happened; it was just as well. They did not want to upset their hosts! After all, they were only there with the military's permission. The cameraman suddenly spoke up: it was bullshit, total bullshit! The military did not give a damn about these people! Her producer asked why the military would help them if they did not care.

The cameraman snorted. Could her producer really be so blind? What did he think was causing the famine? Did he think it might have something to do with the civil war between the U.S.- backed rebel forces and the Soviet-backed government that had crippled Ethiopia's economy? Did it have anything to do with the fact that relief supplies could not get through the combat zones to the people who needed them? That the rebel forces - which the United States government had supplied with weapons and train-ing! – regularly raided relief supply convoys? That's all this was about to them! It wasn't about starving kids, or people fighting over which bowl they would take in their one suitcase; it was about emptying the northern region so that the supply convoys would stop, and the rebels would be starved out!

The cameraman folded his arms, looked away from them, and fell silent. Her producer finished his lunch, and asked her is she was going to finish hers. She said that she could not eat, thinking about those poor children. He re-minded her that it was important to eat; she had not had any breakfast either! It was important to eat and stay hy-drated. This environment could be very taxing; he knew that he did not have to tell her what a toll it could take, both emotionally and physically! He began to eat her lunch. She asked him how he could eat at a time like this. He shrugged. There were two kinds of people in the world: noble people and practical people. He had figured out a long time ago which one he was!

The soldiers began to clear out. There was the sound of barking from behind the kitchen area. The cameraman ex-cused himself and took his camera. He came back a few minutes later, led by two soldiers. One of them was carrying the camera. He set it down on the table in front of her producer and the cameraman sat back down in his chair. One of the soldiers said that the captain would like to speak to her producer at his next soonest convenience. Her producer set his fork down and followed the soldiers out of the tent. The Newscaster asked the cameraman if he got any footage. He shook his head and said that they had grabbed him the second he put the camera on his shoulder. It was such total bullshit; it made him sick! The government wanted them to film miserable people in the depths of despair, and then show the military sweeping in like some savior angel... They were not here to bring awareness about the famine: they were here to unwittingly craft a piece of Soviet propaganda! He could not believe that he had not seen it sooner. It was his fault, really; it was his own stupid, self-satisfied, American blindness!

She nodded but wasn't really listening; she was beginning to feel very tired. She wondered if she had time, before they went out again, to go back to the tent and take a nap. God, it would be wonderful to be home, to be in her own bed! She was already convinced: when she got home she would apply for a change of position. No more field work for her! She'd had enough. Who did she think she was? This life was not for her; she belonged in the city! She belonged in the city and she belonged with him. That was the life she wanted; why hadn't she realized it sooner? She'd been at odds with herself for years, taking assignments around the globe out of duty: to herself, yes, but also to the audience that looked to her as a shining example of an ambitious woman, to her producer and the hours he had spent battling for her, even to him, afraid that if she stopped she would no longer be the woman he fell in love with... She was done with it; she was done with it all! She had no more passion for the suffering peoples of Ethiopia than she had for the innumerable and anonymous masses huddled elsewhere.

Yes: when he saw her again he would see that she had changed. Why had she gone on this assignment in the first place? Why, when the only important thing in her life was slipping away? And yet the thought of not going had not even occurred to her! No: she had been a good little soldier, marching bravely forward; she was tough and driven! She could not help going on the assignment! Why, when all she really wanted to do was chase after him? God, she hated herself sometimes!

Her producer came back and said that after a careful review, the commanding officers had decided that it would not be feasible for them to film the meeting that was to take place that evening. There would be no room and besides, they could not imagine that the meeting would be of much interest to them, seeing as how it would be in another language. They suggested that the crew spend the time filming something else instead. Her producer picked up his fork and set back to eating her lunch. He would very much appreciate it if the cameraman would clear any dumb ideas he had with him before he went and did them. The cameraman did not say anything. She asked if she had time to take a nap before they went out again. Her producer checked his watch and said that their escort would be by in half an hour. The cameraman said he would walk her to the tent.

She stretched out on the cot and closed her eyes. After a while she heard the cameraman go out. She woke up a while later with the panicked certainty that they had left without her, and that she would not be able to find them. But then she remembered that the cameraman's equipment was still in the tent, and that the soldiers could not have come to retrieve it without waking her. She realized also that she had a stomach cramp. She took a drink from the canteen and then went back to sleep. She woke up upset; she knew that if one was dehydrated one retained all of the water one drank! She felt her face, and was certain that it felt puffier than before.

She wished that they would film her already! Why did they have to do it against the backdrop of the loading convoy? There was no good reason: a report delivered before the village of tents would be just as compelling. But she knew as well that she was barely showing the effects of her hunger: no, those would not be evident until well into tomorrow! And her producer was right: reporting with the loading convoy as a backdrop was much better. She would have to remain vigilant: yes, vigilant against herself, vigilant against her own mind and the tricks it played! She would not eat until tomorrow evening. What was one day, in the vast scheme of things? Nothing! She strengthened her resolve. The cramp in her stomach had worsened; she rolled to her side, thinking that a change in position might lessen it, but did not notice any difference. She reminded herself that the cramp was the promise of future renown; yes, this report would certainly be among her finest!

Her producer came in. Was she feeling all right? She did not look well. And she hadn't eaten any of her lunch! Perhaps it would be better if she stayed behind and got some rest. She shook her head and sat up, but felt dizzy and did not stand. She was fine; really, she was fine! She would go with them. Her producer shook his head. No, it was best that she stay. They would not be long; they only needed to film a few houses, and then whatever else the cameraman saw along the way. It would not take more than a couple of hours. He would have their escort send over some shirts for her to try on while they were gone. It was actually better this way! She apologized; she did not know what was wrong with her! She did not have to apologize! She'd had a few drinks, had not slept well on the plane: he understood! She did not need to explain herself. But she should get caught up on sleep while she had the chance.

He left the tent and she lay back down on the cot. A few minutes later the soldiers came in to collect the cameraman's equipment. Afterwards she heard them talking outside, and heard her producer explain that she was not feeling well, and would not be coming with them. She closed her eyes and tried to sleep, but was brought awake each time she was close by the cramp in her stomach. She again wished that she was home; how nice it would be to be home, and in her own bed! How nice it would be to be home, watching her report on television; it would all be worth it then! Thinking this, she managed to ignore the cramp in her stomach long enough to fall into a shallow and fitful sleep.

It was dark inside the tent when she awoke, and it seemed to take longer than it should have for her eyes to adjust. She looked for the cameraman's equipment at the foot of his cot, but did not see it there. She sat up and, feeling only mildly dizzy, stood and left the tent. The lights strung from the tent posts were lit, and glared white against the darkening sky. There was no one around; she walked towards the meal tent. A half-dozen soldiers sat around a table in the center of the space. When she entered they turned to face her and stopped talking. She asked if they knew where the cameraman and her producer had gone. But as she was speaking two more soldiers were attempting the enter the tent and she moved awkwardly out of their way, having failed to notice them until they were directly behind her. They went in and joined the others and she repeated her question: the two white men: had anyone seen them? One of the soldiers pointed and said something that she did not understand. She thanked him and hurried out. Her producer and the cameraman were standing outside their tent when she returned and she hugged them both; she was so glad to see them! Where had they been? She woke up and they were gone! She'd gone to find them; she'd gone into the meal tent and everyone had just stared at her; it was like being back in high school! They couldn't imagine how stupid she'd felt.

The cameraman explained that they'd gone to the meeting; it was just as well that she'd missed it. He was not allowed to bring the camera inside and anyway nothing had happened. The officer in charge of the operation talked for a long time and when he was finished everyone just left. Nobody had the energy to say or do anything; it was so sad! There would have been nothing worth filming, even if they had let him bring the camera inside. He sat down on his cot. Her producer asked if she had already eaten. She told him that yes she had eaten a few hours ago. He said that he was going to see if there was anything left in the meal tent. He was starving! He asked the cameraman if he wanted anything. The cameraman said sure. Her producer went out. The cameraman put his head in his hands. She sat down on the cot beside him and put her arm around his shoulders. He really mustn't take it so hard: she'd been in this situation a hundred times, and knew what he was going through! It was easy to get overwhelmed sometimes; it was hard to see these things and not get caught up in them! People did not understand how hard it was to be in the news industry, to see the things that they saw! He had to remember: what they were doing was helping these people! They were bringing awareness, and awareness would bring help, real help! They were telling the story to people who really could make a difference in these people's lives, if they only knew! He could take comfort in that.

The cameraman lifted his face to her: he appreciated what she was saying! For as awful as the things he had seen today were, he was glad he had seen them. Seeing them meant that he was here with her. He kissed her and then pushed into her, and she surrendered to his intention and lay back on the cot. She felt his hands sliding along her stomach and sides, and was glad she had not eaten. Her producer called from outside that dinner was already cleaned up, but that he had been able to pull a few things together. The cameraman stood quickly and sat down on the opposite cot. Her producer came in bearing plates: he hoped this was all right, but there wasn't much to choose from! The cameraman said that it did not matter: he was starving, too! He gave a nervous laugh and took the food. Her producer sat down on his own cot to eat. The cameraman offered her some of his. She declined.

She gave a yawn; she did not know why she was so tired! She lay down and faced the tent. She wanted nothing more than to sleep, to leave the room, to be somewhere far away! She closed her eyes and implored sleep to take her. It was no use; she could hear them chewing in the dark beside her. How she hated the sound of them chewing! The thought that her mouth had been pressed to one now making such revolting sounds disgusted her. For a moment she thought that she was going to be sick; yes, she had to rise and leave the tent immediately! But the feeling passed quickly. Besides: there was nothing in her stomach to vomit! She congratulated herself on her resolve. What had she been thinking about? She was having trouble focusing.

Of course one always had trouble focusing before sleep! That was all it was. Ah: kissing the cameraman! What had she been thinking? He was just a child! Oh well: it hardly mattered now! There would likely be no other opportunity for that mistake to repeat itself.

They had finished eating, and the tent was quiet. In the new silence she began again to compose her report: she was reporting from northern Ethiopia, where the starving residents of the village they saw behind her were finally getting the help they so desperately needed. A new government initiative was transporting residents from famine-plagued villages like this one to the country's more fertile southern regions. What they saw behind her was hope: hope that less dire circumstances were waiting in the country's southern regions. But for many families the promise of relief was bittersweet, as thousands of lives had already been lost in what some were calling a biblical famine in the twentieth century. In northern Ethiopia the starving residents of villages like the one they saw behind her were finally getting the help they so desperately needed. An initiative was underway to transport residents of famine-plagued northern villages like this one to more fertile spots in the country's southern regions. What they saw behind her was hope: hope for the future, hope that less dire circumstances awaited them. But for many the promise of relief was bittersweet; thousands of lives had already been lost in what some were calling a biblical famine in the twentieth century. But for many help had arrived too late: thousands of lives had already been lost in what many were calling a biblical famine in the twentieth century.

She had not tried on any of the shirts. Had they even brought the shirts for her to try on? She needed to try on the shirts! What if none of the shirts fit? What would she wear then? She thought of waking her producer to remind him. Perhaps he had forgotten! It would be stupid for her to keep quiet then. She rolled over, but felt that she did not have the energy to deal with waking him, explaining, making a plan… She rolled back and closed her eyes. Soon after she was asleep.

She awoke to the sound of trucks moving nearby. The cameraman and her producer were already up and gone. She left the tent. Her producer was coming towards her with a bundle of shirts over his arm. He called something that she could not hear over the noise. She shook her head; he reached her and yelled that this was all he could find. He handed her the shirts. She asked him where the cameraman was. Her producer said that he had gone to film the convoy getting into formation. He checked his watch; she still had some time to eat, if she was hungry. She asked him to repeat what he had just said; she had sort of spaced out for a minute! He repeated that she had time to eat if she wanted. She told him that she was fine.

She went into the tent to change. She tried the first shirt, but did not like the way it fit. The second fit much better, but she decided to try the third for good measure. She had the second one off when the cameraman came in. She held the shirt up to cover herself and turned her back to him. He apologized and turned to face his own cot. He was sorry; he just had to pick up one thing! She felt acutely the nakedness of her back; it seemed unbearably horrible that her bra strap was exposed to him, and that she could do nothing to cover it! The cameraman fumbled in his equipment and, apologizing, went out. She put on the shirt, in a panic that someone else might enter.

It made no sense! How many times had she been forced to change on location, right out in the open? Why had her exposed bra strap so pained her? Certainly because he had kissed her: yes, the kiss permitted his look, permitted whatever he felt at the sight of her naked back and bra strap! When she changed clothes on location it was out of an understanding of necessity: it was the height of professionalism, the emblem of her total commitment! The thought that her naked back and bra strap could become part of someone else's thoughts about her, could, indeed, become an object of erotic fixation, the seed of a fantasy in which she played a starring role and over which she had no authority, deeply troubled and annoyed her. Kissing the cameraman – or, rather, allowing herself to be kissed! – was a mistake: an obvious mistake! Hunger and dehydration were obviously catching up with her! Had she been thinking clearly, she certainly would have stopped him. Confident that she would not make the same mistake again, she buttoned the third shirt and left the tent.

The villagers stood in line, waiting to load their luggage. A pair of soldiers walked the line, repeating instructions. The cameraman stood filming. Her producer was beside him, and waved her over. Could they get some footage of her in front of the line? He wanted to film her in as much as possible today. She should say something about these people had been waiting since early morning to load their possessions onto a truck, with only the military's promise that they would get them back, how it was not unheard of for rebels to attack convoys like this one, netting items of value to sell on the black market. She frowned; did he know that for a fact? Yes: their escort had told him! He led her by the arm to where the cameraman was standing. And even if it was not true, they could edit it out later. He walked her in front of the camera. Was the microphone plugged in? The cameraman handed it to her producer without taking his eye from the lens. Her producer handed it to her. They didn't have much time: they had to get the shot before the soldiers moved the truck and started loading. He knew she would nail it: she was a pro! He stepped out of frame and gave her a thumbs up. The cameraman did the same.

She repeated the line her producer had given her. Her producer clapped; fantastic! He wanted her to do it once more; when she referred to "these people" could she turn her body towards them? And lower her voice when she said "black market"? The cameraman gave the thumbs-up and she repeated the line with her producer's variations. He clapped again; marvelous! Could she do it this way this time? And change the way she said that? He coached her as they recorded a half-dozen more variations. Then the truck pulled up, and the soldiers began to load the villagers' things. She stepped out of frame.

She went back into the tent for shade. She was feeling lightheaded, and sat down on her cot. But her producer came in a few minutes later; what was she doing? He wanted to get a shot of her watching them load. She had to remember: she was the audience's proxy; her experience was their experience! She knew! He did not have to talk down to her! She stood and followed him out of the tent. The meal tent was being broken down, and as they walked past the first row of supports fell. The rest quickly followed. At the far end of the camp another group of soldiers were taking down the sleeping tents. Her producer said that he would get their things out before the soldiers reached their tent. He went back inside and she walked on alone to where the cameraman was filming.

She stopped behind him and explained in his ear that her producer wanted some footage of her watching the loading. He nodded, but did not look at her. She walked awkwardly into frame, then turned to watch the line. She was certain that the shirt, now soaked through down her back, clearly showed the line of her bra strap.

She was profoundly annoyed with herself. Of all the ridiculous situations: to get involved – even a little involved! – with a mere child; what had she been thinking? Was it only her imagination that he was being cold to her? She turned around, smiled, and gave a small wave. The cameraman, looking away from the lens, looked at the line and asked her if she could move a few feet to her left. She took a half-dozen steps and then turned to face him; was this good? He seemed distracted; looking through the lens, he took careful steps in a semi-circle, moving around behind her. She faced the line; she could barely stand it! How much more footage did he need? She stood still for three more minutes, then called the question again. When there was no answer she looked over her shoulder and saw the cameraman and her producer talking; the camera was on the ground at their feet, beside the rest of their things. She walked quickly over to them; who did he think he was? And when there was a cut, she expected him to call cut! And he could not just walk away when they were filming!

But she did not say any of this, because when she reached them she was very out of breath. Her producer looked at her, concerned. This assignment was really taking it out of her! Maybe she should take it easy. She could find some shade, and they would call her when they needed her. She shook her head; this was her report! When there was a shot, she expected to be in it! She closed her eyes, lost her balance, and fell towards her producer, who caught her. She was fine; she was fine! She had just lost her balance. She pushed away from him and stood on her own.

Her producer looked concerned, but nodded. The soldiers were almost finished loading the truck, and the convoy that would take the people was supposed to roll in right after. He thought that they should get a shot of the trucks coming in. What did she think? The cameraman said it was a lot of work for a shot they probably wouldn't use. She said she thought it was a great idea.

An idea had occurred to her: she would make the rest of the trip as unpleasant for the cameraman as she possibly could. The idea had an odd kind of intuitive artistry about it; yes, it was only fair, after what he had done to her! Who did he think he was, leaving while her back was turned? What kind of person abandoned their half of a partnership but allowed the other to foolishly continue, thinking that everything was fine? How long had he been gone before she noticed? She had no idea! The thought of herself standing, alone and unrecorded, while he had already left, filled her with hatred. Who was he, to make her feel foolish? A nobody, someone she would fire and then forget the moment they returned to the city. There were a hundred – a thousand! – like him: not just like him, but better than him! Did he think he was so unique that he could humiliate her? He was expendable, replaceable! She waited behind them and then ran to catch up, hoping that the sweat would make her bra strap all the more visible.

The truck with the villagers' things drove to the end of the camp and stopped, and the convoy moved into position in its place. Her producer handed her a pocket mirror. She tied her hair back and then checked her face; the shadows beneath her cheek bones were clearly defined. She felt an irrepressible happiness; the transformation was so obvious, she was certain, that her viewers could not fail to notice it. All her hard work was worth it!

This produced a strange and disproportionate swell of emotion, and was momentarily certain that she was going to cry. But the feeling quickly passed and she shook her head: she did not know why things were affecting her so much! She checked her face once more, and then stepped into frame. The cameraman shouldered the camera and started filming. Her producer handed her the microphone. She crossed her arms, and felt the shirt pull tight and stick along her back.

She was reporting from – what was the name of this village? She laughed. She did not even know the village's name! Her producer told her the name. She was reporting from this village, where a new government initiative was underway: the military convoy they could see behind her was transporting residents from Ethiopia's famine-plagued northern villages to her more fertile southern regions. She stopped to ask if "her fertile southern regions" sounded too suggestive. She laughed again. Her producer told her it sounded fine. Would she take it from the top? She started over.

A soldier began calling instructions to the crowd of villagers. Her producer stopped her: they had very limited time, and had to get this right! She should not look like she was enjoying herself. He asked her to start again. She was reporting from this village, where... He waved his hands and she stopped. Her producer told the cameraman to stop filming. All right: they would go through it together. Pretend he was the camera! She was reporting from – Chin down! – where a new government initiative was underway: the convoy they could see behind her – Pause! Gesture! – was transporting residents from Ethiopia's famine-plagued northern villages – Diction! Diction! – to her more fertile – Pause! – southern regions. Good: that was very good! He crossed his arms and told her to start again.

She had it; why didn't they just film it? He held up his hands in surrender: she wanted to film it? He told the cameraman to start filming. She was reporting from this village in northern Ethiopia, where a new government initiative was underway. Her producer threw up his hands and looked away. She stopped: what was wrong with that one? Did she really want to hear what he had to say? The truth was that she did not speak clearly: he could not understand a word she was saying! Every report was a battle to squeeze an ounce of diction out of her.

He wanted diction? She would give him diction! She told the cameraman to start filming. She was reporting from This Village, where a new government initiative was underway: the Military Convoy they saw behind her was Transporting Residents from Ethiopia's Famine-Plagued northern villages to her more Fertile Southern Regions. There, how was that? He said that it was much better. She said that she was glad it was up to his standards.

They did the lead five more times. She grew rapidly tired of fighting him. The cameraman's expression never changed. The first truck in the convoy moved in line behind the truck carrying the villagers' things. Her producer spoke to the cameraman, but she could not hear what they were saying. He asked her to do the lead twice more, changing key phrases. On the second take she forgot her line, and they had to start again from the top.

She wanted very much to be finished, to be back at the hotel, to take a shower and eat something. Her producer asked her to take it once more. She groaned: God, didn't they have it already? What was wrong with the last three? She didn't want to do another one! Her producer shrugged. She didn't want to do another one? Fine! That was just fine! They would move on to the close. She hesitated, and explained that she did not have the close quite worked out.

Her producer threw up his hands. When was she planning to work it out? When the convoy was already gone, perhaps? Or back in New York?

What did she have? She was going to say something about how for many it was too late, how only time would tell if... He interrupted her, and told her to speak up. He could not understand her! She repeated herself, louder.

How she hated him! What did it matter that he could not hear her? She was speaking into the microphone; her voice would be loud on the tape! Besides, he had no business talking to her like that! She had poured her blood, sweat, and tears into this report; how dare he talk to her as though she was little more than a model, propped up before some atrocity? This was *her* report! He had no business treating her this way! And in front of the cameraman; it was almost too much to bear. Yes, it was too much to bear: she was going to say something; she was going to set him straight!

She began to speak; he held up a hand and shushed her. Couldn't she see that he was talking to the cameraman? Didn't she know that it was not polite to interrupt? All right, she could take it from the top. Action!

She repeated the lines, then signed off. Her producer shook his head: again, with diction! She repeated the lines; again! Chin up! More volume! Pause here and here! Look back at the convoy when she said this! She repeated the lines. Better, but still awful! She began again, but the second truck started its engine and drowned her out. The producer waved his arms. What was she going to do: shout over a truck engine? There were only a dozen more people to load, she had to get this one right! The truck reached its position in line and the driver shut off the engine. She repeated the line. Her producer tapped his wristwatch. Once more, from the top! She closed her eyes; in a few hours she would be back at the hotel. She could eat and drink and bath and sleep and then she would be on a plane home and he would meet her at the airport. She began to repeat the line, but then remembered that he would not be meeting her at the airport. No: he would not be there glad to see her, nor would he be at their apartment. He would not be there to listen as she told him about her trip and he would not be there when she awoke the next morning. She realized, also, and just as absolutely, that the pleasant memories of their life together were somehow equally lost: that in his absence their happiness served only as a reminder of her own folly, stupidity, and failure. How had she let him get away? And why? And what was she doing here, in the middle of Africa?

Her producer tapped his watch. Time: they were short on time! What the hell was she waiting for? She began again, but found that her voice had grown weak; she felt a tear run along her nose and she quickly wiped it away. She took a deep breath and finished the close. Without bothering to look at her producer, she immediately repeated it. As she was finishing the third truck's engine started. She handed the microphone to her producer, and went to change out of the shirt. She did not bother turning her back to them as she did so.

Their escorts carried their bags to the truck. She asked them if it was possible to get to any of the food. They apologized and explained that the food was already loaded, and packed beneath the other equipment. But if she liked, he would see if he could get to it. She told him not to bother; she was not hungry anymore anyway. They climbed aboard the truck and sat, waiting for the convoy to start. Her producer congratulated them both on their fine work. She had delivered a fine performance out there!

Finally the trucks started moving. After a while their truck split from the convoy. They followed the road into the city, and their escorts unloaded them at the hotel. The elevator, in their absence, had been restored to working order. The bellboys carried their luggage into the room. Their producer checked his watch. They had a few hours before they had to go to the airport; what did everyone feel like eating? He would order some food while they were getting cleaned up. She said that anything would be fine. She went into the bathroom, where she drank two glasses of water and then got into the shower.

It certainly was a relief to be finished! But there was still so much to do: yes, she would have to be in early the first day back in New York. She would start composing her voiceover material on the plane. It would be hard to do without first seeing a rough edit, but whatever changes needed to be made would be simple if the body of the text was already composed. Shorten, lengthen, change the or-der: all of this could be done easily. But it would probably take a long time to get it just right. Yes: there was a lot to do to finish the report; she would likely barely have time to set foot in her apartment. Oh well: at least they could not say that she was not committed! It occurred to her that, since she was going to sleep on the plane, she might not have to go home first at all.

2

The ballroom was still being prepared for the dinner. The Newscaster moved around between the tables, dodg-ing caterers and indicating to the cameraman where she wanted him to stand. If he stood here the audience would see the B-listers sitting at the back tables; if he stood here they would see the stage and the flowers! Now which did he think was better? Oh, good for him: he'd guessed the right answer! And if he stood here she would be backlit by the stage; he would have to stand off at a slight angle. How would it look? The cameraman said that it would look fine. Would she just relax? He'd been in this business longer than she had; she didn't need to tell him how to do his job! She replied that if he was any good at his job he wouldn't still be a cameraman.

The caterers began spreading the tablecloths. The florists, finished with the arrangements around the podium, left the stage to distribute the centerpieces. The Newscaster said that she needed some air, and went outside to smoke. She stood under the awning outside the door, deciding where she would stand when the limousines arrived. She would have to be close to have any chance of interviewing anyone, but did not want to wait outside until then. She should hire a bum to sit there for her, and save the place for her when the others arrived! She laughed at the idea. Yes: she would hire the hairiest, smelliest bum she could find! She thought of the other reporters retreating in disgust, at the thought of their faces as she paid him and took his place beside them. That would show the bastards who she was! She rose and went into the alley beside the hotel, but did not see anyone. She went back under the awning to finish her cigarette.

Four years: four insufferable, maddening, depressing, frustrating, worthless years! And now, to be stuck covering this: it really was funny; the prizes on the shelf in her office were funny! God, what she wouldn't give for another famine in Ethiopia! But then again: what did they say? Every challenge was an opportunity! Perhaps she would be the first Newscaster to win an award for her coverage of a dinner party! She laughed and lit another cigarette. If God would only send her some bloated babies, she promised that she would go to church every Sunday! If only He would help her, she would never ask for anything ever again! If only He would strike down those who got the assignments she wanted: yes! She laughed again. She finished her cigarette and went back inside. The tablecloths had all been spread, and half of the centerpieces were in place. Through this minor alteration the ballroom had been wholly transformed. She stood and watched the florists hurrying between the tables, holding the bouquets before them. In no time at all the rest of the centerpieces had been placed. She had to get going if she wanted to be ready by the time the guests arrived. She went up to the room to change.

The cameraman was sitting on the edge of his bed, watching the television. He stood as she came into the room; had she heard what was happening? She winced and waved a dismissive hand; she did not care what was happening. She did not want to hear about what was happening. It was enough that she knew what was happening tonight; that was what he should be most concerned with as well!

She went into the bathroom and closed the door. The sound of the television was muted behind the wall, and disappeared almost entirely when the shower came on. She undressed, but could find neither her soap nor her shampoo. She overturned her toiletries and sorted through the pile; her soap and shampoo were absent. She sat down on the edge of the tub in abject exasperation. There was nothing to be done; she took the hotel soap and shampoo from the tray and got into the shower. The television was a low mumble through the wall. She washed her hair, but was certain that the hotel shampoo had not rinsed out clean.

She got dressed and left the bathroom; keeping her back to the screen, she lifted the remote from the nightstand and turned the television off. She did not want to see or hear or talk about anything having anything to do with news, reporting, world events! She did not want to see the big important things that other people were covering while she sat in a hotel ballroom, covering a dinner to honor some has-been actor that no one remembered! She just wanted to get through the evening and be done with it. But she could only do that if she was not reminded of how stupid the assignment was, or of the fact that the report would probably be cut to make time for whatever else interesting and important was going on in the world. All right? Could he go along with that?

He shrugged and said that he could go along with anything. All he needed to know was which way to point the camera. She thanked him and asked him to zip up her dress. She turned her back and pulled up her hair. And while he was back there, would he do her a big favor, and strangle her with her necklace? He zipped up her dress and she let her hair down. It was just as well; still, he couldn't blame a girl for asking! Did he want a drink? She was going to have at least three before they had to go downstairs.

They went downstairs. A half-dozen other reporters had now gathered in the lobby. The cameraman went outside to set up. The Newscaster went into the ballroom, but found that since the caterers were still arranging plates there was no one at the bar to serve her. She went back out into the lobby and then followed the group outside. The cameramen, who had been standing in a knot up against the building, shouldered their cameras and dispersed. Her cameraman asked her where she wanted to stand. She said that it did not matter: there were not enough of them there to make a difference.

The attendees began to arrive. The Handsome Actor with his wife the Beautiful Actress emerged from a black limousine, waving. People passing by on foot stopped to watch. The reporters shouted their questions. In his last movie he had worked with the Honoree; had the Honoree taught him anything? Of course: just being in the Honoree's presence was a lesson! His warmth, his charm, his sense of himself in a scene were things that other actors spent their careers trying to learn. And did his wife, the Beautiful Actress, have a chance to meet him? Yes: one day she'd been working on the same lot, and came over on her lunch break to visit her husband; she'd bumped into the Honoree at the coffee table and been so starstruck that she could not remember why she had come in the first place! The Honoree was the acme of humility, and had directed her to where he'd last seen her husband. That was the thing about the Honoree: he stayed genuine, even when everyone around him was falling all over themselves! That was what made his performances so great, she thought: he never made himself the center of attention; he let the other actors have the big dramatic moments! Her husband suggested that they go inside.

The Actor with the Attractively Ruined Face arrived. He had worked with the Honoree on Broadway: what was it like to work with a legend? The Actor with the Attractively Ruined Face shook his head; what could he say? He would say this: never once during the entire run of the show did he see the Honoree's dressing room door closed. Not once! If the door was closed, it meant the Honoree had gone home for the evening; if he was there then the door was open. That was the kind of man that he was! He wanted to hear the other actors running lines; he wanted to get a feel for the timing and the rhythm of the ensemble that night. He wanted everyone – from the lowest tech to the director! – to feel like they could come to him with notes, problems: anything! In fact: he just remembered! He'd gone one night to ask the Honoree to join him for a late supper, and when he got to the Honoree's dressing room he found the Honoree talking to a sound tech who had come in, wanting to fix a problem with one of the cues. The Honoree had asked the Actor with the Attractively Ruined Face what he wanted, and when the Actor asked him to dinner he agreed, and invited the sound tech along! The three of them had gone out together; everyone who saw them must have thought that the sound tech was quite a big shot, to be with the two of them! But that was the kind of thing the Honoree did! He was a special man: a wonderful man!

The Well-Respected Movie Director arrived. He had worked with the Honoree on more than a half-dozen movies; no one in the business knew the Honoree better! What did he think of the event tonight? He thought the event was long overdue: he and the Honoree were getting old! But seriously, he could not be happier for his friend; so many others in the business owed so much to this man, and he was just glad that the Honoree was getting some of the recognition that he deserved. And he was glad that his friend was being recognized also for his work outside of the business: the media and the general public had a tendency to look at the body of work and only at the body of work. But here was a man who had devoted himself to dozens of environmental causes, had befriended politicians, had invested his time and effort into his community, and at the same time remained a devoted husband and father! Yes: the life they were honoring was a life that deserved honoring, and he was just glad that he could be there to be a part of it!

The Lieutenant Governor arrived; a half-dozen security men secured the area. The Lieutenant Governor waved to the cameras. How long had he known the Honoree? And when had they first met? Oh gosh: he had known the Honoree forever! It must have been fifteen years ago he was working on an initiative to plant community gardens in the inner city, and one day he got a phone call that his secretary said was from the Honoree. Now, at this time the Honoree had just been nominated for an Academy Award, so he'd assumed it was someone pulling his leg! But sure enough: he picked up the phone and there was the Honoree on the other end, calling him to voice his support of this program to plant community gardens in the inner city! They got to talking and struck up a friendship: the Lieutenant Governor had been planning a trip to California later that month, and they'd actually managed to have dinner together. He remembered being so impressed with the Honoree: he remembered wondering how this man managed to do all that he did, while staying so informed on environmental issues, advances in environmental policy, the actions of his local government: they'd talked for hours! And that, as they said in the movie business, was the beginning of a beautiful friendship! The Lieutenant Governor and the reporter who had asked the question laughed.

A dozen others arrived. The Honoree arrived last. He waited as his wife exited the limousine, and closed the door behind her. How did it feel, to be honored in this way? He was very blessed to have such wonderful friends; he was blessed to have been able to live the life he had lived! He was blessed and he was humbled; he was overwhelmed! If he said anything else it would ruin his acceptance speech! He laughed and they went inside. The cameramen followed and the reporters stayed outside. The ballroom erupted with applause when the Honoree entered. The Newscaster had left her cigarettes up in the room, and asked if anyone had one. One of the others produced a pack and a lighter. The applause subsided, and the other reporters went inside. The crowd that had gathered across the street to watch the arrivals dispersed.

She finished her cigarette and went inside. Her seat was at one of the press tables at the rear of the room. She went to the bar instead and stood in line. Up on the stage a string quartet was playing something familiar. She could not quite place it. Then it was her turn at the bar. The second bartender was also ready, and called to the man behind her. She moved to give him room. The bartender brought her drink. She faced the stage and watched the quartet, trying to place the song. The man who had been behind her in line spoke to her; they had really pulled out all the stops, hadn't they? She turned and was surprised to see the Lieutenant Governor. He pointed to the stage: the dinner, the flowers, the ballroom, the string quartet; they weren't messing around! He laughed. She agreed: the string quartet was a nice touch! She was having the hardest time placing their music. She knew she had heard it before! The Lieutenant Governor laughed again. Well, she had if she had any taste at all! Their pieces were from the scores of the Honoree's movies; but she should not feel bad! He'd only recognized them because he'd seen the movies so many times!

Wasn't she the Newscaster who had done that report from Ethiopia a few years back? He thought so! He could not tell her how much that report had changed his life. And that was from the heart! In fact: was she here with anyone? And where was she sitting? Would she like to come sit with him at their table? He would love to have a chance to talk with her. But was there room at his table? Certainly: all he had to do was tell one of his security men to go eat in the kitchen! He laughed again. They didn't like it when he did that but hell: she wasn't dangerous, was she? Would she do him the honor? He offered her his arm. She took it, and he led her across the ballroom to his table.

One of the security men rose when he saw them coming; he would have the caterers bring a fresh place setting. She laughed; did he do this at every social function? Only when he met someone interesting. No one was going to shoot at him: he was the Lieutenant Governor! What did anyone care about the Lieutenant Governor? She would be surprised who he'd managed to have dinner with, just by offering them his bodyguard's seat! Or maybe it made people feel like he was risking life and limb, just to have a conversation with them. He didn't know; it seemed to work, and he wasn't about to change something that worked!

She laughed and sat down. She recognized several of the others at the table: across from her sat the Actor with the Attractively Ruined Face and his date. Beside him were two less well-known actors who nevertheless had costarred with the Honoree in several of his films. Their dates seemed to know each other, and sat talking side-by-side between them.

The string quartet began another piece, and the Lieutenant Governor challenged her to name which film it was from. She closed her eyes and listened; of course: it was from this film! The Lieutenant Governor applauded. So she was a fan of the Honoree's work, and not just here to hobnob with the stars! She laughed; if he had not invited her to sit with them, the closest she was going to get to the stars was if she had to ask one of the other tables for butter!

He laughed and turned his chair, slightly, to face her. He could not express how grateful he was for this opportunity to speak with her; her piece on Ethiopia really had a profound impact on his life! At that time he was just leaving private practice to run for public office; his thoughts were occupied by a hundred different things! He'd had no idea – and to be honest, he'd had no interest in having an idea! – what was going on in the rest of the world. He'd thought it was enough just to worry about his own life, and let others worry about theirs! What could he say? He was young, ambitious, had a successful law practice; he'd thought that all of his success was God telling him how happy He was with the Lieutenant Governor's life! He laughed again. Anyway, he was supposed to speak at a town hall meeting; it was his first big chance to speak with the voting public! He'd come down with a terrible stomach flu, and had to cancel only hours before the meeting was to take place. He was sitting at home, feeling sorry as hell for himself, convinced that he had just lost the race for office, and had turned on the television and happened to catch her report, just as it was starting. It was the punch that he never saw coming! Right then he'd realized: God was not happy with him at all! He'd been calling himself a Christian, but was running around worshiping false idols: success, power, money, things! He sat before her one hundred percent convinced that God made him sick that day so that he would see her report: it was God's plan to make him see and realize just what kind of a selfish, self-exalting life he was living! It was God saying, Look! The path he was on was not the One True Path!

So what did he do? What could he do? He called his campaign office and dropped out of the race. Then he had his secretary do some research to find out what kind of relief organizations were available for civilian volunteers who wanted to help in Ethiopia. Three days later he was on a plane! He was certain that he did not have to tell her: he was a man who did not hesitate when he saw the path before him! She could call him crazy! He just felt that a life spent waiting was a life wasted. Did she know what he meant? She said she thought she knew just what he meant.

That was why he admired her: she was still out in the world, making a difference! He'd spent eighteen months in Ethiopia, and then a few months here and there, and still he'd never felt like anything but a tourist. He knew that when it was over he would go back to his practice, or his campaign; he knew that he had a life waiting for him back in America, as soon as he got this impulse worked out of his system! And what did he do? He came home and went right back into public life! She shook her head: he really shouldn't think of it that way! Whatever his reasons, he'd done real good for those people! In the end, wasn't that all that mattered? He placed his hand on hers: it was sweet of her to say so! But no: he shook his head and turned away. She began to speak, but at that moment the Well-Respected Movie Director stepped up onto the stage and approached the podium. The audience applauded, and the Movie Director held up his hands in protest.

He just wanted to say a few words about his friend, the Honoree! When he'd first met the Honoree he'd expected to meet a man who was an amalgamation of the characters he played; he was wrong! It was true that the Honoree was warm like this character, and wise like that one! But one thing that was present in all of the Honoree's characters was wholly lacking in his personality: the director spoke, of course, of the effortless way the Honoree inhabited the screen, inhabited each role. Nothing about the Honoree was effortless: the Honoree put great effort into every role, every new undertaking! In his entire career, the Movie Director had never worked with anyone so meticulous, so concerned with craft, so dedicated to his art! Any tribute to the Honoree that did not acknowledge his tireless devotion would be incomplete. It was a devotion he displayed on and off the movie screen: a devotion whose fruits had touched the lives of far more than the few dozen who sat in this ballroom! It was a devotion he had never seen equaled. He was honored to be with his friends and peers to celebrate the Honoree's life: a devoted life!

Everyone applauded, and the caterers came out of the kitchen carrying the salads. The Movie Director, still standing at the microphone, explained that a short film would be shown in tribute to the Honoree's life while they ate their salads. Toasts would follow during the meal, and everyone should feel free to continue eating. The Handsome Actor, seated near the front, called for him to stop directing. Everyone at the forward tables laughed and the Lieutenant Governor's table laughed as well. The Movie Director laughed and, acknowledging, stepped down from the podium.

A screen was lowered behind the podium, and the lights dimmed. The caterers moved carefully in the dark. The string quartet returned to the stage and began playing. The screen filled with the image of the Honoree as a young man. This was followed by a series of clips from the Honoree's best-known roles. These were followed by images of the Honoree with his family. The silverware sounded noisily against the plates as the audience started eating. The Honoree, on the screen, was shown engaged in a number of causes. One of the caterers tripped in the dark, and a pair of salads fell to the floor. The music swelled to its finale; the screen showed the Honoree in his most famous role. The character, condemned by his own actions, stared out from the screen as one determined to face with poise the inevitable future. Then the screen went dark and the Handsome Actor, deeply moved, stood from his chair and applauded. The lights came up and the other attendees, seeing him standing, stood as well. A pair of caterers, crouched in their midst, were gathering the remnants of the overturned salads. The Lieutenant Governor, standing to applaud, shook his head and said that he still could not believe he was at a dinner with these people.

She had been struck by his apparent naivety; now, as she watched him turn his starstruck gaze from the Director to the other famous guests she felt an almost maternal twinge. He was so guileless, so genuine; he was an innocent, thrust in with the false and the disingenuous! Did he really think that the others in attendance shared his admiration for the Honoree? She could wholeheartedly assure him that, were it not for the presence of the television cameras, the ballroom would have been empty.

Yes: she had seen the other side of these lives, had seen the ugliness the cameras managed to erase! She had long since lost her fascination with the famous and the beautiful and the powerful; she had been jaded by life and experience! How many interviews had left a bad taste in her mouth? How many objections had she silenced when she saw that, in the final cut, the subject kept his dignity? How she had come to loathe their discretion!

She was certain that this information would break his heart. And yet with each passing moment the ugliness threatened to reveal itself: at any moment, it seemed, the Actor with the Attractively Ruined Face would unmask – with a word, a look, an anecdote, a gesture! – his true nature and with it, the entirety of the evening's hypocrisy. And she would be his betrayer: she whose reports he took for truth, in whose tears he saw a sensitive soul crying out! She was as false as the worst of them; her greatest triumph was a lie, a misunderstanding! She had felt nothing for those children; the sight of their starving bodies had touched her not in the least. Could she make herself feel? Of course she could not! She'd seen a half-dozen other atrocities in that year alone. A person could not feel for each of them; one reached one's limit, became saturated, became drained!

And yet none of that held argument against their deliberate misrepresentation: she had wept because she was tired, because she was hungry, because she was thirsty, because she wanted to go home! She had wept because her boyfriend had left her, had wept because the cameraman had kissed her! She had not wept for the starving children or their starving parents, had not wept for the lives they were leaving behind! No suggestion that she did not understand her own emotions – perhaps she merely had not realized how much the things she had seen affected her! – nor argument that the ends now justified the means – think of how many people saw the report, and were moved to help! – could lessen her private certainty that whatever trace of humanity remained within her was erased when she stepped up to the dais and accepted the award for her compelling and heartfelt report.

The thought of the Lieutenant Governor seeing her in this way seemed wholly unbearable. She wanted suddenly to rush him from the room; she wanted to cover his eyes and ears! She wanted to leave him now: now, while he still admired her; now, while he still thought that she was out in the world, making a difference! She wanted to protect him; she wanted to shelter him from all that was false, affected, hollow!

The Actor with the Attractively Ruined Face rose and asked if anyone wanted anything from the bar. She answered that they were fine. She was relieved to see him go! She pressed her hands to her temples. The Lieutenant Governor looked at her with concern; was she feeling all right? No: she was afraid she was not feeling very well at all! She was a little overwhelmed by everything that was going on. Maybe it would be best if she went up to her room to lie down. She stood and he stood as well; he would be happy to escort her! She thanked him and, taking his offered arm, said that she would like that very much.

They left the ballroom and got into the elevator. It was very sweet of him to go with her! She was sorry to make him miss any of the dinner; it sounded as though they had a wonderful evening planned for the Honoree! One never really got the chance to see what movie stars were like when the cameras were turned off; she'd covered a dozen events like this, and still could not get used to the sight of the Handsome Actor buttering his rolls!

They left the elevator and walked to her room. She invited him inside. He came in and she sat down on the bed. He went into the bathroom; did she have anything for her headache? Maybe he could call down to the desk and have them send something up. He came out of the bathroom with a glass of water; did she want him to call? She shrugged and took the water. Could she admit something to him? He sat down on the bed, facing her. Of course she could: anything! She didn't really have a headache; she'd made it up so that she could get him away from those people. He laughed: how sneaky of her! She groaned: she knew! That was exactly it: she was sneaky and underhanded and phony! He laughed again: she was not a phony! He met a lot of phonies in politics, and knew how to spot them!

She shook her head: he did not understand! He was so good; he was a genuinely good person! He cared about things and he cared about people and everybody in the ballroom only cared about themselves! It was all a big lie: the whole evening was one big lie, where everyone pretended to care so much about the Honoree! But they didn't; they really didn't! She would bet money that the Lieutenant Governor was the only one in the ballroom who could really call himself a fan. Like how he'd known which movies the string quartet was playing pieces from: she was certain that no one else in the room with the exception of the Honoree himself could do that! But everyone would get up and give their speeches and the television cameras would record them saying what big fans of the Honoree they were and that would be the truth to everyone watching!

And she was part of it: that was what she did! And she hated it; she hated it!

She suddenly covered her face with her hands: she knew that she was being ridiculous! She looked at him, embarrassed. Here she was, telling him all this, and she didn't even know him! He was very sweet for listening to her go on and on about it. But God, he must think that she was crazy! She laughed. It was funny, really! She'd be totally convinced that she had to get him away from all of those people, that being around them would ruin him somehow! They laughed together.

It was very sweet of her to want to look out for him like that. But he was a big boy, and had been in the game for a long time! He knew what these people were like. He pushed an errant strand of hair behind her ear. Was there some other reason that she'd brought him up here? Some other reason she wanted him all to herself?

Afterwards, as he was getting dressed, he explained that it would be best that they not be seen returning to the ballroom together. He knew that she understood! He would leave one of his security men posted outside the door, and he could get her anything that she needed. She laughed but he did not laugh, and she realized that he was not joking. She was thrown into confusion. Why was he treating her in this way? She had given no indication that she would create a problem for him; she'd raised no objection to his request that they return to the ballroom at different times! She understood the sensitivity of the situation; she would handle it with the utmost discretion! Or did he assume that she would use their encounter to her own ends?

There was no time to ask him: he was already putting on his coat. He spoke to someone standing outside, then stepped out into the hallway and closed the door. She waited for him to return: he had not even said goodbye! She wrapped herself in the sheet and went to the door; one of the security men from downstairs leaned against the wall opposite, and the Lieutenant Governor was nowhere in sight. The security man took a step towards her; how was she? Was there anything that he could get for her? The Lieutenant Governor regretted that pressing matters required his attention elsewhere, but wanted to express his gratitude for a wonderful evening. Was she hungry?

Thirsty? Anything he could do for her he would be more than happy to do. Confused she could only murmur that she was fine. She went back inside and closed the door.

She got dressed and opened the door; the security man, moving towards her, regretted to inform her that he could not allow her to leave her room at this time. She laughed, incredulous: did his boss think this was charming? She had a job to do! She stepped out into the hallway but the security man moved to block her path. He needed her to do him a big favor and stay in her room. She laughed again: or what? He held up his hands; he did not want to give the impression that he was threatening her! He just needed her to stay in her room until the Lieutenant Governor had vacated the premises. And how long would that be? The security man did not know. Was there anything he could get her in the meantime?

Yes: there was something he could get her! She wanted a job in Washington. She had fantastic PR skills, and a natural on-screen presence! Certainly his boss had to know somebody that could use her. The security man laughed; he meant was there anything he could get her like a sandwich, maybe some flowers! He laughed again; he could see why the Lieutenant Governor liked her!

She went back inside and sat down on the bed. She had to hand it to him! She began to cry but realized that it was ridiculous to cry: she did not even know why she was crying! She stopped crying. She thought, momentarily, of going to the security man and asking him to pass on her admiration to his employer. She quickly thought better of it. She wondered who was speaking now, and what they were saying, and if the cameraman was getting any decent footage of it. The Lieutenant Governor would likely stay until after dinner was served, and she would not have a chance to film her sign-off with the departing crowd as a backdrop. But what the hell did that matter? She could just as easily do it in an empty ballroom. She just had a certain way she wanted it to be, that was all. What was that? Talent: for better or worse that was talent. And one did not pick one's talents!

She went back into the hall, and told the security man what she wanted for dinner. He relayed the order into a walkie-talkie. She shook her head: no, she wanted this, not that! He apologized and amended the order. Also there was a bakery on this corner that had the best cheesecake! Did he want some? She told him to order a piece for himself as well. The security man said that he appreciated the offer, but was trying to watch his diet. She told him to take a piece home to his wife and he thanked her and said that he would. He relayed the information.

How long did he think that would take? Probably no more than fifteen minutes. She went back into the room and took a shower. While she was toweling off there was a knock at the door, and she let in the security man carrying her food on a tray. Was there anything else she needed? If there was, she knew where she could find him! The security man nodded and went out.

She sat down on the bed and turned on the television. Several checkpoints along the border between East and West Berlin had been opened, allowing travel between the divided sectors for the first time in forty years. Too excited to eat, she rose from the bed and picked up the telephone. Was her producer there? There was an intolerable pause as her producer was located. How was she? And how was the dinner?

Who gave a shit? Was he watching the news? Berlin: they had to send her to Berlin! Yes: the station was sending someone. Someone who? Someone else. No: she would fly to Berlin herself if she had to; this was the story she'd been waiting for! This was her chance; this was her last chance! For eighteen months she'd been working these damned dinners! This was the story she'd been waiting for! She needed this! She needed to know that he was going to fight for her on this! She didn't care what he had to do! She didn't care, did he understand? This was her story! This was her story!

Her producer said that he would talk to the execs. Was she still in the hotel room? He would call her in an hour. She hung up the phone, but was still too excited to eat. She got dressed and left the room. The security man, still standing outside, asked her where she thought she was going. She told him that she had to speak with her cameraman immediately. The security man said that he would call down and have her cameraman come up. She shook her head: never mind! She would talk to him later. She went back into the room to wait for her producer's call.

The last four years were a vaguely miserable dream from which she was now awakening; yes, she was certain that her best work was still to come! How ridiculous that, only hours before, she'd seriously considered leaving the news profession. She was an award-winning journalist! She was talented and well-respected! She had no doubt that, within the hour, her producer would call to tell her the good news.

3

Earlier in the day she'd seen the Famous Actress laying out on the beach, not far from the hotel where she was staying. Although the Actress had received much critical acclaim early in her career, she had fallen out of favor in recent years over a series of bizarre incidents stemming from her increasingly reclusive behavior. It was, in fact, a rare thing to so much as see the Famous Actress, and the Newscaster had left the beach giddy with excitement. Later she congratulated herself: she would never see the Famous Actress again, and was glad that she had not ruined their encounter by forcing a meeting.

The street leading back to the hotel was crowded with vendors selling faux Mayan statuary. She stopped in several of the shops, and eventually purchased a sarong which the seller assured her was one hundred percent handmade. Back in her room she put it on and went out onto the balcony to watch the sun go down over the ocean. But this scene somehow troubled her, and instead she went back inside and closed the blinds. Still, she found that she was unable to sit still. She decided that she was hungry, and called down to the front desk for a taxi. The man who answered did not speak much English, and she hung up the telephone certain that he had not understood, and no taxi had been called. But when she got to the lobby the taxi was waiting outside.

She got in and gave the name of the restaurant where she'd eaten dinner the last two nights. Did he know where that was? Of course: a lot of people from the hotel went there! It was a very popular restaurant. Did she have a reservation? She replied that she had not needed one for the past two nights, and had not thought to make one. The driver told her not to worry: a beautiful woman never needed a reservation! Did she need anything for the evening? Perfume? Makeup? He held them up from a box on the passenger seat. Good brands, cheap! He had everything, anything she needed!

The perfume he'd held up was a brand she'd worn for years. She asked to smell it. He removed a bottle from its box and handed it back. She sprayed it into the air above the empty seat beside her. The scent was very similar, and she could not tell if the difference came from the cab or the perfume itself. He asked her if she liked it; he would give it to her at a very good price! She said that if he picked her up after dinner she would buy two bottles from him. He asked her to promise: beautiful women were always telling him lies! She laughed and promised.

At the restaurant he gave her his name and told her to call the company and ask for him. He would be waiting for her call! She went inside. There were no available tables, and she went into the bar to wait. A while later the Famous Actress came in, sunburned and alone. The host was very pleased to see her; a table had just opened up! They disappeared together into the dining room. When the host came back the Newscaster asked if her table was ready yet. The host said that it would just be a few more minutes.

Senora, Senora! They were ready for her, if she would just follow him! He led her across the room to a small table beside the Famous Actress. He stepped back and frowned: what had gone wrong with the world? Two beautiful women, eating dinner alone? Where there no *hombres guapos* left in the world? Didn't they know it was not good to eat alone?

The Newscaster asked the Actress if she wanted to sit together. The Actress considered and then rose from her table and sat down opposite the Newscaster. The host clapped his hands: this was much better! He went away to fetch their waiter.

The Newscaster knew who the Actress was. The Actress nodded: she knew who the Newscaster was! She'd seen several of her reports. Which ones? The one about Ethiopia and the one about the Berlin Wall. And there might have been another one; she could not remember. The Newscaster had seen several of the Actress' movies; she really was a big fan of the Actress' work! Did she have any new projects coming up? No, did the Newscaster? No. Why not? The Newscaster did not know; there was nothing going on that sparked her interest! Which was not to say that there were not interesting things going on; she did not mean to say that! It was just: she did not know! She was waiting for something to really grab her attention.

Why didn't the Actress have anything coming up? Oh: for more or less the same reason! She had not come across anything interesting. She was at a point in her life where she could not get up for just anything! When she was younger she had put so much of herself into each role. But she could not do that forever, and certainly could not do it for two or three or four movies a year! Once every couple of years was all she had energy for anymore, and that was only if she found something really special. The Newscaster knew just what she meant! The waiter came, carrying water on a tray. Did they want anything else to drink? The restaurant had an extensive wine list! The Actress asked to see it. Did the Newscaster want to split a bottle? Several of these were very good. The Newscaster said she trusted the Actress to pick one. The Actress ordered and the waiter went away.

The Newscaster had to admit: this was very strange! The Actress was so familiar to her, and yet she did not know her at all! But the Actress must get that all the time; God, she must hate it! The Actress shrugged; she had hated it when she was younger. In the beginning it was just odd to have people – strangers! - treat her with so much unabashed affection. But very quickly it became obvious that their affection was not for her but for who they had imagined she was. It was an odd kind of prejudice: treating another not as the person they were but as the person one imagined them to be!

So yes: for a long time she had been very upset by it! But a lot of the upset came from feeling like she was the only one who experienced it, or that celebrities were the only ones who experienced it. That was not the case! She'd felt like there was some inner self that was being denied by everyone's insistence that she was this person they imagined her to be. But she was not the only one who felt that way: everyone felt that way to some degree! Every thinking, feeling person at least! Didn't the Newscaster think so? Didn't the Newscaster feel that way?

Yes, but she'd never even thought of it like that! No, the Actress was right: she felt exactly like that! She'd spent her entire career with this anxiety about what she was doing with her life: the only times she really felt anything at all was when a report was well-received. She was entirely dependent on that praise to keep her going! Sometimes she wished – and she'd never told anyone this! – but sometimes she wished that she had never done the report from Ethiopia. She was ready to quit! But then everywhere she went people were telling her how wonderful it was, how talented she was! If it were not for that she might have walked away and found something that made her happy!

She felt like – God, this was ridiculous! – she felt like Tarzan, swinging from tree to tree on vines. Each time that she'd been praised or awarded was like a vine that carried her over some huge empty space. And every time she reached the end of one swing, when the last success was too distant a memory to make her feel like she was doing what she was supposed to be doing, the next vine had come along and carried her for another month, two months, six months, year...

The waiter arrived with the wine and the glasses. They watched him pour without looking at each other. Then the waiter went away. The Newscaster thought of offering a toast, but was somehow disinclined to speak. They looked over their menus. The Newscaster could hear some of the other diners whispering about the Actress and was certain that the Actress could hear them, too.

The thread of the conversation, broken by the waiter's intrusion, could not be resumed. The Actress seemed suddenly tired. The Newscaster wondered if she had said something wrong, but then reminded herself that the Actress was known for her manic behavior. This comforted her momentarily, until she realized that this was only one of a number of perceptions about the Actress she had borrowed from public knowledge, that the truth was likely deeper, more interesting, and wholly inaccessible. The false feeling of familiarity was suddenly replaced by an extreme sense of alienation, and the Newscaster realized that she'd spoken not as one person to another but, despite her best efforts, as one in the presence of celebrity, forever and unconsciously relegating herself and her experience to a place below, holding them up to the Actress for affirmation.

Yes: she, and not some misunderstood mania, was the cause of the Actress' silence!

The Actress yawned: God, the sun had made her sleepy! The Newscaster commented that the Actress was very sunburned. The Actress laughed: she'd fallen asleep in the shade, but then the sun had moved and she wasn't in the shade anymore! Impossibly relieved, the Newscaster laughed as well.

❖

After dinner the Actress asked how long the News-caster was staying. She had three more days until she flew back to New York. Did she have any plans for the next day? They should have lunch: the Actress knew a great place just a short walk up the beach. They parted with plans to meet in front of the hotel at noon. The Newscaster went into the bar to call for the taxi, and asked for her pre-vious driver by name. She went outside to wait. A few minutes later the taxi arrived. The driver seemed glad to see her. He had two bottles of perfume set aside for her! How much did he want? For her? He told her the price and she paid without hesitation. On the drive back he asked her if she in a hurry to go back to the hotel, if she had seen a specific spot along the shore. They would pass by it on their drive, and it was very beautiful at night. It was a full moon tonight; the time to go was when there was a full moon! The view of the ocean was just incredible. Where was it? Not too far! It was right on the way to the hotel. The Newscaster replied distractedly that she was in no hurry.

An idea had occurred to her as she was leaving the res-taurant: she would cultivate this new familiarity with the Actress, and once they were both back in New York she would interview the Actress on television. It was the natu-ral progression for her own career: it was time to let the younger, hungrier newscasters establish themselves by running around the world chasing crises. She would re-main in New York, interviewing people of interest. She would lobby for time on the news show on which she worked, and depending on the segment's success would petition the network for her own show. New York had a never-diminishing supply of visiting dignitaries, under-ground artists, respected actors: in this way she would cre-ate the next phase of her career.

The driver pulled off the main highway onto a smaller road, then off again onto a bumpy dirt road cutting through a dense growth of foliage. Then this foliage subsided and he stopped the taxi and turned off the engine. He got out and she did the same. They were on a rise overlooking the ocean. The moon was low and shone in a long silver streak across the water. The sound of the waves on the beach mixed with the low hiss of the wind through the grove be-hind them. She walked toward the ocean and he told her to watch the edge. Did she want a beer? He had some beer in the trunk. She said that she had to be getting back. Just one beer? With her back to him she heard him go into the trunk. That perfume that she had bought: he loved the smell of that perfume! The sound of the bottle opening was close behind her, and then his voice was in her ear: when a woman wore that perfume, he just about lost his mind!

She'd dismissed him as harmless, and was staggered by her miscalculation. She wanted to go back now; she wanted to go back to the hotel right now! She had plans for tomorrow morning, and had to get back. She really had to be getting back. She appreciated him showing her this spot, she really did! It was beautiful, he was right! But she needed to be getting back. She got into the backseat, and he got into the backseat beside her. He wasn't going to hurt her; she didn't need to be scared! She wasn't scared. She just really wanted to go back to the hotel right now. He would take her back to the hotel! He just needed some-thing from her first.

She opened the door and got out, but tripped on the uneven ground. Certain that he was right behind her, she rolled away from the car and began running. Her hair was in her face and she was crying; she heard him call out to her but did not stop. Then there was nothing beneath her feet and, opening her eyes, she saw the moon and its long streak of silver. She thought, briefly, that she could not be falling: she had plans with the Actress for the following afternoon! But then she hit the sand below, and that thought and all other thoughts ceased.

The driver turned around and drove back onto the highway. Stopping at a gas station, he made a telephone call. An hour later a small fishing boat carrying the driver and another man made its way along the shore to the spot beneath the overlook. The passengers climbed out into the surf and pulled the boat ashore. They looked for twenty minutes, but could not find her. The other man suggested that perhaps she had been only knocked unconscious, and by now had come to and wandered off somewhere to get assistance. The driver said that that was worse, that then the whole thing would come to light, and his wife would find out. They continued to argue as they looked. Then the other man said that it was a moot point: he'd found the body. The driver hurried over, and together they dragged her down the beach and loaded her onto the boat. The driver went back and kicked sand over their track. Then they pushed the boat out into the water and climbed on-board. The other man lowered the motor and they headed out towards open water.

A few miles out he stopped the motor. The driver tied the anchor line to her ankles, and then working together the two men pushed the body overboard. It sank, slightly, and then bobbed back to the surface: the driver was still holding the anchor. Then the driver threw in the anchor.

The body jerked as the line came taut, and then sank. The full moon cut streaks through the clear water and they could see to a terrific depth, and it took what they agreed was a surprisingly long time for her body to completely disappear.

The other man asked if the driver was satisfied. The driver said that he was satisfied. The other man said that the driver owed him an anchor. The driver said that he would get it to him when he had the money. The other man started the engine and headed back towards shore. They stopped a half mile from shore, and the other man handed the driver a fishing pole. They threw their lines over the side and waited. The moon went down, and the sun began to come up. The other man started the motor and they headed in. On the dock the others asked what they'd caught and the other man spat blasphemously and said that they'd caught nothing, that the ocean was a bitch that morning! To make it worse, the driver hadn't tied off the anchor! They laughed and the driver said his goodbyes and went home.

His wife asked where he'd been. He told her that he had worked late, and then had gone out early fishing. She didn't believe him? She could ask the other man! And either way, he didn't care what she believed: he was too tired! He went into their bedroom and lay down on the bed. Soon he was snoring. His wife closed the door so that the children would not wake him.

THE SENTIMENTALIST

"...Yes, sentimentality: that phenomenon by which the emotional need of the viewer takes precedence over the reality of the object; sentimentality: the excessive and inappropriate infusion of meaning, the incorrect alignment of form and content; sentimentality: a child's perception, the stain of immaturity, sister to stereotype, father of prejudice, the soul of dramatic irony!"

My friend was reading the English newspaper when I arrived. "Listen to this," he said. He waved me toward the vacant chair opposite. I was tired and glad to sit. "Listen," he said again. "Are you listening? It's the most remarkable story. A tiny fishing village in the South Pacific was destroyed earlier this week when a mountain collapsed and slid into the ocean. Are you listening? The avalanche buried the entire village and sent the residents running into the sea to escape. Geologists say they are surprised because there was no seismic activity to prompt the mountain's collapse. All the men were out fishing when it happened. It is the most remarkable thing I have ever read!"

"Where did you say that was?" I said.

"Some island I have never heard of," he said, "in the South Pacific somewhere." He threw the paper down on the table and called the waiter over. "Do you know what you're having?" he asked. "I always order the same thing. I've known what I was having since yesterday. I was only waiting for you."

"I'm sure that whatever you're having is fine," I said. "Just order for both of us."

My friend ordered. I didn't speak the language. The waiter made a comment that I didn't understand, and my friend replied with a phrase that I knew, meaning that what the waiter had said was fine. When the waiter was gone I asked what the trouble was.

"He said," my friend said, "that the haddock hasn't come in yet today, and he wanted to know if I would prefer to order something else or if we would mind eating yesterday's. I told him that yesterday's would be fine." He turned back to the newspaper, but then stopped and said, "you don't mind, do you? I took it for granted that it would be fine with you. What you have to remember is that, even being yesterday's, it's still fresher than anything you usually get to eat back home."

"I don't mind," I said. "I was just curious, that's all. These people loathe me for not speaking the language, anyway. I'm sure they've been serving me day-old fish the whole time I've been here."

"You're probably right," he said, apologetically.

A girl turned the corner and came down the boulevard toward us. We watched her cross the street and come into the shadow of the building.

"Do you know who that is?" asked my friend. "That's his girl: that's Galatea!" She took a table a few yards from us and sat looking over the menu. "I'm going to invite her to sit with us," said my friend. "I've always wanted to speak with her!" He rose hurriedly and headed off in the direction of her table.

I took his newspaper and read the story he'd been telling me about. A dozen people were missing and presumed dead; another hundred had been admitted to the hospital with injuries related to the disaster. The only road into the town had been buried when the mountain collapsed, and the wounded had to be taken by boat. But because of the avalanche the coastline was now unfamiliar, and several of the rescue boats had run aground on the shoals. But then I stopped reading, because my friend had returned with Galatea on his arm.

"May I present," said my friend, and introduced us. I stood and we shook hands. I offered her my chair and took the one beside my friend. "I was just telling Galatea that we were planning to attend her husband's opening tonight, and she was telling me about some of his more recent work. It really was quite fascinating. I brought her over because I was certain you would enjoy hearing about it."

"You are a fan of my husband's work as well?" she asked.

"Oh yes," said my friend, answering for me, "a tremendous fan."

"Yes," I said, agreeing with him. "Please, I'd love to hear about it. I'm so looking forward to seeing his exhibition."

"I cannot begin to do justice to it," she began. "After all: my husband is a genius! Any description I could give would be slanderous in its inadequacy. For how can one put another's genius into words? It's impossible!" She continued in this vein for some time, lauding his work and declaring it superior to all others. I soon noticed that my friend had become obviously bored, and was distractedly watching the birds that, coinciding with Galatea's arrival, had begun to circle our table. Soon one of these birds detached itself from the group, dove, and came to perch on Galatea's outstretched and gesticulating arm. A second and third followed. She seemed not to notice, and continued talking. After some time the waiter brought our meals, and this disturbed the birds and they flew away.

"Well," I said, seizing the opportunity to interject, "I certainly am looking forward to seeing his new work."

She did not respond. The birds, returning, landed on her head and arms. She remained motionless, and my friend called the waiter to have her removed. The waiter called two others, who loaded her onto a cart. The birds dispersed with the sudden motion. My friend shook his head.

"Why did I invite her over?" he asked me. "I am consistently surprised by how stupid I become in the presence of beautiful women. After all of these years, you would think that I would know better! They never have anything to say, and what they do say they have no ability to say succinctly. She was nothing before she met him, you know," he added. "She wouldn't say anything if he didn't tell her what to say. She doesn't even understand what little there is to understand of his work. Still: perhaps now she will introduce us to him at the reception. How is your haddock?"

"It's fine," I said, chewing and swallowing. "But tell me: you seem to despise her husband. I am curious to know why."

"Her husband is no more offensive than most," he said. "All of the artists I have ever known have had such insufferable regard for themselves, and reverence for their own work. But I have never met an artist deserving of this demeanor! Her husband lives upon a claim of unsubstantiated genius. He has yet to produce anything of note, and yet he perpetuates himself based merely on his and his wife's assertions that he is in fact a brilliant artist whose unique vision, et cetera et cetera. In so far as that is concerned, I find him no more offensive than any other fraud who chooses to ply his trade on the public, so long as that public does not include me. But where it is possible to ignore artists in most cities, to do so here would be to effectively recluse oneself. I am not complaining! I love this town and the life I have here. But at times the rendering unto Caesar becomes exhausting." He sighed and took a large bite of fish. "In any event," he said, chewing, "tonight should be a fabulous party. I'm glad you are coming. If you're going to be in town very long, it will be helpful for you to meet some of these people. Are you going to be in town very long?"

"I haven't decided," I said. "I suppose I'll see how it goes tonight."

He nodded. "And have you had any letters from home?"

"No," I said, "not since the last one. But I changed rooms at the hotel, and it is possible that one has merely been misplaced. I'm certain that I will hear from them soon. They've written to me every week since I came here. I can't imagine that my silence would inspire them to stop, since it has not already. In any event, I imagine that my mother is writing for her own sake as much as mine."

He nodded again. "And how is your own writing?" he asked. He had finished his meal and called the waiter over to order drinks. He ordered for both of us.

"No worse than before," I said, once the waiter was gone. "It's funny: in some ways this has been the easiest book to write. But I can't shake the feeling that it might be so much better, if not for certain troubling aspects. My trouble is that I can't tell what in the troubling aspects troubles me, and so cannot correct it, and I worry that on account of this the book will be a failure. It will be finished, and still I will not have discovered what would have made it so much more! A very personal failure, for only I will know that the book was not what I had hoped it would be. Perhaps it doesn't matter. Only I had great hopes that this would be the best of all my work thus far, and instead it seems indistinguishable from the rest."

My friend laughed. "That is the difference between artists and writers," he said. "Artists are full of self-regard; writers are full of self-doubt. People lump them in together, but they are very different! Hemingway spent his last years in a state of endless horror, convinced that he could no longer produce the quality of fiction he expected of himself. Now Picasso: ha!" The waiter brought our drinks, and my friend took his and drained off half. "In any event," my friend went on, "I am certain that it isn't so bad as you think. Tell me what you have said, and tell me what you are trying to say. I am certain you will find that, simply by virtue of you being its author, your intentions found their way into the text."

"Perhaps," I said. "Something just feels wrong. I just can't quite figure out what it is."

"You need to get out more often," said my friend, sympathetically. "You spend all of your days cooped up in your room, staring at your pages. What can you hope to write about, having no experience to draw upon? You will end up writing about our lunches together if you are not careful!" He sat forward and said, "I'm glad that you have decided to go to this opening with me. At the very least it will be good for you to get out of your own head for a while."

"That's just it, though," I said. "I don't believe in all of that. I don't believe that one must have experience to write well. Too often I read work that seems stitched together of anecdotes which found their way into the narrative only through the author's refusal to dispense with them, having an affinity for these stories from his own experience: anecdotes which add nothing and do not fit at all! Further, reality is owned by all: each person who experiences an event claims ownership of its memory. To claim final authority - as one does when one writes about it - is to me an intolerable self-indulgence. It is only what one produces wholly from oneself that one can call one's own! More often than not the fallacy that one acquires experience leads one to pursue innumerable distractions which take the artist further from himself; and of course the purpose of art is to express oneself, to know oneself! For myself, I find offensive the suggestion that experience makes the artist!"

"Come now," said my friend. "You cannot actually believe this. After all, you came here! What were you hoping to find in coming, if not some enlightening experience?"

"I was hoping to find distance," I said. "That is all."

"Still," he said, "there was no limit to the number of places you could have gone. There are plenty of places farther still; why not go there? You must have imagined that this place held something those others would not."

"Perhaps you're right," I said. "Still, the impulse to accumulate experience is a dangerous and destructive one: one which I would rather not give rise to, if given the chance. To regard one's own experience with reverence is to commit the most fundamental of artistic sins. I have always felt that one can know the world more accurately if one understands one's own perception of it: to see the world you are writing as your own creation is to acknowledge its insignificance. Too often one writing his own experience falls into a repulsive sort of self-exaltation, taking his experience's foundation in reality as an affirmation of its Truth. One reads stories of an author's profound, life-changing, miraculous experience and emerges only with the clear understanding that the author thinks very highly of himself and his own perceptions. The author writing from imagination makes no such claim."

"But then the world you are writing is not the world at all," said my friend.

"No," I agreed, "but then neither is the world one writes when one is writing from experience! Experience is merely a form infused with meaning: the events themselves merely occur. Reality - true reality - is necessarily devoid of meaning. It is only in the context of the author's mind that it becomes substantial. Read his version of the events and you do not experience the events but experience his experience of the events. One can never write reality: one cannot relate events devoid of meaning! Word choice, the order in which events are related, every variant in a given passage is an expression of the author's opinion: an opinion which even the most vigilant author cannot help but write into his story. The earth, the universe, infinity, all remain indifferent to a mountain sliding into the sea and destroying a village in the South Pacific. But even to write that it destroyed the village is to acknowledge the importance of the destroyed village over the destroyed forest, the destroyed reef: one cannot escape one's own opinions! To write well, one must be aware of this fallacy. One must either write as the universe or else as a speck of dust in infinity, absolutely aware of the unimportance of its experience. To do otherwise is to participate in and give into the worst sort of self-exaltation and regard, the true and final enemies of Art."

"What you are saying is ludicrous," said my friend. "If one writes with full awareness of one's own insignificance, then why write at all? If one feels that one's thoughts have no value, then why spend such time and effort in relating them?"

"You are of course right," I said. "I do not devalue my own insights. I cannot escape a needling suspicion that I am, in fact, a brilliant thinker whose works will inspire to enlightenment the hordes huddled in the darkness. I am not proud of this fact! But I can no more deny its truth than deny the fact that his wife is now coming across the plaza towards us."

"Oh God," said my friend with a groan, "tell me you are joking!"

She sat down in the chair left vacant by her departure. "As I was saying," she went on, "he has moved away from sculpture and is now working exclusively in refuse.

He scoured the city from morning until night for months, searching through dumpsters. I hardly saw him during the day! My God: you should have smelled his workshop! I insisted each day that he bathe twice, and still he could not get the stink of garbage off of his skin. I told him - listen to this! - that I deserved as much credit for his art as he did, for putting up with the smell of it! Isn't that funny? But when it was finished I was so embarrassed for having bothered him about it: the work justifies every moment of the process! It never ceases to amaze me: he can look at the city's gathered refuse and see something so beautiful. That is his gift: to see such beauty in the world, and to help it to reveal itself! That is why I have learned never to question him: he has a plan and a vision!"

She sat back in her chair, speechless with admiration for her husband. I looked above her, expecting to see gathering birds, but saw none; her lapse into statuary seemed to have been a momentary one.

"Your husband is lucky to have you," said my friend. "I know how he hates to shout his own praises. Still: the world might not understand, were it not for your irrepressible explication. I thank you for taking the time to explain to those of us without the privilege of your insight! But please," my friend went on, "I am curious about you. You have spoken only about your husband! Tell me: how did you two meet? Are you also an artist? How did you spend your days, when your husband was laboring over refuse?"

"Oh, there isn't much to tell," she said. "It's like I always tell my husband: I didn't really start living until I met him! I mean sure I was there, but I wasn't really there! I was just a body going through the motions of a life! When I met him the world became vibrant, dense, rewarding to know! Before I met him things were just things; now I see things for what they really are! Do you know: before I met him I had never read a book for pleasure, or been to a museum! I had never stayed up just so that I could watch the sunrise, or been moved to tears by the playing of Bach!" Again she sat back in silent admiration. "Do you know," she said after a moment, "I can barely remember the time before I met him. I know my family, the town where I grew up, my school, but I know them all as one knows things from a book or a movie: it's almost as if they were not mine at all! Perhaps it was only because I was so passive when they were occurring that it was as though I was watching them on a projection screen. Still, somehow it seems absurd to think that they could actually have happened! For example: I remember the first boy that I kissed, when and where it happened, what we said before and after, how I came home and faced my mother for the first time knowing that something had changed and that only I knew. But that girl's reasoning, her behavior, seems so foreign to me: I cannot imagine that it was me who said or did those things! Isn't that funny? And I was so certain that I loved him, that I would spend my life with him! Now I can barely remember his name. That has been my husband's greatest gift to me, intentional or not, and one for which I am eternally grateful: he has helped me to realize that my former life does not define me, that I am no more bound to the self I am in memory than I am to the clothes I wore on my fourteenth birthday. That is why I say that I was not alive before I met him: I was someone else before that day, a girl's body buffeted by the winds of influence. Now I am free to fully realize myself!"

She leaned over the table so imposingly that both my friend and I sat back.

"Well," said my friend, "it sounds as though your relationship with him has been a revelation. Let us hope that his art will do the same for my friend and I!"

He raised his glass and toasted the artist. His wife drank with us and then, explaining that she had a million things to do before the opening, excused herself.

"My God," my friend said when she was gone, "have you ever met such a bore in your entire life? I cared almost nothing for her husband before she sat down; I am close to hating him now! To fill her head with such ridiculous - such pompous! - ideas: to revel in her exaltation! One would think he would collapse with shame. And refuse? We are to attend a gallery filled with garbage?" He laughed. "I had assumed, since he is an artist, that her husband is an ass," he said. "I had not imagined he would be an insufferable one. To fill her head with such garbage, and then send her out into the world to dispense it! Can't you just see him, instructing her on which moments in Bach should inspire her tears? It would be funny, were it not so tragic."

"You are quite right," I said, shaking my head, "the poor girl does not see it. Such profound delusion! To imagine oneself becoming more fully realized, while in actuality becoming realized into someone else's creation: you are quite right to call it tragic! No doubt she feels that there has always been a beautiful soul within her, longing to weep to Bach, needing only his kind guidance. Imagine!"

We laughed together at the artist's wife. The waiter came back, and my friend ordered another round. We were still laughing when the waiter returned, carrying our drinks. My friend wiped his eyes and raised his glass to give a toast, but collapsed into laughter as he opened his mouth to speak. I could no longer remember what was funny, and so drank without his toast, and waited for him to finish.

"And the birds, the birds!" he said, gasping for breath. "My God, she did not even notice!"

He struck his fist upon the table, which upset our glasses. I called for the waiter, and ordered another round. The waiter was someone I had been to school with: we spoke at length about what each of us had been doing, and I told him about my father. He expressed his deepest sympathies and assured me that if there was anything he could do, anything at all, I should not hesitate to call upon him. I thanked him and he went away.

By that time my friend had stopped laughing, and we drank to the artist's wife. I wished her health and rapid realization, and my friend did the same. I was unsure whether my friend had stopped laughing at the mention of my father, and so was uncomfortable in the silence that followed our toast. I considered several subjects with which to break our silence, but dismissed each one as too obvious, too forced, or too trivial to elicit a lasting exchange. The last among these was, perhaps, the worst: I thought of again mentioning the birds which had descended upon the artist's wife, thinking that perhaps we could share a laugh at the memory. But I knew that such an exchange could only be followed by a more profound silence, harder to shake, resulting from an understanding. The understanding was an understanding about what the silence meant. It meant that we were not speaking about my father, but could think of nothing else to say. For some reason I was certain that I could not bear such a silence, that at that moment such a silence would result in my total collapse. I had not been feeling well all day, and was thinking of excusing myself so that I might return to my room to lie down for a few hours before the opening.

I was also curious as to whether I had received any word from home. I invariably neglected to write in response; nevertheless the possibility that my mother had stopped writing altogether wholly horrified me.

I watched a group of men and women enter the plaza from one of the side streets and leave through one opposite. They were talking and laughing, and I wished suddenly and intently that I was with them, that I was friends with them. They seemed to be such nice people. Knowing nothing at all about them, I nevertheless had the feeling that knowing them would make me profoundly happy.

"Do you know those people?" I said.

"I know two of them," he said. "I met them at another of these things. They'll probably be there tonight. I would be happy to introduce you."

"They seem like such nice people," I said. "Are they nice people?"

"I don't really know them," he said. "I couldn't say." He sat up suddenly in his chair. "My God," he said. "That's him: that's Pygmalion himself!"

They were being seated at a table on the other side of the patio.

"Who is that with him?" I asked.

"His mother," said my friend. "She goes everywhere with him. He is still very much a child, you know."

Pygmalion, in the form a child, rose from the table where he sat with his mother and ran up beside me. He took the scraps of food left on my plate and hurled them with great force against the ground. He stood back to admire his work; his mother rose from her seat to get a better view.

"It's wonderful," she said. "Beautiful. Magnificent. Visionary. Truly, there is no one else like my Pygmalion.

Who can be like Pygmalion?" The child Pygmalion beamed with pride. He lowered his trousers and defecated on the sidewalk beside us. His mother clapped her hands and, taking my napkin, tenderly wiped his bottom. "Wonderful," she said. "Brilliant, incredible!"

"You see?" said my friend. "It is no noble thing to be an artist. Look!" He pointed across the open patio to where the adolescent Pygmalion wept, huddled beneath his sculpture. The sky darkened over and began to rain. The wait staff quickly erected umbrellas above the tables. Pygmalion continued his weeping.

"That is no kind of life," said my friend. "Think what a burden such ceaseless gravitas would become!"

Pygmalion's mother, rushing from the shelter of the awnings, ran to her son and sheltered him with her body. "Oh cruel Gods!" she cried. "Why do you delight to torment my son in this way? Why do you make all earthly women so base? Surely one such as Pygmalion deserves better! Why do you ignore my prayers? Are my offerings unfit? Please: a mother lives only to see her son's joy!" She clutched the weeping child to her breast and ushered him beneath the shelter. All present shifted uncomfortably in the awkward silence prompted by their presence.

My friend shook his head in disgust. "This is the ideal to which you aspire?" he said. "It is as though you have given it no thought at all. The artist works to produce something essentially internal, to which his audience will respond with praise. How is that different from a child producing shit and delighting in his mother's tender affection? To be an artist is to live in an endless regressive state, courting more and more the attention of a maternal proxy! My God! That which you call Art is merely a sublimation of the shit disallowed by social stigma! If they could, artists would defecate upon the world, as this child has, and then bask in the glow of renown!"

"I could not disagree with you more," said Pygmalion. We were startled by his arrival; he had aged since we'd seen him last, and it took me a moment to recognize him. We rose and shook hands, and my friend offered him a chair. The rain had stopped, and the wait staff came and removed the umbrellas. My friend ordered three coffees and something stronger for himself.

"Is your mother here?" my friend asked. "We could ask her to join us."

"Heavens, no!" said Pygmalion. "I have no idea where she is. I see her so rarely now! My wife does not care for her at all. It puts me in quite an awkward position! But I suppose it is difficult for any new wife, living in the shadow of her husband's mother! My Galatea is a wonderful little wife, make no mistake! But there are things a man's mother understands about him that a wife cannot; of course you know what I am talking about!" He removed his black beret and drew from inside a pack of cigarettes, which he offered around. "Yes," he continued, blowing a thin bead of smoke, "a man's best friend is his mother! Do be good enough to tell me if you see her coming: she hates it when I smoke, and I would rather not have a scene!"

"Of course," said my friend, "but please continue! You feel that I am mistaken in my estimation of art and artists?"

"Oh, horribly mistaken!" said Pygmalion, returning the beret to his head and adjusting its angle. "An artist yearns to express something profound, something essential, spiritual, transcendent! It is true that he produces both Art and shit, but what of it? You produce arguments as well as shit and yet your arguments do not suffer, are not dismissed, because they spring from the same source, namely yourself. But of course the mind produces arguments, not the stomach: just as the soul, not the intestines, produces Art! You see?"

He sat back in his chair, looking very pleased with himself. The waiter brought our coffees and my friend's drink.

"I was mistaken," said my friend. "Truly, I know nothing of art! It must be a terrible chore for a great artist such as yourself to explain his craft to a simpleton such as myself, whose uninformed-yet-espoused opinions litter the air like so much debris. I thank you - enthusiastically! - for your time! But now I fear that I see your mother coming, and suspect that her arrival heralds your departure."

"I thank you for the warning," said Pygmalion. He took a hasty sip of his coffee and then rose and hurried off in the direction opposite the one my friend had indicated, calling his farewells over his shoulder. I watched him go. His bohemian uniform was like a smudge of dark paint against the sunny promenade. When I could no longer discern him from the background I turned, expecting to see his mother approaching. But after several moments I had failed to locate her. I turned back to my friend who stared, disinterested, into his coffee cup.

"I thought you said his mother was coming," I said.

"Don't be ridiculous," said my friend. "I merely said that to get rid of him. I can't stand him. When I met him for the first time he spoke at such length about music I was certain that I would have to dispense with my records the instant I returned home. He had me so bored with the very *idea* of music that I was certain I would be unable to listen to them ever again! The next time it was the Dutch masters and the time after it was some sculptor

I had never heard of, whose work consisted exclusively of smashed television sets. I find him wholly insufferable!"

"You are being unfair," I said. "Surely it is a chore to sit and talk with him, but as an archetype he is without parallel! There is no better example in myth or literature of a character who so completely refuses engagement, who so readily trades sentimental understanding for truth. And to make him an artist - ah! Having no firsthand knowledge of the world, he nonetheless ordains to speak with absolute authority, producing works he regards as more true than reality itself. He is the sentimentalist in true form!"

"I see that you are right," said my friend. "Still, I do not enjoy speaking with him, and would rather you warned me the next time so that I might excuse myself before his arrival."

Being in agreement, we drank our coffees in silence. The plaza was growing crowded with early afternoon shoppers. They walked beneath the facades of buildings that predated their births and would survive, barring any catastrophe, long after they and their children had expired. Watching them hurry past, it was easy to imagine that I saw the world as the buildings saw it, with all human activity blending in its frantic and progressless pace. I imagined watching as, over eons, the buildings themselves began to fade and crumble. It was comforting to contemplate the insignificance of my life, with all its pain and failure.

"I do love Europe," my friend said. "History is so present here. One gets the sense, living in America, that everything has sprung newborn from the earth at every moment, and that it will collapse again as soon as one leaves the room. Over there history is something outside of ourselves, something completely removed from our experience. Here one is forced to live among its artifacts. Do you know that the church beside my flat is over four hundred years old? Amazing! I am certain that, when Mother America turns four hundred, there will be very little of the old left standing."

"You make an interesting point," I said. "I wonder."

He looked up at the buildings and said, "I suppose it is because we like to imagine that we are ourselves an infinity that predates and will outlive the world around us. I can find no other explanation for the horror that rises within me each time I conceive of my own life as a brief interval in the life of a building. I am forced to assume that it comes from a lifetime spent among disposable objects."

"Perhaps you are right," I said. "Still, I find it hard to imagine that anyone enjoys being reminded of their own insignificance. More often than not, I fear, preservation becomes a misguided attempt at immortality: one imagines that one's name may be essentially joined to that which is unencumbered by the limitations of a human lifespan. I have always imagined that we erect statues of the noble dead in the hopes that the trend will catch on, and one day a statue will be erected of us. Such is the stupidity born of fear!"

"I am surprised by your bitterness," said my friend.

"If I sound bitter, then I apologize," I said. "It is only that my father spent many years wholly invested in acts of historical preservation, and I am hard-pressed now to see the good in it, or find any trace of him in the objects he preserved. He viewed history with such profound sentimentality, such overwhelming nostalgia! We quarreled once because I said that history was self-exaltation, that the earth itself had no memory, that to the trees and mountains our movements were frenzied and without meaning. I meant it as a blow and he took it as such. Still, it did nothing to alter the course of his affections."

My friend nodded. "As children we take for granted that our parents' first love should be ourselves," he said. "Sadly, that is not always the case. Although it should not be overlooked that he attempted to include you. You have told me on several occasions how he dressed you all in period costumes, and paraded you down the streets of historical villages. There is something to be said for such attempts at inclusion!"

"Hardly," I said. "There is no difference between that and a child with his toys, begging his mother to play along, insisting that she take on a role in his elaborate fantasy. If there is a difference, it is that the child may be forgiven his domineering love, his demands for compliance, having a child's limited understanding of the autonomy of others. He cannot be blamed: the child, we know from Lacan, sees the mother as a part of himself! But to see one's children in this way, to see one's wife in this way, and further, to become angry with them when they express their essential autonomy: my God! What way is that for a grown man to act? What way is that for a father to act?"

Without intending to I had begun to cry, and stopped speaking so that I might regain my composure. I had resolved to change the subject entirely when the silence was interrupted by a terrific clamor: a great crowd came around the corner and moved past us down the street. It was the funeral parade of history: the collected dead of the world's wars, famines, and disasters marched in an inarticulate mass. Roman soldiers walked beside the slain moors; knights in armor strode noisily alongside felled

Luftwaffe; feeble Africans staggered beside those crushed beneath the rubble of the mountain's collapse.

"You see?" said my friend. "What have I been telling you? History is so present here!"

"But this is not history!" I said. "This is something else; this is the propaganda of history! This is sentimental history: these dead march forever in the garish and inaccurate light of nostalgia!"

"Not so!" said my friend. "These honored and mourned dead have gone to glory!"

"But that is just my point," I said. The cacophony from those marching was fantastic, and I had to shout to be heard. "These dead have never done an unclean thing, nor slept, nor doubted! They are inaccurate portraits of men, redrawn in the image of Titans! But by becoming Titans they cease to be men: they lose their claim upon reality! These dead never died, nor ever lived! They never ate nor yearned, they never shit; yes! That is exactly it! There is no shit in history: a dead man is absolved of his faults, becoming a caricature of himself! We remember them distinctly as they were not, because when the dead are dead they lose their power to disappoint us: we look upon them with whole-hearted reverence, with no fear that one day our hearts will be broken by a base act! There is no shit in history!" I was out of breath from shouting, and stopped to collect myself. I had more to say, but it was clear that there was no point: my friend was no longer listening. A military band was at that moment passing our table, and my friend was clapping his hands in time to their song.

I signaled to the waiter that we wanted another round. He brought it quickly but did not clear any of the plates or empty glasses. I called to him, but he was not looking and my voice was drowned out by the approaching cavalry.

"Perhaps you are right," I said. "Perhaps it is not history's inaccuracy which bothers me, but rather its ceaseless progress. There is something unpleasant in the sensation of being carried along by an irrefutable and indifferent current. Still, I would prefer some assurance that upon my death no one will feel any undue charity toward my memory. I would hate for my children to go through life suffering the sentimental reminiscences of my acquaintances, and their misguided assertions that I was a wonderful person! Yes: better still to be forgotten altogether, for my existence to disappear entirely upon my death. To have all the benefit of never having been born, with only the unpleasant but brief interval of life to trouble me. No ghost left to haunt anyone!"

"What?" said my friend. "I am sorry; I could not hear you over the sound of the parade."

"It was nothing," I said. "Never mind."

The parade was nearing its end. A few final stragglers moved past us. I looked away in disgust: how I loathed the parade of history! I longed for a country with no past: a country like a person walking in the sand, dragging a bough behind, erasing his footsteps as he progressed. I was tired of memory. It was not life that was unbearable, but its ceaseless record. One relived his own life countless times, with no ability to alter or correct it. It was a terrific joke.

"Should we have another drink?" asked my friend. "I'm still terribly thirsty."

"Not me," I said. I was feeling sleepy and unwell, and was concerned that I would become unable to attend the opening that night. "Perhaps a coffee. Another drink, and I'm afraid that I will fall asleep before the opening."

My friend checked his watch. "We still have several hours," he said. "Have another. If you have to go, I will wait for you here. I can find some way to entertain myself. I have not finished reading my newspaper. I still don't know what happened to all of those people in the South Pacific."

I shrugged my acceptance. My friend called the waiter over, and ordered our drinks. I had nothing more to say to the waiter, and so I looked away when he approached and did not look back until he had gone. My friend was rubbing his hands.

"You will like this one," he said. "You've never had it before, have you? I did not think so. A miraculous drink. They say it was what Descartes was drinking, when he wrote all of his best work. One of these and you will see everything clearly."

"I'm half blind now," I said. "One of those, and I do not think I will see anything at all."

"Perhaps," said my friend. "But tell me - and please forgive me if it is imprudent of me to ask! But you have hardly spoken of your father since our first lunch together. I cannot imagine that your silence is due to a lack of things to say! Further, you say that you are not writing at the moment; I assume from this that you are greatly troubled. Am I correct in thinking so?"

"It is nothing," I said. "In any event, I am certain that I will begin writing again soon. It is only a temporary blockage, no doubt linked to the change of scene. To say that I am greatly troubled seems to overstate the fact."

"Come now," said my friend. "Or will you keep lying to yourself in this way? I say nothing but what you have me say: I am servant to the clickity-clack of your typing! Or did you have me ask so that you might feign stoicism?"

I was startled: until that moment we had never spoken of my friend's unreality. It had gone unstated in each of our previous conversations.

"God created man with free will," I said. "To say that he is still God's creation does not state the whole fact. Given his free will, man is also his own creation. You say and do many things which I do not decide, but merely type. Your autonomy is overarched by my own, that is true enough. But my autonomy is nearly boundless: you can say and do whatever you wish, and still remain beneath the domed sky of my thoughts. I did not command you to bring up my father: you did that of your own accord."

"Did I?" he said. He shrugged. "I suppose I would not know the difference. Either way, I will take responsibility for the question if you will admit that your autonomy is anything but boundless."

"Hardly," I said. "Watch." The sea rose from its banks and flooded the rivers; the sky turned the color of raspberry jam; the dead rose from their graves and ascended to heaven, leaving gaping holes in the earth. "You see?" I said. "Anything is possible. I give you complete freedom. Wish something done, and it shall be done."

"I wish to exalt your father," he said. "May I exalt your father?"

I recoiled. "Never!" I said. "My father was a sentimental fool, incapable of showing any but the most garrulous love. His love for me centered not in myself but rather in some abstract estimation of father-and-son: he invented a bond between us which in no way reflected the reality! Myself he despised, could not tolerate, became annoyed at, wished to alter! It was only in my absence, when he was free to invent me to himself, that he felt anything resembling affection. It drove me nearly mad! He claimed to be proud, and yet could not suffer even the briefest explanations of my work or interests. He claimed to love me, and yet took issue with most of what I said. What conclusion can I draw but that the me he loved was not me at all, but a sentimental construction, mimicking me in form but wholly divested of content? Can you imagine the horror: being loved and despised in the same moment? Can you imagine what that is, when your heart aches only for your father's attentions?"

My friend nodded. "You see?" he said. "You are not nearly so boundless as you think. I am limited by your allowances, which force me down a corridor you no longer see, having lived within it your entire life. Were I truly free, everything would be allowed and nothing would have any meaning. But this is not the case: inside of your autonomy everything has meaning and nothing is free. I am a prisoner inside your sentimental world."

"Exalt, exalt," I said, throwing up my hands in surrender. "I release you: you are free!"

"Thank you," he said. He began to wail his lamentations, but suddenly broke off and said, "You do not have to harden yourself to your heart's response. If you wish to wail as well, I invite you to join me."

"I do not wish to wail," I said.

"Someday you will regret these years you spend feigning stoicism," he said. "You are not avoiding the suffering, but only delaying it."

"I am not feigning stoicism," I said, growing embarrassed and a little irritated. "Further, it is impolite and cruel to shine such a harsh and unsympathetic light on another's sustaining illusions. What would you have me do: break down in public and weep openly? This I cannot do! I am so tired of this demand: I am so tired of the fallacy of appropriate grief! How am I to act, having no experience with this sort of thing? I have lost no other father; it is all I can do to understand my own feelings, without trying to make others understand them as well! Should I have played the mourning son to those at his funeral? My unchanging countenance does not void my emotions! But it was none of theirs: who were they to me, for me to reveal myself to them thusly? Why would I bare my soul to strangers?"

"I just hate to see you unhappy," he said. He was silent for a moment. I expected him to say something else, but instead he resumed his lamentations.

The waiter arrived with our drinks, and I drank mine while I waited for my friend to finish. I was unsatisfied with all that I had said, and wanted very much for him to stop wailing so that I might explain. I wanted to explain the difference between my father's sentimental world and my own. But beyond my own certainty that they were different, I could think of no concrete meaningful deviance. My father's sentimentality rose like a wall behind which he retreated from the encroaching and dangerous world; I was certain that my friend would see my sojourn abroad and subsequent writing as more of the same. I could have shown him that it was not, but I did not feel like it.

"I think I will go back to the hotel," I said. "I am certain that there is a letter waiting there for me, and I would very much like to read it before we go out for the evening." I rose from my chair and began counting bills onto the table.

"Don't be ridiculous," said my friend. "It's almost time for supper. Stay and eat it with me. Your letters will wait for you. We will eat a pleasant supper and then go to the opening. Please. I did not mean to upset you. Sit down. We will talk about something else. Put your money away."

I sat back down. I was feeling very tired and a trifle unwell, and was not certain that I could manage the dozen or so blocks from the patio to my hotel.

"That's better," said my friend. "Now: what shall we order?"

"I feel like Hamlet," I said. "It may be bad writing to say it, but that is how I feel."

"And therein lies the problem!" said my friend, laughing. "All of your talk about the *noblis oblige* of art, and in the end you only want to tell us how you feel. That is why you remain hopelessly mired in yourself, yourself surrounded by yourself! Even this - having me dictate your failings - is only another manifestation of your work's egocentricity. This is a gesture towards an authorship outside of yourself: a gesture which in no way attains its goal! You would have me ask for an explanation and then, in judging you harshly, allay your audience's anxiety about allowing a mere character final authority. But this is false surrender: my criticisms only give you the opportunity to more accurately state your case. And no one cares what your case is; the world is indifferent to your sorrow!"

"But it is my sorrow!" I said. "How can I keep within me that which clamors to be expressed?"

He laughed. "You are speaking of excrement again!" he said. "In your sentimentality you feel that your experience contains some essential and universal truth, which will resonate among the masses and assure your place beside Hemingway and Kafka. But this is not the case! The singularity of your being makes impossible its universality. You say that you feel like Hamlet, but indeed you are nothing like Hamlet. Your mother has not married your uncle, nor was your father slain by treachery. You are just a sad little boy, living by fiction because you are afraid that the world will hurt you, producing work like excrement in the hopes that it will discover some maternal haven in the world beyond your own thoughts. But no one has time to play mother-savior to you: there are wars and famines and mountains sliding into the sea! What possible reason would someone have for subjecting themselves to your demand for affirmation?"

He looked at me with hatred. I knew that he did not want to say these things; they made impossible a pleasant supper, one of his life's greatest joys. I felt exhausted, and no longer even a little bit like Hamlet. There really was nothing alike between us. I didn't know why I had said it.

My friend had turned back to his menu. "My God," he said. "May we talk about something else? Please let us talk about something else."

We looked at our menus and did not say anything for a while. The waiter came and my friend ordered wine with our dinner. The waiter commented that the wine was an excellent choice. It was almost evening, and the sun-beams that escaped into the plaza between the buildings made a rainbow above the fountain. I knew that when we were finished eating we would take a walk and then find our way to the gallery. It was everything I had always imagined Europe would be, and I felt just as I had always hoped that I would in Europe. It made perfect sense that I had left America: in the decades to come such episodes would comprise my legend. All of the events of the pre-vious year lost their ambiguity and became instead part of a larger meaningful progress, leading me inevitably here. And I would continue on from here: yes, the future was impossibly clear and bright! Looked at in this way, it was no great tragedy that my father's body had been placed in a kiln and burned until only his charred bones remained; it no longer broke my heart to think that the bones were then put through a grinder which pulverized the remaining ash into a fine powder. His physical absence seemed now no more substantial than any other fantasy I mistook for truth.

"You will like this wine," my friend said. He looked up from his menu with a concerned expression on his face. "Are you feeling all right?" he said. "You are looking terribly pale."

"I was thinking something really unpleasant," I said. "But it is over now. I am looking forward to the wine. I was hoping that after dinner we would have time to walk around the town a bit. I have explored some, but have been by myself and invariably lost interest after a while and became distracted by my own thoughts. You know how I am: when that happens, I might as well be on the moon! I hardly see or hear any of what is going on around me. I would love to walk it with someone who knows the town, and who can tell me something about it as we go. I have this nagging fear that I will leave with no memory of the town, only memories of what I was thinking and writing during my time here."

"Of course, of course," said my friend. But he was not paying attention to me: the waiter had brought the wine, and was pouring it into two glasses. My friend watched with increasing annoyance as wine from the lip caught the edge and ran down the outside of the glass, blushing the tablecloth. "Idiot," said my friend, "simpleton! Tell me: have you no sense at all? You are worse than incompetent! Leave both the bottle and my sight!"

"My God," I said after the waiter had gone. "I never thought you capable of such cruelty! I myself would never speak so harshly to a stranger. You shame your-self!"

"Hardly," said my friend. "Your sentimental world, confined as it is, nonetheless contains such cruelty. The shame is your own. Your father, at his worst, was no more sympathetic than I, and perhaps much less: do you delude yourself so far as to claim that you would never act thusly?" He laughed suddenly. "I was wrong," he said, "you are just like Hamlet: sending your father to his judgment, with all his sins upon his head!" He finished pouring the wine, careful to make the turn as he finished, and held out my glass. "There you are," he said. "Try some of that. I will bet you dinner that you've never had better. Come now," he said, when I did not take the glass, "don't be that way. Or I will be disinclined to introduce you to the girls I know."

"You don't know any girls," I said, taking the glass.

"Still," he said, raising his own glass, "you will spoil the wine, being upset with me. And it is too good a wine to waste on such pettiness. I give you permission to be upset with me, but only after the wine is gone."

I agreed and we drank. The wine was indeed exceptional. I again had the sense that Europe was everything I had always imagined it would be, that I felt just as I had always hoped that I would, and that it made perfect sense that I had left America. But I was surprised to find that I could not remember my departure, nor my trip, nor what country it was where I had arrived. I could not recall if I had stayed there and if that was where I was now, or if I had left and traveled to another location. I could not, in fact, remember arriving at the hotel nor checking in. I could remember nothing of my time there before my walk to the café, where I had come to meet him for lunch and where I was now sitting.

"Are you certain that you are all right?" said my friend. "You are looking worse and worse. Is it the wine? Perhaps it is an acquired taste! Maybe it would be best if you went back to your room and slept for a while before the opening. My God! You are as pale as the tablecloth!"

"I am all right," I said. "I just need to use the restroom. I will be back in a moment." I rose from my chair but immediately fell forward, striking my head on the table. My father had fallen in just this same way: one of the as-yet-undiscovered tumors growing in the secret darkness of his brain had burst, causing blood to collect in the tight caverns of his skull. It was quite a surprise to everyone.

"Help, help!" cried my friend. Two waiters hurried to my side. Together they pulled me back into the chair. I had knocked over our glasses, but my friend had recovered the bottle.

"I'm fine," I said. "I was only dizzy for a moment. Please. There is no need for you to be concerned." I touched the place where I had struck my head and discerned that I was not bleeding. I made an effort to smile. "Nothing at all to worry about," I said. "It happens to me all the time. Thank you for your help, but I really am fine now."

The waiters shrugged and left. I did not want to explain, and so I closed my eyes and put my head back against the chair. I could hear my friend refilling our glasses. I thought about returning to my hotel, but realized I could not remember the way. I was certain that I had a room, but could not remember what it looked like. I wondered if I was dying, and if I died in this country, what they would do with me. Probably the authorities could locate wherever it was that I was staying. In any event, I realized, it would not matter very much to me.

"Would you be good enough to walk me back to my room?" I said. "I cannot seem to remember where I have been staying, and would like very much to lie down before we attend the opening."

"I have not been to your room," said my friend. "Besides, our dinner should be arriving shortly. Perhaps if you eat something you will feel better, and then you will be able to remember the location of your room. You hardly touched your lunch: I would not be surprised if that, at least in part, is the cause of your unwell feeling."

He turned back to his newspaper. I was surprised to see two of my childhood friends approaching our table from across the street. They waved in unison and then came over and embraced me in turn. I was very glad to see them, and called for the waiter to bring two more glasses and a second bottle. They shook hands with my friend and sat down. They had heard about my father, and expressed their deepest condolences.

"It is as well for him," I said.

"Come now," said one of my friends. "You needn't be glib with us."

"Surely your heart is hurting!" said the other.

"I do not think much on it," I said, "I am busier at my work than ever!"

"Your work will wait for your grief," said the first. "You must not deny yourself this period of mourning! I have seen men divorced from themselves: maladjusted, ignorant of their own motives, a mystery to themselves! I have watched these men as, over years, they become poisoned by the seeping truth of their disallowed sorrow. Holding back your tears will only bring disaster!"

"He is right," said the other. "Why not talk with us? I am certain that you will feel much better when we are finished; why persist with such self-hating stoicism?

There is no audience which applauds your efforts; such gestures disappear into indifferent infinity, and bring only pain during their tenure!"

"What would you have me do?" I said. "It is not so simple a decision!"

"Talk with us," said one of my friends. "Help us to discern the nature of your calamity, and by so doing shoulder some of your burden! You think that you struggle through this alone, but you mistaken! Your friends and those of your father are eager to embrace and comfort you. It is no weakness to desire such an embrace! Would you disallow such relief?"

"What would you have me do?" I asked again. "I cannot face them! Then intone to me my father's pride, mounting his virtues upon his head! They tell me how much he loved me! They know nothing: they know only the illusion my father presented! They know our public lives and mistake them for truth! Their illusion is a prison which I cannot escape: I cannot face their intrusive assertion of such blatant falsehoods! My father was not my friend! His every living breath caused me pain. I tried endlessly to please him, yet he remained indifferent to my actions! He established precursors to his affection: endless precursors, the body of which I could never traverse! And they speak to me now of his affection, of his pride; I could tear out my heart by its roots! No, I cannot face them; I will not face them!"

"Your mother misses you," said one of my friends. "She would like you to come home."

"Ah," I said. "And so, your misdirection extinguished, you turn now to truth as your salvation!" I laughed. "How did it happen? Did she make your travel arrangements, pay for your hotel? What did she hope to receive in return for her investment? Was it only my return? I hope, for your sakes, that there is no penalty should you fail!"

"She wants only to see you," they said in unison, "it pains her that you are away!"

"Then she might have convinced me to stay with her actions and words!" I said. "She might have done a million things to prevent my leaving. She would have me weep in the embrace of family? I laugh at the very idea! Perhaps she hates me because I do not mourn, but I cannot mourn for him whose death I do not lament!"

"So you would revenge yourself upon your mother thusly," said the first, "and take comfort in her sorrow?"

"Her sorrow was my sorrow," I said. "For twenty years, my sorrow was the sorrow of one left alone! And now that he has died, am I required to feel differently about him? Is it expected that I forget my pain and forgo my claim to resolution?"

At that moment my father's ghost appeared, walking upon a parapet which had suddenly arisen in the middle of the street. The cars swerved around it and crashed into each other, making a terrific racket over which I could not hear the words I could plainly see him speaking.

"I see," I said. "I understand." I wrote something upon a napkin, folded it, and handed it to one of my friends. "Would you two be so kind," I said, "as to take this to the waiter? It is a private joke, and it is important that the contents be presented in a secretive manner."

"Right away," they said, rising. They took the napkin from me and hurried across the patio to where the waiter stood, leaning against the wall. I watched him take the napkin and read over what I had written, and I watched the three of them disappear inside. My friend lowered his newspaper.

"What on earth did you write?" he said.

"I asked the waiter to execute my messengers," I said.

"My God," said my friend. He shook his head in indifferent disgust. "It is hardly their fault that they were sent for," he said. "It is your mother who is to blame. And you can hardly fault her for her concern!"

"It is of no consequence," I said. "I am mad and know that I am mad and can only hope that such madness will run its course while I am sojourned here. But then again, such realizations make impossible the continued belief that I am here. Ha-ha! Yes, it is a pleasant fantasy, but I feel that for my own good I must decline our plans to attend the artist's opening."

I looked around but, having no memory of how I had arrived, could not quickly discern which path I should take to leave. I nevertheless rose and hurried down one of the many alleys leading off the plaza. I walked briskly through, and was surprised to find that it opened onto the plaza where my friend was sitting, quietly sipping his wine. I tried another alley, and achieved the same result. I tried two more, but each time I emerged onto the plaza I had just vacated. I was feeling out of breath, and sat back down at the table.

"I'm glad you have returned," said my friend. "I hate to eat alone."

"How did I get here?" I said. "Where did I come from? Where am I now?"

My friend shrugged. "How should I know?" he said. "If I had to guess, I would say that you are seated in a dark room somewhere, poring furiously over these pages, ignoring telephone calls and pretending to be out whenever anyone comes to the door. I expect that there is a pile of slowly spoiling food on your front step; I expect a pile of cards have been slid under your door."

"Would you have me do otherwise?" I gasped. "You have heard my reasons! I will not put on the performance of grief before strangers: it is highly inappropriate! I would sooner lecture them on politics, chastise their taste, advise them on childrearing! Such private beliefs should admit no discourse with public life!"

"But I hardly think that is why you retreat," he said. "You continue to make the case that your grief, belonging to no one but yourself, has no place in common parlance. But that is hardly the truth: you are surrounded by friends who gladly offer you their time, their compassion, their comfort! No: I think you retreat because, when you are here writing this, your father's death is only ink upon the page. It loses its reality; it can no longer wound you. He is no more absent now, when you are writing, than he was a year ago, two years ago, three years ago. He is as present to you now as he was when you were merely apart. Here in this fanciful mess you have created your father is no more deceased than he ever was. That is why you do not go outside; you cannot face the reality of his absence!"

"Papa," I wept, "papa, papa, papa, papa!"

My friend offered me his napkin, and I dried my eyes. I began to think on other things, and found that I felt almost immediately better. Our food arrived, and my friend refilled our glasses. I was certain that there would be plenty of time later to think about all that my friend had said, but for the moment I was feeling very hungry, and was not interested in getting into it. Dinner was excellent, and the wine made a perfect compliment. I ate everything on my plate.

The waiter came back and informed me that, as per my instructions, my two friends had been executed. The sun had gone down while we were eating, and the plaza was lit now by a row of spotlights surrounding the central fountain. I looked for my father's ghost, but did not see him. I wondered what it was that he was saying when I had seen him earlier. As the tumors in his brain progressed he mouthed words nonsensically: I wondered if, as a ghost, he was bound to enact more of the same, or if he had been restored, in the afterlife, to his full faculties. I was not at all certain which I preferred: his words invariably rose like arrows shot o'er the house which, in falling, found no target save my heart. His descent into that final confusion was, for me, characterized by an odd ignorance: striving always to understand the intention behind his words and actions, I found myself disoriented and lost inside a series of behaviors which made little sense and which, in retrospect, I know meant nothing.

I was yet more heartbroken by this fact: to realize that I been so completely conditioned by two and a half decades of manipulation that now I could not watch his death throes without feeling that they held some attack. This struck me as the greatest tragedy, the greatest loss, of all. But that loss did not begin with my father's death, nor did it end: I was nevertheless certain that, had I heard the ghost's words, I would have found in them some fundamental criticism. But this hardly made it the case: it was certainly possible that, tilting so aggressively at these meaningless gestures, I was as much a sentimentalist as my father, and perhaps more of one than he ever could have been, inventing content which I assigned to the form of his actions. I could not be sure, however: the moment this thought arose I cast it from me with adequate force as to lose its shouted claim to truth in the vast distance between us.

"What are you thinking?" said my friend. "You looked a million miles away just then."

"Nothing," I said. "I am thinking nothing at all. And I have come to a conclusion: I do not care if this is only a sentimental fantasy. It is a pleasant fantasy, and one from which I would rather not awaken. There is no mandate that grief be handled in a timely manner. I will stay here until I feel that I am ready to do what is expected of me, and not a moment less."

"Are you certain that is wise?" said my friend. "What you are describing is a knowing and willful sojourn in madness! Who is to say that, having given yourself over to such delusions, you will know your way back? Even now you can hardly discern the path, even with the world outside your mind still fresh and foremost in your thoughts!"

"Yes," I said, interrupting him, for I felt that I finally knew exactly what it was I was trying to say. "Sentimentality is a kind of madness: it sees the world as it decidedly is not! To be sentimental is to live in the world as a pleasant dream, free from the anxieties of ambiguity. Here I know every cobblestone, every droplet which rises from the fountain! There can be no mystery if I hold final authority."

He threw up his hands. "I can do nothing more for you," he said. "No argument I can mount can hope to breach the fortress of your self-satisfaction. You are just like your father!"

"I hardly think my revelation or resolution deserves your insults," I said.

"You are an ass," said my friend. He called the waiter, and asked for the bill. "I hope you are very happy in this life you have chosen," he said. "But I hardly plan to participate. If you insist on living in this ridiculous way, then you must forgive me if I choose not to spend the evening with you. When one becomes an object in someone else's world, one very quickly loses any interest in stating one's own case."

"Don't be that way," I said. "You are simply upset that we do not agree. You will see in time, however, that I am right: the world is only what you make of it! Nothing is either good nor bad, but that thinking makes it so! The triumph of the self is the triumph of final and autonomous subjectivity, a subjectivity unbounded by intrusions from the objective world! I might find myself bounded in a nutshell, or prisoner in the trunk of a hollow tree! Yes: that which you would call madness is merely enlightenment!" But then I stopped speaking, because my friend was weeping.

"And what of those you hurt?" he said. "What of those who long for your attention, your affection, your interest, your affirmation? What of those of us who speak to you only so that you might hear us, who value ourselves only as you value us? What of us?"

He broke off into howling lamentations. I wished to comfort him, but could not understand why he was upset. Further, I was annoyed by the implication that I should change: as father to his being, I could not help but feel myself the post 'round which his perceptions should tailor themselves. Who was he to feel hurt by me, when I did not act to hurt him? Who was he to find meaning in my actions? It seemed a dangerous and easy slide from honoring his feelings to giving myself over wholly to his wishes.

With this in mind, I sat back in my chair with the intention of doing nothing. I was certain that, one day, he would merely accept me for who I was, and no longer ask more of me than what I already gave without effort. But my friend continued weeping, and I felt suddenly exhausted. It was a terrible strain to continually invent and interpret. I longed to return to my room and lose myself in my writing; I was certain that, as I sat before the pages, the words would come easily. I was certain, even though I knew this certainty to be a lie: I had been unable to write for the past week, and did not know what to write now. The sentimental image I had of myself poring over pages emanated peace and satisfaction, it promised a profound disambiguation. Yet I knew this feeling to be a lie: doubtless I would sit before the pages feeling nothing, thinking nothing, becoming mired again in conflicting ideas with no ability to discern a path through them. One sentence seemed as good as another, and nothing that happened seemed to matter. My friend had stopped crying.

"Ah," he said, "I see you have discovered the flaw in your plan. It is no easy thing, to be both Alpha and Omega of one's own existence! Many collapse under the weight of such burdensome authority."

"Spare me your reprimands!" I said. "That is hardly the issue."

"Then explain," said my friend.

"It is my writing," I said.

"What about it?" he said.

"I am having a very hard time putting it into words," I said. "It is something like this: I set out to write a very simple book about sentimentality. But my father was dying while I was writing it, and the book became something I had not expected. Now I have pieced it together with overt structural references to Sartre and Joyce and Kundera, and am still no closer to capturing the thing I set out to describe."

"Surely," my friend said, "it cannot be as bad as you think."

"But it is!" I said. "I have been deluding myself, thinking that this place is my own production, that this fantasy is my own! But it is obvious to me now: at this very moment we are trapped in what I can only describe as an imitation of certain passages from Kundera's later work."

"I have read Kundera," he said. "You are no Kundera!"

"I know it!" I said. "As myself I am passable, but as an imitation of another I cannot help but fall woefully short."

"Tell me," he said, "what was it that you were trying to say?"

I threw up my hands in exasperation and said, "I was trying to describe sentimentality! I wanted to show what a destructive force it is; I wanted to show that it is a retreat from the world, a refusal to engage! I wanted to show how those who love the sentimentalist are condemned to heartbreak, as one who loves a stone is condemned to heartbreak! No: far worse! For the sentimentalist speaks the language of affection, and does so convincingly! But he is speaking a foreign tongue; he is a banker in a currency whose value he does not understand!"

He shook his head. "But you have said all of this," he said. "You, in fact, said much more in the very first chapter: why write a book to expand upon - or rather, fail to expand upon! - what has already been said?"

I again threw up my hands. "Because what was said in the introduction was not all that there was to say! I had something more to say! It was only that, as I was writing, my father was dying, and I was very distracted. It is hard to think about fiction when reality so aggressively imposes itself!"

"And yet you did," he said, giving me a smirking smile.

"What does that mean?"

"Don't you know?" he said. "It should be obvious! As your father lay dying you hid in your rooms thinking only of fiction, pretending that fiction was more true than true life! You imagined that the issues that remained - your anger over your father's distance, his sentimental removal, his worthless and affected affection - would find their resolution in the ether of prose. But it was only a dodge! And now you limp toward the close, with no idea how to conclude! And why? Because there is no conclusion! To conclude satisfactorily would require growth, progress! Now that you have brought yourself into the narrative, the only fitting conclusion would be for this conversation to end mid-sentence, for you to leave off fiction, and for your book's remaining pages to be left blank. But we both know that you will not do it: you are too comfortable here, yourself surrounded by yourself! You will not speak to others: you will stay here and speak to me. And I do not even exist: these arguments I put to you are your own! How will you get beyond yourself, with only yourself to guide you? Yes," he stood from his chair in triumph, "this book is a portrait of your refusal to engage with reality, of your sentimental inner life where all quantities are known and all meaning is fixed! You are a laughable contradiction!"

"But I have written this already," I said. "This is my Girl's speech to her Student. Do you think that you can sway me with my own words?"

"No!" said my friend in final, triumphant exasperation. "This is exactly my point! I can say nothing that will inspire alteration: nothing I do can affect you in the least! Here," he said, "I will show you." He drew a gun from his coat and fired it at my chest. Nothing happened.

"That proves nothing," I said. "The gun is filled with blanks."

"Not so!" he replied. He opened the cylinder and removed two of the bullets. "You see?" he said, holding them up. "You toy with life and death, and imagine that you have touched on Truth! But fiction is fiction is fiction: fiction never killed anyone!" He set the gun on the table, and looked at it with disgust. "And again you resort to half-realized imitations of Kundera. I'm surprised you did not have me shooting at car tires!"

"I know, I know!" I cried, putting my head in my hands.

At that moment the Newscaster emerged from the sea, dragging rope and anchor behind her. She sat down at the table beside ours and set to untying her ankles.

"That was a lousy thing you did," she said, "sending me to the bottom of the sea. And for what? For failing to cry for the right reasons? Who are you to judge anyone?"

"If only I could see the problem clearly," I said, "I feel certain that I could make some progress. But it is impossible to see it clearly: one can never arrive at any starting point that their own perceptions do not color or preexist! I would that I could describe sentimentality, and yet my opinion of sentimentality is a sentimental one, waxed o'er by my hurt, imbued with meaning uninherent to the form! That which I have mistaken for objectivity in these pages is my own agenda in disguise: a little boy's hurt, clamoring for the world to notice! My God: this novel is a pathetic jumble, a hopeless mess! You are wrong in your assessment: the only fitting conclusion would not be for the narrative to end mid-sentence but rather for me to hurl these pages from me, to never again admit that I wrote them, to cast the memory of them from my thoughts! My father is dead, and our history admits no revision! To trumpet my pain from the rooftops does nothing to reduce it, and less to alter its cause. It is my cross to bear, but I would that I were noble enough to bear it in silence!

"Come now," said my friend. "You are being too hard on yourself. You deserve respite!"

"But this is exactly my point," I said. "No one deserves anything! Nowhere is it written that pain must not become intolerable, that suffering must cease! There is no heavenly mandate which declares that every man face only burdens which he is suited to carry. Life may grind us into the dust and make no apologies for it; it has broken no guarantees which it need apologize for breaking."

"All that you say is true," said my friend, "and yet I beg you to reconsider. Sustaining illusions are not a weakness! To live always with the certainty of one's own insignificance, to belittle one's demand for heaven's acknowledgement - a demand which seems to spring universally within the human heart! - is to live a life without value, a life devoid of pleasure: in short, it is to live no life at all!"

"What good is pleasure?" I said. "And of what value? Life has no value!"

"Perhaps," he said, "but one's life having no value to heaven and having no value to oneself are two very different things. Would you so readily cast your life from yourself? Can you really tell me that you count your life lowest among your possessions?"

"What value has my life?" I said. "It is a seemingly interminable slog through pain and sore travail, defined at every moment by my father's undying presence. I am intelligent enough to see it, and yet stupid enough to live beneath its yoke!" I laughed. "I spoke earlier of realizing the self, of the triumph of subjectivity! You could have cut me to the quick! In my years of speaking I have never said anything more untrue. I can no more realize myself than I can slay my father's persistent ghost; I see him now, armed at point exactly, cap-a-pe! Would that I could please him! But the heart, as we know, does not go where it is commanded; further, I sense, it was not his disapproval but rather his indifference which wounded me most. What horror: to be intelligent enough to see, but impotent to alter! I would laugh were my energies not already wholly expended by my tears."

"I have been listening to you very closely," said the Newscaster, "and please forgive my intrusion! But I fail to see your crisis. You father is dead: rejoice! Turned to ashes he is incapable of hurting you further. No longer will his satisfied smiles flaunt his blindness; never again will he mistake the dogmatic incantation of nonspecific affirmations for a display of fatherly love! He cannot disappoint you: he is dead! Why are you not rejoicing?"

"Because he is my father!" I said. "Because all that I am I owe to him! Because he is my flesh and because he is my mirror; because he was a Titan to me when I was small! Because, for good or ill, I know nothing of myself save what I know through him! Because there is a hole in the world where he stood: because my mother's heart is broken! Because despite his failings he was a wonderful man, a beloved man! Because the failures between us belong as much to me as they do to him; because in spite of all I loved him! In short, because he was my father!"

The Newscaster shook her head. "And yet you write this now to slander him, to state your own case, to parade your hurt; truly you are an awful son, if this manifesto is the only tribute you can muster! What right do you have to speak ill of the dead? On what grounds do you ordain to preach? Your father saw the world from behind fortress walls: that much is clear! He fell helplessly into falsehood when he attempted to speak genuinely. How can you fault him this? You are guilty of the same! You run from inarticulate pain and hide in this palace of fiction, afraid to be seen weeping! You make me laugh. Were you not, yourself, as guarded when addressing him? Yes: doubtless you wished not for true connection but rather to bring him to his knees, to reduce him to tears, to tear down the sentimental walls within which his fragile self sheltered so that you might claim a final and horrible authority over him."

"Silence!" I commanded. "I will not sit idly by while you dispense with such accusations! I loved my father, and wanted nothing save his friendship! But his sentimentality presented an intolerable and ever-present barrier through which I could find no path."

"And that is the greatest sentimentality of all," she said bitterly. "You place yourself in the role of the incorruptible altruist, whose motives were always pure and whose goals were above reproach. Do you mistake this for truth? Ha! The truest mark of sentimentality is the inability to admit ambiguity! How hopelessly lost you are!

"Everything you have said is very interesting," I said, "but I am afraid that my friend and I have plans for the evening, and will be late if we do not leave now."

"Not at all," said my friend. "The opening is not for another hour, and I have no intention of leaving my seat until it is absolutely necessary."

"I thought you were going to show me the town," I said.

"You have seen it already!" he said.

"You are no help at all," I said.

A man and a woman had arrived while we were speaking, and now sat at the table behind ours. Their clothes were in tatters and their faces were heavily coated with makeup. They eyed me with obvious disapproval.

"How insufferable you are," said the man, "how you have misrepresented me! I, who wrote for years on the failure of fiction, wrote calling for people to engage more fully with their lives, to avoid fiction's escape, to awake from its disengaging dream! Who are you to accuse me of sentimentality? And why? Because I wrote once that the sight of a bare arm or a half-exposed breast might stir one's desire? You obviously understand nothing of my work!"

"Yes," said the woman, nodding, "and you seem to understand even less of mine! Honestly: to you women are either praising or disparaging; they have no existence save in relation to the men they orbit! Just once I would like to read something of yours which does not incite repulsion within me."

"Yes," said the man, shaking his head, "it is clear that you have strung together anecdotes from our lives, and permitted yourself to invent the rest! Did you read *Being and Nothingness*? Or *The Mandarins*? Scour back issues of *Les Temps Modernes*? Consider any of the fine - or even any of the poor! - biographies written about us? Or the book of our letters? It is almost laughable! It is as though you made no attempt to represent us as we truly were. Yes," he said, growing excited, "you call me sentimental, but it is you who are sentimental, inventing content for the forms of Jean-Paul and Simone, and functioning as though these delusion were fact! In all of my years

I never saw a more deliberate affront to reality; you are just like your father!"

"You see?" said my friend. "We are all in agreement. The apple does not fall far from the tree."

The Student, my great defender, came hurrying from the bathroom and leapt up upon our table.

"Simpletons!" he shouted. "Do not confuse your limited understanding, however widely agreed upon, with truth! The portrait he has drawn of us is unpleasant, perhaps, but this does not make it false! Truth is never easy: it takes strength to stand and face it! I applaud him for his efforts!"

My friend lifted the pistol from the table, took careful aim, and fired; the bullet struck the Student in the stomach, causing him to crumple. Falling to the concrete, he cried out; the Girl - beautiful, radiant, unlike any other - emerged from the ocean, born of the sea foam, and ran to him.

"I cannot die," said the Student, "there is so much I have not seen, realized, experienced, learned, written, spoken!" But then he died and the Girl, weeping, held his body. His parents arrived in their car, and lamented that his life was cut short, tragically short! The waiters had hurried over at the sound of the gunshot, and were restraining my friend. The gun lay, smoking, upon the table beside the unpaid bill. Policemen came, and took my friend away. Jean-Paul and Simone watched the proceedings with disgust.

Jean-Paul, lifting his shirt to remove a rat nesting betwixt his ribs, said, "Disgusting, Wholly reprehensible."

The Student's father, shaking with rage, his arm in a sling, turned to me and said, "You bastard. How could you let this happen? My son: my darling boy! The great things he might have done!"

I laughed and said, "You knew nothing of your son! If you had any inkling of the things you did to him you would hurl yourself into the sea, or put out your eyes! You have no right to call him darling, your pride and joy: you, who have caused him so much pain! All that gave him pleasure you dismissed or worse, devalued! So intent were you on playing father that you failed to make any relationship with the son you had, chastising him always for the son that he was not! Your smile made him sick! Every word that spewed from your mouth was a conde-scension, an affront! By attempting to make your son into the man you thought he should be you made him ashamed of the man he was! Don't you understand that thoughts of you caused him only pain? Don't know that it broke his heart to hate you?"

The Student's father looked at me in bewilderment. "You do not understand," he said. "You do not under-stand what it is to have a child! How do you tell him anything? There are no words! A parent's love for his child is inarticulate; what words should I have said? What words would he have heard?"

The Student's mother interrupted on her husband's behalf, saying, "My husband loved his son; how dare you speak thusly to a grieving man? Think of all he did for our son, the opportunities he provided! His own father never did so much for him! And what thanks did he re-ceive? None! Our son (may he rest in the bosom of the Holy Mother!) regarded us as philistines, too simple to understand his sensitivity, his pain: pain with which he justified his ceaseless assault! Just look!"

The Student's father, arm unslung, hanging upon the cross, his eyes turned skyward, said, "Forgive my son, Father, for he knew not what he did!" The Roman sol-diers, returning to the plaza, prodded him with their spears. The Student's mother, weeping, held the chalice to collect the blood.

"Such selflessness!" intoned the earth's gathered masses. The creatures of the sea dove and then rose rapidly to the surface, bursting forth in magnificent tribute. The cloth, rent, cried out in pain.

"In nomine Patris, et fillii, et Spiritus sancti," responded Simone and Jean-Paul in unison. "And lo, he made many miracles upon the earth including but not limited to the provision of food, clothing, and shelter, the payment of tuition, the signing of permission slips, the negotiation of a second, low-interest mortgage…"

The Girl, looking up from her fallen Student, nodded in agreement. "That is not it at all," she said. "What you have stated is blatantly untrue. I knew him better than anyone. You have entirely missed it. These statements belong to no one but yourself; further, I refuse to let you slander or misrepresent the dead."

The Student, beautiful in death, became whole and ascended into heaven on a cloud. A chorus of angels, bearing the standard of St. Stephen, sang *In Praise of Innocence*. The great golden gates swung wide; all present turned their eyes skyward and were amazed. My friend returned in the garb of a coffee maid, humming the hymn as he poured.

"How did you escape?" I said.

"It was simple!" he replied. "I told them that I was Joan of Arc, and required immediate martyrdom. None of us had a match. When they stopped at a tobacconist's I escaped. I hid in an attic for two weeks, surviving on coffee beans. Remarkable improvement to my complexion. I see," he said, turning from my cup to consider the empty place where the Student had lain, "that they have removed the body."

"Not so," I said. "Ascended into heaven. Chorus of angels. You caught the last bit as you were coming in. Dolce et decorum est."

"Of course, of course," my friend said. "Only fair. God is great, God is good, we must thank him for our food. Amen. Presto!" He cast the carafe down upon the table where it shattered, covering our plates and staining the tablecloth with coffee.

The table grew and gave birth to flatware; the flatware begat china and the china begat a feast. All present were seated. My friend, in a priest's collar, bowed his head.

"Now at this most holy time," he said, "we thank the great and holy God: the eternal father whose love we cannot earn, whose grace we cannot deserve, the keeper of the objective light, to whom all must finally render forth the spirit just as Christ rendered forth even under protest rendered forth the spirit nonetheless. How sweet it is: to wallow in the pleasant certainty of faith!"

No one waited for him to finish: the food was being handed around and rapidly devoured. I could hardly believe my own hunger; I had finished supper not more than an hour earlier. My friend, unable to continue with his blessing, resumed his chair. There was a crash as the great gates of heaven swung shut, but this noise was barely audible over the clamor from the table below. I had never heard such bestial eating sounds.

"Excellent!" everyone agreed. "Marvelous, delicious, wonderful!"

"Will you cut this for me, mother?" the Student's father asked the Student's mother. "My arm is giving me a terrible pain!"

Wine spilled through the hole in Jean-Paul's stomach. All in attendance laughed. The Newscaster lifted food to mouth with fish-nibbled fingers, saying, "I feel as though I have not eaten in ages!"

My friend excused himself and, wearing an artist's smock, set to work behind a massive easel. All present called for him to show. My friend demurred; the crowd demanded. After much cajoling he turned the canvas to reveal a painting in the fashion of da Vinci's *The Last Supper*, with the Student as Christ. The Student's mother began to weep. His father, arm slung, comforted her.

"Fear not," said my friend, "for He is with you always!"

The situation, which a moment before had held the lucid reality of a dream, seemed suddenly divorced from the events which had precipitated it. I was struck by the absurdity of the scene, and wondered how I had managed to stray so far from my original thesis. The world of forms had been wholly liberated from the world of content: the plaza was crowded with what amounted to a jumble of meaningless symbols. I knew that I was mad, that in attempting to deconstruct my own impulse to explicate I had instead arrived at the more essential truth: that whatever content hid behind form remained essentially and eternally unknown and unknowable, that there was no meaning save my own, that living in the world demanded a kind of reprehensible sentimentality, that my father deserved nothing but forgiveness. I opened my mouth the speak, to command them all to stop. But I lost suddenly the will: nothing I did could move me one step closer to reclaiming what I had lost: barring that, nothing else mattered. I resumed my seat, indifferent to their celebration.

"I saw you start to speak," said my friend. "What is it you wanted to say?"

"Nothing," I said. "I wish now to say nothing. My father is dead. Long live my father."

All present grew silent at these words, and fell immediately to weeping. My friend wept loudest of all, saying, "You see what poetry is in the world, if only you do not hinder it with semantics, or disguise it with dodges!"

"I had no idea," I said.

"No," said Jean-Paul, "of course you had no idea! You who live only in your head: and why? Not because you are such an academic; no! It is only because, in your head, you are free to interpret events as you wish, free to harbor hurts which have little basis in fact, free from others' incantations of the shining truth which, like a lightning bolt, cuts through your delusions and calls your wounds false! You imagine that your injuries justify you, that as victim you hold power over those that have hurt you! And yet you lose all credibility when every word is a slight, when every gesture holds some hidden meaning which only you can ordain! You are too sensitive, and your sensitivity carries an agenda! You wish the world to cast itself at your feet, begging your forgiveness; your weakness disgusts me! Your father loved you more than any other; how could you spend his dying hours protesting, demanding his apologies, claiming hopes for an improved relationship as your sword and shield? You did not want a relationship with your father; you have presented facts only in evidence of your hatred! It was not love you wanted, but subservience! You wished to force your father to prostrate himself before you, and beg your forgiveness! You are a cruel and petty child: your father's life is worth a hundred, a thousand, of your own!"

"Yes," said Simone. "I have listened very carefully to everything you have said. It is clear that your father's sentimentality presented an intolerable wall not to your love, but to your ceaseless assault. Removed as he was, your words could neither reach nor dethrone him. It is not at all surprising: boys must always compete with their fathers! But to take it to such lengths, chastising and insulting him as he lay sick and dying: my God! Would that I could draw down thunder and lighting upon you!"

The Student's parents and his Girl, the Newscaster and the waiters all murmured their agreement. The Girl took a turkey leg from the remnants of the feast and hurled it at me. The others followed suit. Soon the table was bare of food, and the assembled began to throw plates and flatware. One serving bowl struck me in the head as I turned, and I toppled forward onto the pavement. Dishes and glasses continued to rain down upon me. I longed for the Student's return; I imagined him descending on a cloud to shield me. But soon there was nothing left for them to throw, and he still had not arrived.

Someone overturned my friend's easel, and the large painting fell and covered me entirely. I lay beneath, and listened to them leaving. When I was certain that they were gone I crawled from beneath the canvas and resumed my seat. My friend was sitting opposite, looking much the same as he had when I arrived earlier that afternoon. He filled my glass from a fresh bottle the waiter had brought. I looked around and saw that the splattered food, the broken dishes, the overturned easel, the painting, and the empty table had all been cleared away. I looked to the sky and saw that even the golden gates of heaven were gone. I had a terrible headache, and wished to return to my room before the opening. I was certain that if I could get some sleep I would feel much better. Somehow I could make neither head nor tails of the world around me, and I was growing exhausted with the effort. The cobblestones, the fountain, the tables, the waiters, the new bottle and the wine in my glass seemed wholly unintelligible.

"My God," I said, "I'm irreparably mad."

"Not at all," my friend said casually. "You are simply not yourself today. I am certain that you will feel better tomorrow. Here: try some of this wine. I am certain you have never had better."

I tentatively lifted the glass, uncertain that I had ever lifted a glass before. The wine was indeed excellent, although I could think of nothing with which to compare it. I drank it down and felt my headache lessen with the first swell of alcohol rising in my blood.

"I think I'll take a walk," I said. "Just a short one, just to clear my head. I'm in a rotten mood, and would rather not meet people as I am. I won't be long, and when I return we will go to the gallery. All right?"

"That sounds fine," said my friend. "Try not to get lost."

I walked away from the table, past the fountain, and down one of the side streets leading off the plaza. I knew that each street opened as well onto the plaza, that each plaza had other streets leading onto the plaza, that I would leave and return in an endless loop from which I could discern no escape. But halfway down one of these streets I noticed a narrow passageway leading between two of the buildings: I turned into this alley, and followed it beneath an arch into an enclosed corridor, and then along an impossibly convoluted series of passages, all of which seemed to be leading down. Soon dirt began to show in the places where the brick was falling away, and I knew that I was moving beneath the earth. I continued further and further down, and there seemed to be no end to how far I could go.

I had left the table with the intention of finding my father's ghost: I wanted to ask him what he was trying to say to me on the street above, when his voice was drowned out by the traffic noise. Then I wanted to ask him what he had been trying to say in those final weeks, when it seemed that he could find no words at all. I wanted to ask him what he thought of me, if he was proud, if he even liked me. I wanted to ask with the full knowledge that I would refuse, as I had when he was alive, whatever answer he gave: that he was proud, or that he loved me, or any of the phrases that had by now lost their meaning through repetition and unsubstantiated use. I wanted to insist until he admitted that, if he had not been my father and I had not been his son, we would not have been friends.

Then, I imagined, we would talk for a while: I would explain how hurt I was that, despite my best efforts, he always refused to hear what I was saying: that he could not see me through the sentimental facade he had erected between us. He would explain how hurt he was that, despite his earnest attempts, his labor and sacrifice, I was always upset with him: that I assumed the worst about him, that I did not understand his intentions and so took umbrage with his every effort. We would argue and curse each other, and not speak for days. Then we would come gradually back, speaking to each other parsimoniously, sure to impart with our manner and words that by returning we admitted nothing: that our return held no surrender to the other's view. But in this fantasy our conversation did not halt at this first estrangement and reunion, as it did invariably during his lifetime: it continued until we had exhausted all arguments, and arrived at the threshold of understanding: that we simply did not and could not see eye-to-eye, that we viewed the world and ourselves differently, but that this difference held, finally, no discourse with the love each bore the other. By this admission we would come to see each other clearly, and we would weep and hold each other, and our hearts would be filled. Then he would lead me out of the labyrinth of streets and plazas and back to the world where my mother mourned alone, fearful that to express her grief to me would only draw down the fire of my ongoing polemic against him.

But despite my earnest and exhaustive search I could find no trace of him. The finality of this refusal infuriated me, and I cursed him loudly. But I knew, of course, that his absence was no refusal, nor was it his fault: he was merely dead, and could no more respond than I could ordain to speak with him. Having been for so long ever-present in my mind, his absence now arrived as an impossible shock. I knew suddenly and finally that there would never be any resolution, that I would continue through life bound by an anger to which I would admit no progress, awaiting a catharsis that would never come.

I sat down on the earthen floor and wept. But after crying for some time I felt ridiculous, and I broke off laughing. It seemed impossible that he was gone: how could he be gone? My existence seemed overarched by his, seemed to progress beneath the domed sky of his eternal presence. Yes: and beneath his gaze I remained hopelessly fixed and muted, subjugated and ignored! How I hated him in that moment! I rose to my feet, resolved once again to find him. I had more to say! My case had not been made!

But instead I found myself climbing, and soon I emerged into the alley from which I had strayed. The sky had grown dark, and the lights from the fountain shone like a beacon into the sky. I moved toward them, and achieving the plaza saw my friend waiting for me at the table. He waved when he caught sight of me, and I hurried to join him. The bottle was empty, but our glasses were full. He rose, and together we toasted the artist and the vision he held in store for us. Then, our glasses emptied, we left the plaza and started down the street toward the gallery. Soon we had walked beyond the reach of the fountain's light, and the world was obscured by opaque darkness.

Yet I had no trouble finding my way, for even in this darkness I knew the shape and circumference of every thought and form.

STAVROS STAVROS lives and works in Cleveland, Ohio. His first novel, *THE SIRENS,* was published by The Artless Dodges Press in 2009. More of his work may be found at www.StavrosStavros.WordPress.com.

www.ingramcontent.com/pod-product-compliance
Lightning Source LLC
Chambersburg PA
CBHW050026180626
46810CB00002B/592